BILLION DOLLAR DISPUTE

SHARON WOODS

Content Information

This book contains spicy descriptive scenes and language. There's mentions of struggling to conceive, breast cancer, and drug use.

PROLOGUE

JEMIMA

"Dad, can we go play some basketball?" Chad asks, bouncing his orange ball excitedly as he reaches my bedroom. Following behind him, I look over Chad's shoulder to see my husband, Butch, lying on the bed, partially covered by blankets, wearing just his black boxers and a stained white T-shirt. Lately, he hasn't been taking care of himself. His beard is matted, and his blond hair, streaked with gray, hangs long and unruly.

The same man who used to get up at the crack of dawn for morning gym sessions...who once cared. He started slowly, missing a workout here, canceling plans there. I told myself it was just a phase, that the stress at work would pass. But months stretched on, and the man I loved faded, replaced by someone I barely recognized. Because of that, we've been fighting about everything lately.

He rolls over, mumbling something incomprehensible, and my blood boils. It's Saturday. He used to love Saturdays. Now our apartment room's a mess, there's clothes thrown everywhere, and it smells stale. He's changed…become lazy, showing no care or attention toward me or Chad anymore. I'm about to say something about it, but Chad beats me to it. "Please, Dad," Chad tries again, his voice softer this time. Hopeful.

"Just give me a minute, kid," he slurs after another late night. I bite the inside of my cheek so hard it hurts. A minute? He's been giving us the bare minimum for a while now. Nights out with friends instead of being here. Missing dinners, missing bedtime stories. Missing us. The distance is making it hard to want to stay together. He's forty-five, yet for the last twelve months, he's been acting like a twenty-one-year-old.

I walk out, head to the kitchen, grab the bottle of Tylenol, and return to our room, tossing the bottle onto the bed next to him. "Get up and go hang out with him."

He doesn't even flinch or look at me…not even for Chad. My heart breaks a little more, but I push it down. I can't fall apart. Not now.

I grit my teeth to prevent myself from yelling at him for stumbling in at three a.m. When Chad—who's six—woke from a nightmare, the bed was still empty. After I finally got him back to sleep and settled in bed, I heard Butch stomp through our front door. It wasn't five minutes later and he climbed into bed, fully clothed. I have no idea when he lost his jeans, but they're off now. Shaking my head, I go back to cleaning the house, making extra noise to fuck with his headache more.

As I scrub the counters, I think about how this can't go on. I won't let it. I've been telling myself I'll talk to him. That I'll sit him down and force him to see what he's doing to us. To Chad. But every time I get close, Chad is around, or he leaves for *work*.

Half an hour later, he ventures out of the bedroom with red-rimmed eyes and a deep scowl. He looks ten years older today. I look away, pretending it doesn't hurt to see him like this.

"Don't come back for at least two hours. I'd like to finish cleaning the house," I say through a clenched jaw, needing a moment to calm the rage inside me since Chad's in the next room.

"Quit nagging me, woman."

Don't snap in front of Chad.

I take a shaky breath, before replying, "Just go."

They leave, and I sag against the counter. This can't go on. Tomorrow we're having the conversation.

When he returns a few hours later, Chad can't stop talking about all the cool shots his dad took. I put on the biggest, fakest smile and listen as he talks. Butch retreats to our room while I move Chad to the living room to play Chutes and Ladders. Afterwards, I peek into the bedroom, finding Butch still passed out, so I head out to the store with Chad. Not wanting Chad to see his dad in his disgusting state, I make sure to take our time picking out food items, and when we return, I start baking muffins for Chad to take to school next week and then get started on dinner.

A few hours later, I hear Butch bark out, "Are you making dinner?" He's still lying on our bed. With his mood swings out of control, I feel like I'm walking on eggshells in my own home.

"Yeah. Your favorite...pasta bake," I call back.

The TV murmurs in the background with a cartoon our six-year-old loves to watch. Butch mumbles something I can't hear.

"Are you going to get up?" I ask.

"Give me a fucking break, Jem," he snaps.

"Don't swear," I hiss, annoyed he doesn't care about his influence on his son.

A knock sounds at the door. "Are you expecting someone?" I ask, tossing a bottle of beer into the trash.

"No," he replies with a huff.

Realizing Butch isn't going to get up and answer it, I sigh. I stop preparing dinner and move to open the door, but before I can reach it, it bursts open with a crash. I scream as four police officers storm in, weapons drawn, the door now off its hinges.

The officers move inside, and one goes straight to our bedroom. "Butch, on the ground! Hands where I can see them."

My heart slams into my throat. "Chad!" I gasp, my eyes darting wildly around the living room. I spot him frozen near his toys.

"It's okay. Come here." My voice cracks as I rush to him, scooping him up, holding him so tight he's practically molded to me. His little hands cling to my neck like a lifeline.

"Mommy, what's happening?" Chad's voice is high-pitched, his breaths warm and quick against my neck.

"I don't know, honey," I reply in a shaky voice.

There's a loud sound of furniture breaking, followed by grunting and more yelling. I keep Chad's face against me, shielding him from the sight. My breathing becomes shallow, each inhale a struggle against the crushing weight of panic.

I swallow my hysterical sobs, but silent tears flow down my cheeks. The officers quickly handcuff Butch, and there's a heavy bang, likely from him being put on the ground. An officer reads him his rights.

Another officer speaks. "You're under arrest for drug trafficking. Anything you say can and will be used against you in a court of law..."

Drug trafficking... No. No way. Butch? This must be a mistake.

An officer stands in our way, keeping us away from Butch, and I'm grateful for the help in blocking Chad's view of the scene.

"What's going on?" I ask, my voice breaking.

"Ma'am, please remain calm," the officer replies gently. "We're here as part of an ongoing investigation. We just need to do our job, and I promise everything is being handled properly."

I nod, my thoughts a mess of fear and confusion.

"We do need to ask you a few questions, if that's okay," he says. "Officer Kate MacDonald will keep Chad occupied for a bit."

"Okay." I lower Chad to his feet. Officer MacDonald kneels to Chad's level. She offers a kind smile, holding out one of his toy cars.

"It's okay, honey," I say, stroking his hair. "I'll be right here."

Officer MacDonald glances at me. "We'll stay right here in the living room where he can see you," she assures me. She knows what she's doing, and right now, I need someone to help keep Chad safe.

I look down at Chad, giving him a reassuring nod. Brow furrowed, he lets go and walks over to his toys with Officer MacDonald.

The other officer turns his attention back to me, but I keep my eyes on Chad. "Do you know anything about Butch's whereabouts or what he was doing last night?"

"No, I was here with Chad the whole night. I don't know anything about this."

He nods, writing down some notes. Then, he asks a lot more questions. *Were you aware that your husband was involved in selling or using drugs? Have you ever seen your husband use drugs or have drugs in the house? Have you ever helped your husband with any of his activities, knowingly or unwillingly? And so many more...*

My answer to every single one is a resounding *no*.

"If anything comes to mind later, anything at all, please get in touch with us."

"Of course."

"Jem. Chad—" Butch calls out, as Chad returns to me.

I cry again, but harder this time. *What have you done? Why would you do that?* I want to say, but the words are stuck in my throat.

He looks at me, but there's no regret or pain, only defeat.

"I didn't want you to find out like this..." he says as the police lead him out.

The officer turns to me. "Are you okay?"

I nod, unable to speak. My hands are trembling, my head spinning with too many thoughts at once.

The officer must notice my panic, because he asks, "Is there someone you can call to come stay with you tonight? Any family nearby?"

"Y—Yeah," I manage to reply.

When the door closes with a heavy thud, the tears come silently. I hold Chad tightly in my arms, not letting go, even as the sound of the sirens fade into the distance.

How could I not have known?

Pulling back slightly, I brush the hair from his damp cheeks. "Are you okay?"

He nods hesitantly but doesn't speak. I cup his face, pressing a kiss to his forehead. "Everything's going to be okay," I promise, even though I'm not sure how. "I've got you."

"But where's Dad?" he asks, his little face wearing a confused expression. "Will he come back?"

"I don't know, honey," I answer honestly.

His lip quivers as he takes a deep breath, leaning back into my arms. I need to be strong for him, even if I feel like I'm falling apart. After a few minutes, I take him to the sofa and turn on his favorite show. I rub his back as he nestles into the cushions. "I'll be right here, okay? I just need to make a quick call."

He nods again, his eyes already glued to the screen. He's settled and distracted...for now, at least. I step into the kitchen, my hands shaking as I dial my mom, but she doesn't answer. So, I call his parents. They live two and a half hours away, but I need to tell them what happened. When I finally get the words out, they're just as shocked as I am. I try to stay calm, explaining that they're always welcome to visit Chad, but they need to help their son because I can't do it anymore. I share that the front door is now broken, and my father-in-law immediately offers to come fix it. I don't refuse because I can't sleep here until it's done, and I need to keep Chad in the same environment until I figure out what to do next.

While I wait for them to come, I continue making dinner for Chad. I'm no longer hungry though. My mind races, trying to piece together all the little things he's been saying and doing, trying to recall any signs of him using or selling drugs.

I feel so fucking stupid.

Two and a half hours later, my in-laws arrive. They step into the room, and an uneasy silence hangs in the air. I can see the confusion in their eyes, the way they search my face for answers I can't give. I swallow hard. His mother hesitates before meeting my eyes, her lips quivering. I've known her for seventeen years, so I take a step forward, opening my arms. She falls into me, her body trembling as she cries against my shoulder. When she finally pulls back, I turn to my father-in-law. He nods stiffly, his eyes glassy, holding back tears as I embrace him too.

My mother-in-law moves away to play with Chad as my father-in-law replaces the door. I insist they stay for dinner, which Chad loves, because he gets to tell them all about his morning with his dad, making his grandma well up with tears. Once it's late enough, they leave, and I give Chad a bath before tucking him in bed.

"Mom, where did they take Dad?" he asks again, and my heart cracks wide open.

"I'm not sure, honey, but you and I are not going anywhere. We're going to be okay." As I exit his room, I realize I can't keep saying that. Eventually I'll have to explain. But what do I say when I can't comprehend it myself, let alone his little mind?

Ready for a hot shower, I move to the bathroom. I spot Butch's comb, hair gel, toothbrush...all mocking me. The fact that he would bring drugs into our life and house with our son is enough for me to snap. I grab his shit and throw it all in the trash. Opening the cupboards, I clear out his aftershave, razor, and anything else that's his. There's no way I want to look at it. I should've given it all to his parents, but I wasn't thinking clearly, and I don't want them coming all the way back for useless shit they can pick up from Target.

I sit at the edge of our unmade queen bed and feel a little better after throwing it all away. There's a photo of us on our wedding day on the nightstand—a time when we were happy. Tears stream down my face as it hits me. I'm alone. I feel a weird numbness as if I'm empty inside.

How could he do this to us?

I can't seem to stop sobbing until exhaustion takes over, so I put the picture on the side table, facing down. I don't want to look at it. Lying down in the bed, the smell of him hits me hard. I roll over, and looking at his side of the bed makes my chest tight. I imagine him there. It's so vivid that it makes my stomach churn. I get up, grab a clean blanket from the cupboard that doesn't stink of him, move down to the sofa, and cry myself to sleep.

Chapter 1

Jemima

When I open the front door, my mom walks in, full of floral perfume and sunshine. She pulls me into a warm hug, her arms wrapping around me tightly. "There's my girl," she says, her voice soft and full of love. "You look beautiful, as always."

She's wearing a flowing, multi-colored kaftan that shimmers in the light, white oversized sunglasses on top of her head, and gold bangles that jingle with every movement. Her hair's styled in loose waves, and she's grinning like she's won the lottery.

"Guess who's finally taking life by the reins!" she announces as her eyes sparkle with excitement.

"Mom?" I blink at her, trying to make sense of what she's saying.

She drops her purse on the counter, then spins around like she's on a stage. "Me, darling! I'm talking about me.

Your dad has been gone for a while, and I've decided I'm going to sell the house. I can't sit around waiting for life to happen. Nope! Your dad and I always talked about going on a cruise to Alaska, so I booked one. I leave in four weeks!" She beams.

My smile freezes on my face as my heart sinks into my stomach. Of course I'm happy for her, but it's like the universe decided to pile on just one more thing. "That's... great, Mom. I'm happy for you."

"I knew you'd understand," she says, oblivious to the strain in my voice. She's already pulling something from her bag. A small silver key, which she places on the counter in front of me. "But before I head off, I've got something for you."

I stare at the key like it's a puzzle I'm supposed to solve. "What's this?" I ask slowly, glancing up at her.

"It's for the office, silly. Recaredo Events is yours now." She's smiling like she's handing me the world's best gift. "I've had people sniffing around, wanting to buy it, but I thought, 'Why sell it to a stranger when my brilliant daughter's right here?' You've always had a better head for business than I do."

Mom helped with setting up events, but otherwise, it was my dad's company. Mom and dad had been together since they were twenty-one. Forty-two years with the same man, and then suddenly he passed away a year ago from a heart attack. It's the first time she's been on her own. I can imagine she wants to be busy all the time and not be surrounded by reminders of Dad every day. I know that feeling well as I stand in the kitchen I once shared with my ex-husband. The night of his arrest replays in my mind daily. The only reason I haven't left this apartment is to keep Chad's life as normal as possible, which includes our lovely landlords, Jade and Pedro, who help me with Chad. The judge decided to deny Butch bail, which is a relief because I couldn't afford to bail him out anyway.

My stomach twists at the reminder that I was recently laid off from my in-store job at Macy's due to restructuring. I've been applying for other jobs but haven't had any call backs yet. I've been desperate for something. Anything. Butch didn't just leave a broken little boy; it turns out, he also left me a mountain of credit card debt and no savings, too.

Late notices are coming in thick and fast. I've been calling around and asking for a grace period until I'm back on my feet. I've managed to get more time, but I'm angry that he hid it all from me. What kind of marriage is that? *One that's been growing apart...*

"Mom, I don't—"

"Listen," she cuts me off, eyes bright with that carefree energy that's so very her. "I'm not a businesswoman. Never was. Your father was the brains. I was the heart, the one who set up the parties, decorated with balloons and flowers, and made sure the playlists were fun. People loved me, but I'm not going to pretend I'm cut out for spreadsheets and payroll. And since your dad's been gone...well, it's been a mess. I've let some of the staff go. The business is just... It's not what it was. But you? You've got a mind for this stuff. I've seen it." She taps her temple like she's had some grand idea.

I haven't set foot in the office since I met Butch.

I'm still staring at the key, my fingers itching to pick it up, but my brain's screaming at me not to. "Mom, this is a lot. I—I've never run a business."

"So? Nobody's born knowing how to run a business. You'll learn. You're smart, Jemima. Smarter than I ever was when it comes to this stuff. Your dad always said so, didn't he?" Her eyes soften, and for a second, she's not the larger-than-life social butterfly in neon colors, she's just my mom, missing her husband.

Her confidence in me makes my throat tighten. "Mom, I—"

"Look, darling." She places her hands on my shoulders, eyes locked on mine. "I'm not saying you have to do it. But it's a chance. If you don't want it, I'll sell the business. But I'd rather see you make something of it. I know you can. I've seen you fight through so much already."

Tears sting my eyes, but I blink them back. I'm not going to cry. Not now. "Okay," I say softly, my voice sounding more sure than I feel. "I'll give it a shot."

"That's my girl!" she says, and then she's back to grinning, arms thrown wide. As she hugs me tightly, her bangles clink against my back. "You're going to do great things, I just know it."

Her eyes twinkle with excitement as she pulls back. "Now, where's my grandson?"

"In the living room," I answer.

Mom heads off. I watch her go, and warmth spreads through me. I hear Chad giggle as she must've scooped him up into her arms.

I pick up the key, my thumb tracing its cool, smooth surface. It's small but full of so much potential. My chest tightens with something between fear and hope. I'm not ready for this. But I can't keep crying myself to sleep every night hoping things will change. I have to be the one to change them.

"Mom," Chad calls, his voice piercing the early morning silence.

My eyes snap open, adrenaline spiking as I rise from the sofa. My feet shuffle across the creaking wooden floors as I head toward his room. As I rub the sleep from my eyes, the wall clock glares back at me. It's only five a.m.

"Hey, honey," I murmur, lifting his blankets and sitting beside him. "Shh, go back to sleep." He comes closer, his small arm wrapping around my stomach, seeking comfort. I gently stroke his messy brown hair, in a soothing rhythm, and watch as he drifts back to sleep. I close my eyes and lean back against the headboard. It's not as uncomfortable as the lumpy sofa, but I can't seem to bring myself to sleep in the bed I shared with Butch; his betrayal hurts too much. Closing my eyes, I attempt to grab a few more hours of sleep before the day pulls me back into reality.

I'm unable to fall back asleep, so I quietly slip out and watch his little body curl up peacefully for a moment. With a soft smile, I move to the bathroom to take a shower. The persistent drip from the leaky faucet reminds me of yet another repair in my future. I can't ask my landlords to fix it because I still owe them rent. The two-bedroom apartment in Melrose is falling apart, but it's all I can afford. I push aside my worries, taking a quick, warm shower before heading to the kitchen to make some coffee.

Sitting on the sofa, I sip my warm coffee, cherishing the rare silence. Nights here are disrupted by my next-door neighbor, who brings home a new woman every night.

As the quiet surrounds me, memories of the last few months flood my mind. *The police, drained bank accounts, credit card debt, etcetera...*

Just as the image of my ex in this apartment flashes before me, Chad shuffles out of his bedroom, rubbing his sleepy eyes. I lower my coffee cup and open my arms, ready for our morning hug, the start of our new routine. I'm dressed in black pants, a black top with lace trim, and a black jacket. I prepare his breakfast and our lunches, tidy up, and choose his outfit for the day.

As he finishes breakfast, I add a touch of mascara, and some blush to my cheeks and lipstick before telling Chad to get ready, so we can head out.

In the lobby, Jade and Pedro, the apartment owners, who are both in their late sixties, warmly greet us. I smile and they wave me over.

"Morning." The lump in my throat grows, remembering the amount of money I owe these lovely people. Not me... My ex. I thought he was paying the rent, but it seems all our money, including our savings, was used for his secret addictions. I expect them to ask me for the money but instead, they surprise me.

"We can take Chad to school, if you'd like?" Jade offers with a warm smile. "It's your first day at the new job."

I shake my head. "It is, but I don't want to bother you."

One thing I was never prepared for was how hard it was going to be as a single parent. I literally have to do everything. I don't get hobbies or time for myself because, one, I don't have money, but two, I have Chad all on my own. Butch wasn't a great father, but I could at least leave Chad to head to the shops, clean the house, or get my hair colored.

"Nonsense. We love it." Jade smiles.

Chad is smiling beside me, unfazed by our conversation.

"It's on our way," Pedro insists.

I contemplate the offer because it means I won't be late meeting Mom. "If you don't mind."

Jade touches Chad's shoulder. "We'll look after you. Kiss Mom goodbye so she can go to work."

I squat and give Chad a big cuddle and kiss. He scrunches his face up as if he's embarrassed about getting a kiss from me. Rising again, an older guy with black and grey hair approaches.

Jade's face beams as she rushes out, "Oh, Jemima, this is my son Haiden."

The one they—including Chad—keep mentioning to me. Haiden's expression tightens, his eyes briefly flicking to me before settling somewhere into the distance. He barely nods, lips pressed into a thin line. Disinterest radiates off him, and I'm relieved. I'm glad he isn't interested in me either, because I couldn't think of anything worse than trusting another man again.

At first, I was reluctant to have Haiden around Chad, but Jade assured me she'd always be there, and that it was just for basketball since it's too much for Pedro at his age. "Could we play some basketball?" Chad asks, shoving his ball toward Haiden.

Haiden shuffles in his black work shoes and crisp gray suit. "I can't today. I've got work, and you have to go to school."

Moments like these fill me with anger. I wonder if Butch ever thought of us while he was doing God knows what, selling drugs to strangers and putting his family at risk. I doubt we ever crossed his mind. I doubt he thought about his wife and child having to watch him be taken away by the police. Our bank accounts drained. Now I'm left alone, stuck in this apartment with nothing but painful memories keeping me up all night.

I swallow the nasty words I want to call Chad's asshole father and focus on the good times. There was a point when I loved him, and he was a good father. I just wish I knew why and when he picked up his drug habit. However, I'm not willing to waste my time looking for those answers either. He chose drugs, and I chose my family.

"I'll play with you." Pedro winks at him.

Chad punches the air. "Yesss."

"Okay, I better get to work, and you need to go to school."

Haiden is talking to his dad, and I spot a piece of paper between them. I can't help but wonder if it has anything to do with the plans to sell the apartment complex in the next few months. Jade has been hinting at it lately.

This reminds me that I need to get to work, where I can focus on saving my parents' business so I can afford a new place.

On the subway to Lexington Ave, I pull out my notepad and make a to-do list. I have zero experience in events, and even less running a business. Now, here I am, wrapping my head around my new business, or what I like to call my life raft. I exit the subway to a building in Carnegie, walking the steps dreaming of a new life for me and Chad.

"Mom," I say, hugging her.

She pulls back but keeps a firm grip on my arms, her gaze on me, searching my face. "You ready, darling?"

"More than ever."

CHAPTER 2

JEMIMA

"THIS TIME IN THREE weeks, you'll be off to Alaska," I say to Mom, forcing a smile and ignoring the way my stomach twists into knots.

"Can you believe it," she replies. "I've already packed my sequins and faux furs. You can't cruise to Alaska without looking fabulous!"

"Probably because you gave yourself no time," I say with a laugh, though it sounds a bit unconvincing, even to my own ears.

"Oh, darling, spontaneity is the spice of life! I've spent too many years planning everything down to the last napkin fold. Now, I'm all about last-minute thrills!"

As we approach the office doors, my heart is in my throat. I haven't been here for many years, and Mom said a lot has changed since then. The doors are large and the frosted glass panels give nothing away to what lies behind them. Mom pushes the door open with a squeak, and we step inside. The office space is sparse, with simple white walls, harsh fluorescent lighting, and basic wooden desks that have seen better days. As I take a deep breath, the air smells faintly of old paper and something I can't put my finger on. A makeover is definitely overdue.

We continue walking, our footsteps echoing through the empty hallway, until Mom suddenly stops at the front desk. "Molly, this is my daughter Jemima," Mom introduces me to a woman with platinum-blond hair that shines under the light, her roots a darker color. The sight pulls my attention to my own reflection in the glass nearby. I'm in need of a color, as you can now see pieces of gray peeking through my brown hair.

Molly sits in her office chair, her fingers tapping on the computer as she looks up with a curious smile. Her eyes are a bright blue and stand out against her hair. I walk around her desk, extending my hand. "Call me Jem," I say with a smile.

"Nice to meet you," Molly replies, slipping her hand in mine, her grip firm and her smile warm, which instantly makes my shoulders drop away from my ears.

"Molly, I'm showing Jemima around. Do you have time to help?" Mom asks.

Molly jumps up to her feet, her movements quick and eager. "Sure thing, boss."

"Well, Molly, here's the scoop!" Mom announces with an over-the-top sweep of her hand, like she's a game show host. "Jemima's the new boss! I'm finally retiring to sip mimosas and collect postcards. Isn't it fabulous?"

Molly's eyes light up, her lips parting wider. "This is great news."

Her positive energy is contagious, and I can't help the way it ignites within me.

"Let's give Jemima the grand tour, and then you girls can bond over all the juicy office gossip," Mom says, then struts ahead.

As we walk, Mom explains what everything is or what used to be where. So much has changed since my dad died.

The space feels familiar yet foreign. We pause in the hallway, and Molly's hands lace together in front of her as she speaks, her fingers twisting. "I do have to explain my situation because sometimes my life is a little chaotic."

Mom's eyes shine with understanding, her gaze firmly on Molly. "I'm a single mom," Molly announces.

My eyes widen, and I shift my gaze at Mom before looking back at Molly.

"What's the look for?" Molly asks, her blue eyes narrowing at me.

"I'm a single mom too."

Her face softens, and she steps closer as her eyes search mine. "Did your husband cheat too?"

I shake my head. Her putting herself on the line in such an innocent way makes it easy to confess. "I don't know if mine is better or worse," I snort. "But he was arrested for drug trafficking."

"Well, fuck," she says, her eyes flaring wide before she quickly covers her mouth and mumbles, "Sorry."

I laugh, a genuine, hearty laugh that feels good to do. I haven't laughed much in the last few months...if not longer. There's something about Molly that makes me excited about working here. "It's okay, I was as shocked as you."

Dropping her hand from her mouth, she asks, "How old is your kid?"

"Chad is six. How about yours?"

"Mine's a boy too. Hugo, and he's four."

Talking about Chad makes my chest swell with pride. I never had a mother's group or friends when I had Chad. We moved when he was two, and I found it harder than I had been expecting. Butch was not a very present father because he worked a lot, and I felt lonely and defeated, never really having the time to actually focus on myself.

"This is going to be fun." Molly rubs her hands together.

I smile. "It is."

The sound of a door opening catches my attention. Turning, I see a man in his early fifties confidently walking in.

"Here's Danny. You remember him, don't you, Jemima," Mom says, and Molly mumbles something I don't catch before returning to her seat.

Danny strides over.

"Hi, Danny. It's been a long time," I say, remembering his face from years ago, only he's rougher now. Thinning slicked-back hair, deep wrinkles etched into his skin, and much slimmer, the suit seeming to swallow him up.

"Sure has, Jem," Danny replies with a warm smile. "You've grown up."

Mom takes a step forward, her bangles jingling softly as she places a hand on Danny's shoulder. "Danny here has been my rock since your dad passed," she says, her voice warm and full of gratitude. "I don't know how I'd have managed without him."

Danny waves a hand modestly. "Just doing my part."

"I appreciate that," I say. "Dad always spoke very highly of you."

Danny's expression softens at the mention of Dad, but there's a flicker of something else... disappointment, maybe?

"Your mom keeps telling me about Chord." Danny smiles.

"Chad," I correct gently.

"Sorry, Chad. I'm hopeless with names," he replies, his eyes slightly red, similar to the way Butch's looked. I shake my head. I'm just paranoid and clearly seeing things. I can't help but have a guard up when it comes to people, especially men.

"That's okay."

Mom clears her throat, commanding attention. "Well, here's the big news. Jemima's going to take over the business."

Danny's eyebrows lift slightly, though he quickly recovers. "That's...unexpected," he says in a neutral tone. "I thought you might be selling."

Smiling gently, Mom shakes her head. "Oh, no, darling. This business was always meant to stay in the family. And who better than my brilliant daughter to take the reins?"

"Of course," Danny says after a pause. His voice is calm, but I catch the way his jaw tightens. "I'll do whatever I can to help with the transition."

His professionalism reassures me. "Thank you. I'll need it."

Mom claps her hands together, her bangles clashing and breaking the tension. "Alright, team! We've got loads to cover, but Danny, I just know you'll be Jemima's rock through it all. You've always been such a star!"

He nods, his gaze lingering on me for a moment before shifting to Mom. "You know where to find me if you need anything."

As he walks away, I let out a breath I hadn't realized I was holding. Mom gives me a reassuring pat on the back. "You've got this, darling," she whispers with a wink.

I hope she's right. The tightness in my chest eases, knowing I have their support, and that Molly and Danny will help me transition.

Mom will be here for the week to settle me in, too. Even though it sounds like she doesn't know what's going on. I guess there's nothing like diving in headfirst.

A few days later, I'm walking along the sidewalk to meet with a potential new client. Molly is with me, because it's my first meeting on my own, and I feel more comfortable with her than Danny. Luckily, Danny had a meeting this morning anyway.

The breeze picks up, tugging at my beige coat and sending a shiver down my spine. Leaves swirl around our feet, and I tighten my grip on my notebook, hugging it closer to my chest for warmth.

The city around us buzzes with activity, a mix of cars, people and construction.

"I filed for a divorce," Molly announces suddenly, her voice cutting through the noise.

"You did!" I beam. "I'm so happy for you."

"Will you apply for one?" Molly glances at me.

"I have. The second he was arrested, I looked into it."

She elbows me. "Not wasting a second."

"I did it so I could change my name and Chad's to Recaredo," I explain. "I worry about any more of my ex's debts coming back to haunt me."

It's one of the reasons I have bags and dark circles under my eyes. I barely sleep four hours a night, worry robs me of sleep. I'm a walking zombie.

"I thought my ex cheating on me was bad, but I think your story takes the cake."

I giggle, the sound surprising me. "It does, right?"

"Still doesn't turn me off men," she remarks with a wry smile, her lips curving up at the corners.

I do a double take. "You're kidding, right?"

"No," she says, shaking her head. "I think it was my mistake, thinking a one-night stand would be a great father to my baby."

"That's how you met?" I ask as I picture the scene in my mind.

"And got pregnant," she admits with a shrug, her cheeks flushing slightly.

"Sheesh," I mutter with a shake of my head.

"Yeah, so I just need to be sober when I date." She laughs.

I laugh too. "And have sex."

"Definitely. Or at least know him sober before jumping into bed with him," she adds with a grin, her eyes sparkling with mischief.

"How are you so positive?" I ask, amazed by her resilience. She's joking and laughing, even though she's been hurt. Meanwhile, just thinking about my situation makes my stomach harden.

"Therapy," she says simply.

The idea of therapy hasn't crossed my mind; I've been so busy since Butch's arrest three months ago.

"Have you seen one?" she asks.

I shake my head. "No."

The glass building we need to enter comes into view. The modern skyscraper stands out against the older buildings around it. We slow our walking pace, then pause on the sidewalk to finish our conversation.

"Are you anti-therapy?" she asks, her eyes searching mine.

"Not at all." I blow out a breath that fogs in the cold air. "I just don't know if I'm ready."

She reaches into her purse to pull something out. "Take my therapist's card for when you're ready to book an appointment."

I take the card, staring at how worn out it is. There's no point in making an appointment now. I don't have time. Every spare moment, I've been pouring over the numbers, and paperwork, scrutinizing every expense and revenue stream. The deeper I dig, the clearer it becomes...this place is drowning in debt. I have to focus on making this business profitable, because it's sinking fast into the red.

CHAPTER 3

HARVEY

"Harvey, let's go again," my latest hookup says, her voice high-pitched and echoing off the walls of her dimly lit bedroom.

"Maybe another time."

"Baby, come on," she purrs. *Baby?* I'm older than her... The nickname is making my dick soft. I clearly drank way too much. Work has been a nightmare lately, and I thought I needed a release.

We met earlier at a bar, and I left my friends, Eriq and Gabino, to take her home.

Technically, not my home, because I don't let anyone come to my place, especially not a hookup. So we're at hers, while her roommates are still out partying. As soon as I came in, I noticed her room was a mess. Everything is in shades of pink, including the bedsheets we're on. Make-up is scattered across the vanity, and clothes are thrown every-where...draped over chairs, piles on the floor, and spilling out of drawers.

"One more round," she begs, her voice like nails on a chalkboard.

Fuck me. I need to get the fuck out of here, and fast.

I stare up at the cracked ceiling. I'll get up and get the hell out of here as soon as the room stops spinning.

Her hand wraps around my middle, and she snuggles into me, her naked body pressing against my side. Her skin is warm and slightly sweaty. The smell of my alcohol and her cheap perfume fills the air, making my stomach turn.

"Feel better?" I ask, not because I care, but because it's the right thing to do.

"Yeah, that was amazing. You're amazing," she purrs, her heavy lashes fluttering against her cheeks.

"Thanks." I make the mistake of looking at her again. She's staring at me, clearly waiting for me to say something nice. I force myself to say the next few words. "You were great." The words taste bitter. That's what I get for lying.

"Did you want to lie on the couch?" she asks, her expression hopeful.

I'm about to say maybe, but then she adds, "Also, are you free tomorrow? Maybe you could meet my parents."

Is she fucking kidding?

I barely know her. She doesn't know a single thing about me, other than I work in an office because I was wearing a suit. At the bar, our conversation was me asking, "What's your name?" and her offering, "Let's get out of here."

She was perfect for a night of distraction. A quick fuck to help relieve some stress, and then I can walk away. But now she's giving me stage-five-clinger vibes, so I need to rush out of here quicker than normal.

"Sorry, I'm busy." I get out of bed and grab my clothes. This time, I don't lie. I need to see my dad about my inheritance tomorrow. I didn't want help starting my business, but now I have my heart set on growing. One taste of entrepreneurship has me thirsty for more.

I pull on my pants and shirt, making quick work of my buttons. Her eyes follow my movements as she whines. "Can't you stay for a little longer?"

I don't look back as I head for the door, "Maybe some other time," I say over my shoulder, not bothering to wait for her response. I need to get out of here and get some sleep. Tomorrow, I'll get back to focusing on my future.

It's Monday morning and I'm looking for my father. When I get to my parents' place, Mom tells me he's at Gram's.

They live around the corner from her since she lives alone and is battling breast cancer. You wouldn't know it though because she doesn't act differently, and if you dared to show her sympathy, she'd tell you off.

Dad spends a lot of time with her, especially since Grams is his mom. He and I are close, but not as close as he is with my older brother, Evan. I often feel like I have to prove myself even more because of it. Being the youngest means my family sees me as the kid who needs to grow up.

I step into Grams's living room, which is quiet, and spot him lounging on the sofa by himself. "Where's Grams?" I ask, scanning the room for her familiar figure.

Dad's head lifts from the TV show he's watching, revealing the aging and tired lines on his face. "She went to take a nap."

I nod and settle onto the opposite sofa. The cushions sag under the weight of me.

"What brings you here?" he asks, his eyes narrowing slightly as he studies me. I can tell he's wondering why I'm not at the office.

I adjust the tie around my neck, the fabric suddenly feeling too tight. I loosen it with a tug to try to ease the pressure, then I pull a folder from my briefcase. "I need to talk to you about my inheritance."

Dad shifts, leaning forward on the edge of the sofa. Setting the TV remote down, he gives me his full attention. "What about it?"

"How can I access it?"

His eyebrows pinch, and he leans back, crossing his arms. "What's changed your mind?"

"I'm happy with where my acquisitions business is, but I want to start a new company."

He raises an eyebrow. "What kind of company?"

"A consulting firm." I hand him the folder, which contains a detailed business plan, market analysis, and projections.

The corners of my dad's lips move, but he holds back from grinning as he flips through the pages. The little bit of a smile means he approves.

"And why would you need the money?"

"I want to keep my current assets intact for the acquisitions to keep growing. But expanding to include a firm will need its own building and staff."

He nods thoughtfully, his gaze steady. "I like the idea."

"So, I can have my inheritance?"

"I'm not going to hand it over without seeing that you deserve it," he says firmly. "Evan worked with me for years before he got his share. Oliver was the same with your mom, and Jeremy donated it to the hospital for taking care of Nova."

I run my hand through my hair, pushing it out of my face. "What do I need to do to prove myself?"

Leaning back, Dad rubs his jaw in thought. The silence stretches, broken only by the soft hum of the TV in the background. I watch as his gaze drifts to the papers.

"I want to help you," he finally says. "But I need to be sure you're ready."

"I am," I insist, sitting forward.

With his eyes narrowed, he taps his index finger on the armrest. "You know, when I started out, it wasn't easy. I had to take risks, make sacrifices. It wasn't just about money; it was about strategy and grit."

I nod, sensing where this is going, but wait for him to continue.

"You want your inheritance?" he asks, his voice firm now. "Here's what I propose." A slow smile forms on his face as he pauses again. "Take a failing business and turn it around by your thirty-fifth birthday."

I blink, processing the challenge. Six months. That sounds easy enough... But before I can let his words sink in, he continues.

"But no cash injections," he adds. "Work with what's there. Get your hands dirty. Understand the day-to-day."

I take a deep breath, steadying myself. "And if I fail?"

"You can try again," he says. "When you turn forty."

Forty. That feels like a lifetime away.

"Your brothers are successful. I know you're smart, and I want you to understand what it was like for me when I started. It's tough, and without money, it's even rougher."

"Can I choose any business to help?"

"How about one you've been pitching to acquire any-way?" Dad suggests.

I mentally go through the list of businesses I've been considering for acquisition, the names and details flashing through my mind. Which one could I help save instead?

"One that you don't really want," he adds.

I tap my chin, thinking of the businesses I'm struggling to acquire. "Like an event planning business?"

"Perfect!"

I think about the woman who owns it. Jemima. Her avoidance of my calls makes it clear she won't sell me the business.

But this plan gives me what I want, and I can offer her what she needs.

I rub my hands together. It will be a challenge to get her to agree...but surely, she'll take the help. I won't stop until she does.

"Keep me updated."

I sense he wants to keep tabs on me.

Maybe due to a lack of trust, or just to ensure I follow his rules. The pressure of it weighs on me like I'm constantly living under the shadow of his expectations, having to prove myself. It's frustrating, but I've learned to accept it, for now.

"Do you want to watch the basketball game with me?" he asks, shifting on the sofa.

"I'll watch the first quarter, but then I need to get to work. I've got a business to save."

Dad chuckles. "Your cocky attitude reminds me of myself. I was the same at your age; nothing would stand in my way."

I grin at that piece of knowledge. It feels like a small but significant shift in how I see my dad. Until now, I've always viewed him through the lens of his success, thinking I could never quite measure up. But in this moment, it's like he's seeing me in the same light he once saw himself in. Hungry and driven.

He grabs the remote and changes the channel, and I ease back into the sofa. We don't usually spend time together like this, but since he retired and handed over Lincoln Media to Evan so he could travel with Mom and care for Grams, our relationship is shifting for the better.

I look over at him. I'm glad I came today. I can't wait to show him how I transform Recaredo Events. I imagine how proud he'll feel, knowing I've earned my inheritance through hard work.

CHAPTER 4

JEMIMA

"HARVEY LINCOLN IS ON the line," my mom calls out from the office, her voice calm yet urgent.

She's helping me out this morning because Molly's running late.

I frown, not recognizing the name. "Who's that?"

"He owns Lincoln Acquisitions," she replies, her tone suggesting that I should be familiar with the name.

"Am I supposed to know what that is?" I mutter under my breath, pulling out my phone and quickly typing his name into Google. The search results load, and my frown deepens. Pictures of a handsome, young, rich, and sleek-suited man appear alongside articles with headlines talking about corporate takeovers and aggressive business tactics. Molly usually handles phone calls like this. I'm trying to figure out what to do when Mom rushes out, "Can I transfer him? There's another call coming through."

"Sure," I sigh, even though I don't like the sound or look of him. Google makes him look like a jerk, all smirks and perfectly tailored designer suits.

"Mrs. Recaredo," comes a smooth, rehearsed voice on the line, dripping with false charm.

I bite my tongue, but I can't stop myself. "Ms. Recaredo," I correct sharply, emphasizing the "Ms." I'm no longer married, and I want to make it clear I'm not tied to Butch in any way.

"Sorry, Ms. Recaredo."

Better. "What can I do for you?" I ask, my voice cool and businesslike.

Assuming he wants to book an event, I find some paper and start looking around my messy desk for a pen. But I have no luck. I'll have to get one from Molly when she finally arrives.

"I want to talk to you about Recaredo Events," he continues, his tone dropping the charm to now all business. "I've spoken to your mother."

I freeze, my fingers curling into a fist. No need to get a pen now. "It's not for sale," I bark out, my pulse quickening.

"I've done some research, and I can see the business is struggling. I want to help," he retorts bluntly.

Asshole.

"That's none of your business. It's not for sale. Don't call me again," I snap, then slam the phone down. My hands tremble with a mix of anger and anxiety.

A minute later, there's a soft knock on the door. Molly pokes her head in, her cheeks flushed from hurrying. "What was that about?"

I shake off the exchange and force a smile. "Hey. Just someone wanting to buy the business."

A wrinkle forms between her eyebrows, and she steps into the room.

Her expression makes me ask. "What?"

"You could, you know," she says softly, taking a seat across from me.

"I don't want to."

"I'll be fine, and Danny will too. Don't think about us," she reassures me, her voice gentle but unconvincing. I appreciate how selfless she's being.

"I want this business, so unless you quit, you're stuck with me."

A large smile stretches across her face. "Single moms for the win."

"Well, that depends on how your date goes," I tease, wiggling my eyebrows at her.

Molly has been excitedly talking about a guy she met on a dating app for the past few days. She's been my co-worker for about two weeks now and we are getting closer by the second.

"I'm not planning to settle down," she insists, though a blush tints her cheeks.

"Oh, I know." I've read their messages, and even now, thinking about them, I can't help blushing. He's so descriptive about how much he wants her and what he wants to do with her. Even if it's a hookup, I'm happy for her if that's what she wants. As for me, I could never. It's just not in me to do that. I'll happily be her cheerleader.

"What if he's catfishing me?" She chuckles, trying to sound nonchalant, but I can hear the underlying worry.

"What makes you say that?"

"He looks too good to be true. What if he's photoshopped all his pictures?"

"I don't think guys do that shit," I reply with a shake of my head.

"You don't think so?"

"No, they're not that smart," I say with a wink, watching as she heads back to her desk. But even as I turn back to my computer, I can't shake the thoughts of Mr. Lincoln's offer. The money would be great. I could move out of the apartment and find something better, a place with no memories of my ex. But I need more than money. I have a goal to make something of myself, to prove I'm worth something, and that even as a single mom, I can succeed without a man.

Five hours later, I'm opening my front door, and my breath catches at the sight before me. Molly stands there, model-like in a tight, long-sleeved black dress that hugs her hourglass figure perfectly. Her hips are the kind I've always dreamed of having. "Molly. Wow."

She looks down, then meets my gaze with a wry smile. "So I take it I look good?"

"Good is an understatement." I admire how the dress accentuates every curve. I remember hoping I'd develop nice curves after having Chad, but it never happened.

She straightens, her eyes sparkling with excitement. I wouldn't be excited for a date; instead, I'd feel dread, but seeing her happy makes me happy.

She peers at her watch, her loose waves falling in front of her face. With a shake of her head, she clears them away. "I better go."

"Have fun," I say, smiling.

"Hugo." She bends to peer around me, catching a glimpse of him running off to the living room. "I love you."

He doesn't respond when she waves, too busy playing with Chad. The room is a mess, filled with Lego blocks, cars, trains, and action figures scattered across the floor.

"If you need to bail, go to the bathroom and call me. I'll come and get you."

"I'll be fine. Stop worrying about me."

"I can't help it."

"I'll call you if I need you."

She turns and walks slowly down the stairs in her black pumps, each step carefully measured. The soft clicking of her heels echoes along the concrete. I watch until she disappears from my view, feeling grateful for our newfound friendship that feels a lot like family.

I close the door behind me and head to the room where the boys have now constructed a large train set. Their little faces are bright with enthusiasm, their hands moving quickly to piece together the tracks while they talk.

Watching Chad play happily with Hugo makes me pause.

I once wished for a big family, more kids...but now, I know that will never happen. Chad will never have a sibling, and I'll never get another child. I'm almost forty-three, and I've only just separated from my husband. I'm not in the right headspace to find another partner. Molly's date doesn't make me want to do the same thing. In fact, the thought of dating makes me want to vomit.

As I stand there, I take in the sound of the boys' laughter, their sweet conversation as they finish building the train tracks and move on to something else. I remind myself that, even if my life isn't what I had once envisioned, there's still so much to be thankful for.

CHAPTER 5

JEMIMA

IT'S BEEN A WEEK since Mom left. Each day feels like a struggle just trying to keep things together. The work is dull but necessary, just a constant effort to figure out where to begin with the mess she left behind. I take a deep breath as I step outside, the cool air hitting my face, when I hear it.

"Jemima," a deep voice calls my name.

I look up and see a thirty-something-year-old with longish brown hair and sunglasses, dressed in a perfectly tailored navy suit. He's leaning casually on the hood of a sleek sports car. Pushing off, he strides toward me, commanding my attention.

My heart skips a beat, panic clawing at my throat. How does he know my name? Is he someone my ex knew?

I straighten, even though my legs tremble. He doesn't look like a guy here to collect money, but what do I know about debt collectors? The thought stiffens my spine even more. No, Butch will not ruin my life and make me worry about every stranger I come across. Not everyone is a bad person or a threat.

I relax slightly when he lifts his sunglasses, revealing his face, which I recognize from my search.

Harvey Lincoln.

Cute and cocky, with piercing blue eyes that sear my soul, causing a weird connection between us.

I blink away the lust-filled haze, remembering he's here to try to take my business.

"What do you want, Harvey?"

He flashes me a megawatt smile. I ignore how hot he looks and focus on his purpose for being here.

"I'm here to talk to you," he says smoothly.

"Stalking is illegal, you know," I retort, crossing my arms.

"I'm not stalking you. I just need five minutes of your time." A piece of his hair falls onto his forehead, and he brushes it away with ease.

"I said no…"

"You said no once, and then you hung up on me before I could finish."

My lips twitch as I remember that phone call. "I gave you—"

"Less than five minutes and you've been ignoring my phone calls since."

"You're persistent, I'll give you that." My arms stay crossed as his gaze drops over me, and I try not to care about what he thinks. Who gives a flying fuck what Harvey Lincoln thinks?

"I won't give up," he says, with an unblinking stare. "Ms. Recaredo, let me help you."

Help me? I don't want help. "I've already got employees. I never put out a help wanted ad. I'll be sure to let you know when I expand."

"Don't expand yet." His words come out in a rush as he pushes his hair away from his eyes again. The intensity of his bright gaze makes me falter.

If I were ten years younger...and didn't have a kid...but that's not my life.

I shake my head. "It's my business, Mr. Lincoln. I make the decisions."

"But—" he starts. I turn and head to my car, not wanting to hear another word.

I don't stop until I get to my car. His raspy voice calls out in the distance, "I'll call you tomorrow."

Inside the safety of my car, I take a deep breath. I don't need his help.

He can keep calling me every day, but I won't give up my business. Selling Dad's company feels like losing a piece of him, and the thought makes my stomach turn. I can't help but remember the late-night calls we shared when he was in his office and I was at home with Chad. He poured his heart into this place, and I can still hear the pride in his voice whenever he got a new event. Letting go of Recaredo

Events feels like I'd be betraying his memory—even if it's failing. I just wish I had his strength and guidance to help me turn it around. But I refuse to let his legacy slip through my fingers and into Harvey's greedy hands. I owe my dad that much, and I will fight for it, no matter what.

I thought my day would get better, but it didn't. I hit the steps at home and see Jade and Pedro standing there with worried expressions. Jade has her short silver hair neatly styled, wearing a bright floral top, and her usual smile is replaced with a somber expression. Pedro stands tall with his arms crossed over his usual button-up shirt and slacks.

"I'm so sorry, love," Jade says, extending a piece of paper toward me with a slight tremble in her hands. "I wanted to give you a heads-up as soon as I knew. It's just too much work. I really think it's time to retire."

I take the paper from her hands and glance down, my heart sinking as I read the words "eviction notice" for six months.

"It's probably the push I need to find a new place," I say, putting on a brave face to not upset her. The building is falling apart, peeling paint, cracked plumbing, and barely functioning heating. It's not her fault they want to retire and give it up.

My fingers grip the papers tightly, the edges bending under my grip. This means I have six months to turn the business around, make enough money to pay the overdue rent, and find a new, affordable, and safe apartment for Chad and me.

Suddenly, I feel lightheaded, needing to sit down. Dizzy spells have been hitting me a lot lately. I need to get upstairs and eat something. I don't remember the last time I had anything to eat today.

"I'm still sorry, love. I feel like I'm abandoning you," Jade says, her voice thick and her eyes glassy.

It seems to be a common theme.

"It's okay." I force my lips to tip up. "I'll be fine."

I'm strong. I can get through anything.

"Chad, are you coming? Your mommy's here," Pedro calls out.

Chad runs to me, his small figure twisting with mine as he hugs me tightly. I brace myself for the impact, not wanting Jade to feel any worse if I fall over.

"Hey, honey. How was school?" I ask, rubbing his back.

"Alright, but after school, I played basketball with my friend Domenic," Chad replies, his face lighting up with excitement.

"Did you win?" I ask.

Jade's grinning from ear to ear. She has no grandchildren, and from what she's told me, Haiden's single.

"Yeah, he sucks," Chad says with a grin.

"Chad," I say, trying not to laugh.

"He does need some practice," Pedro adds with a chuckle, his eyes twinkling at Chad.

Spots dance in front of my eyes, and I start to feel sweaty. I need to get upstairs quickly because I can't stand here much longer without falling over.

"Come on, Chad, let's go. We need to get ready for dinner," I say, keeping my voice steady.

"Bye," Chad says and runs up the stairs.

"See you tomorrow, Chad," Jade calls out.

I force another smile, but it feels brittle. "Thanks again," I say, but the words wobble on the edge of my breath. Gratitude barely covers it.

Her eyes narrow with quiet understanding. "Anytime. I love helping you." Her gaze lingers on me a second too long. I bet she sees it... I'm barely holding it together.

I quickly turn and take the stairs on wobbly legs, gripping the brick wall for support. As I enter the apartment, the scent of last night's dinner lingers in the air, reminding me of how I had stretched the last few ingredients to make it. I head straight for the kitchen before I pass out, my stomach rumbling, and grab a piece of bread, chewing it slowly as I lean my hand against the counter. The weight of the eviction notice, the empty fridge, and Harvey's words press down on me like a heavy blanket, making it hard to breathe but I push those thoughts aside and focus on staying strong, determined to get through the evening for my son.

CHAPTER 6

JEMIMA

THE NEXT DAY, I arrive at the office, standing before the door marked with the bold letters *Recaredo Events*. The second eviction notice in two days ignites a new fire of determination in my belly. This business is mine and will someday belong to Chad.

The fact that I'll now be able to leave something for him when I'm gone feels like a weight has been lifted. Before, to no one's fault but my own, he'd be left with nothing, and the heaviness in my gut at feeling like a bad mom weighs me down. But now I'm taking control, and I'll never let a man take care of me again.

As I walk down the long corridor, I think about the pile of financial problems the business is in, unpaid invoices, cash flow problems, vendor debts, and how much Molly and Danny need me to fix it. I'm working through these problems one at a time.

I pause at the desk, where Molly greets me with a casual, "Hey, boss."

I can't help but roll my eyes. "What did I say about calling me that?" I ask, though it's a reminder I appreciate.

She shrugs as she continues typing away. Her ability to multitask is one of the reasons I value her.

I hold my PB & J sandwich, ready to put it in the fridge. "Is that all you brought today?"

"Yeah, I'm not that hungry," I lie, not wanting her to know I don't have much food for myself. It all goes to Chad.

I don't want her to ask any more prying questions, so I change the topic. "How was your weekend?"

It was the first time that Molly's ex had their child on his own, meaning she had some of the weekend to herself. With a sigh, she pauses her typing and turns to face me. "Exactly what I thought it would be," she confesses, a hint of sadness in her voice. I frown as I wait for her to share more. "Awful," she admits.

My heart drops, imagining what exactly went so wrong. Was it issues with Hugo or her date? "What happened?"

"Well, for starters, I missed Hugo. Every single day for four years, I've had him all to myself. That's over fourteen hundred days..." Her eyes suddenly fill with unshed tears. "Now I'm supposed to share him with my ex. How the heck do I do that?"

"Oh girl, I get it. But you deserve some time to yourself. To just be you. So tell me about that date you looked so amazing for."

A smile spreads across her face, and I can't help but feel so glad it went well.

"It was...interesting." Her lips twitch, fighting a grin.

"Interesting, how?" I prompt, leaning forward. "Details, please."

Molly's eyes brighten as she starts retelling the story. "So the guy was nice. Polite and cute enough. But halfway through dinner, he sneezes so hard a booger lands right in his pasta."

A gasp escapes, and I cover it with my hand. "No!"

"Swear on my life," she laughs. "He's scrambling to wipe his face with his napkin, and the poor guy smears more all over his face."

I'm laughing so hard that my sides hurt. "Did he recover?"

"Barely," Molly wipes her eyes. "He was so flustered."

"Did he try to kiss you at the end of the date?"

She scrunches up her nose. "God no. I would've died if he tried." When she pretends to gag, I laugh again.

"At least he took your mind off Hugo," I murmur honestly, trying to picture not having Chad biweekly. I shake my head. I couldn't do it.

"I guess I'll get used to it," she mumbles.

"Are there any classes or hobbies you've always wanted to try but couldn't?" I suggest, hoping to help her.

"Yoga."

"You should do it then," I say, sitting on the edge of her desk.

She snorts. "I don't want to, but I need to."

I drop my gaze over her figure. She's beautiful. I don't understand the reference to her flaws. "You don't need to do anything," I reassure her.

She touches her lower stomach over her black pants. "I have a pouch."

"So do I."

I have a C-section scar too, so the pouch is a little bigger.

"I'm not ready to let anybody see me naked."

I lean in, my voice firm. "You deserve someone who accepts you just the way you are. That pouch? It brought you one of the most incredible gifts. As moms, we sacrifice our bodies, but we gain more than we could ever imagine. If a man doesn't see the beauty in that, he's not worthy of you."

As the words leave my lips, I have to bite back my disdain and swallow my own insecurities threatening to choke me. This is why I can't waste my time trying to date again. They don't want a 42-year-old single mother who has nothing to offer. Hey, you want some debt? I got mountains of that... Love and trust, though? I have neither.

"I know," she says, quietly.

"You gotta love yourself before loving anyone else," I say.

She raises an eyebrow at me, a teasing smile tugging at her lips. "I think you should take some of your own advice."

"I won't be dating any time soon, so the way I look is not really on my mind right now."

"No, but you're all about work and Chad. Who is Jemima?"

"A business owner." I grin proudly, shoving aside the tired version of me. "Speaking of, I better get into my office and get started."

"Jem," Danny calls out from his office, just as I'm pushing off Molly's desk.

A shudder runs through me at the sound of the nickname, but I brush it off, turning and heading toward his doorway with a smile. "Hey, Danny."

He smiles back. "A new client emailed; I forwarded it to you."

My eyes widen, and I have to stop myself from running into my office and reading it. Instead, I take a deep breath, square my shoulders, and smile. "Thanks." Telling myself to slow down and not to get my hopes up, I take a breath.

"I also came up with some design concepts," he adds yelling down the hallway as I walk to my office.

I take a seat in my cold leather chair and power on the computer to immediately read it.

A small baby shower. Cute. But I can't help but be deflated. It's not going to make the money I need to rent a new apartment. A few extra items of food? Yes, and as if on cue, my stomach rumbles. I drink some water, knowing I don't have a snack, only lunch, so I begin working. I'm picking up the books where I left them yesterday.

Hours later, Molly calls out.

"Jem?"

"Yeah," I say, still reading the old invoice and typing it into the spreadsheet.

"Harvey's on the line."

Harvey?

Oh, fuck off.

I close my eyes and take another deep breath.

"Tell him I'm busy," I reply, irritated.

"He seems adamant," she calls back.

I shake my head, trying to focus on the task before me. "Just tell him I'll call him back."

"He's got a hot voice."

I scoff internally but keep my lips sealed at what he looks like in person.

"Like a phone sex operator." Her voice interrupts my daydream.

It suddenly dawns on me; can he hear all this?

"Is he still on the line?" I rush out.

"Yeah, he's on hold. Why, do you want to talk to him?"

Do I?

"No."

Chapter 7

Harvey

I pinch the bridge of my nose, attempting to settle the rising anger coursing through me. Why won't she answer my calls? We've had one heated argument about me wanting to help her business, yet she refuses to even entertain the idea. She keeps shutting me down at every turn.

Restlessly pacing my office, I'm interrupted by the loud ring of my work phone. I storm across the gray plush rug to my marble and timber-legged desk to answer the call. I run a hand through my swept-back hair, before settling into the chair, and resting my hand on my suit pants.

"Harvey," I answer, my tone clipped as I struggle to maintain composure.

"You have a meeting at one in Manhattan. The driver is downstairs when you're ready."

"Thanks, Esme," I reply curtly, my mind still reeling from thoughts of Jemima.

"Before you go, um," she stammers.

"Yeah?"

"Would it be okay if I left early?"

My eyebrows pull together. "Why?"

"My daughter has a temperature; I need to pick her up from school."

That is the exact reason why I'm nowhere near ready to have kids. They interrupt your life at any given time. Hence why I've stuck with flings. It keeps me focused on my goals.

"Sure," I reply, hanging up.

Attempting to distract myself before I head into the meeting, I turn to my emails, but my mind still drifts to the feisty brunette. I need a game plan to break through her defenses.

Who better to ask than one of my brothers?

The question is, which one?

Jeremy, like me, didn't receive one of our parents businesses. I'm not jealous of Oliver, who took over Mom's gallery, or Evan, who took over Dad's media business, because our parents have money for us to support our own business adventures. Jeremy built his own empire; he started as an ophthalmologist and then become a hospital chain owner. As for me, I started with college, where I completed a Master of Science in Business Administration, and then worked for a company, where I gained industry experience, before venturing out on my own almost five years ago. Where I'm my own boss and buy other businesses to turn them around. We're having a black-tie networking cocktail event this Friday, and the focus will be on mingling, showcasing recent acquisitions, and fostering connections between investors and industry leaders.

Shutting down my computer, I make my way out of my office, nodding to Esme. The car is waiting downstairs, which will take me to my first meeting.

An hour later, I'm walking away after they successfully approved our proposal, so now we can move on to drafting a contract. Next task of the day is Recaredo Events…

On the way, I call Jeremy. He'll help me work through this roadblock with Jemima.

I've never encountered anything like this before. People never say no to me; they're usually willing to do anything for me. But Jemima's different. She's saying no, and I don't know how to change her mind.

He answers on the first ring. "Harvey. What can I do for you?"

"I need some advice."

"Go on."

I run my hand along my freshly shaved jaw. "I have a client who's running out of time to pay their debt to the lenders. Dad's given me an ultimatum. He wants me to turn this small business around, and I only have six months to do it."

"Why are you worried? He gave you six months."

"She's been saying no for fucking weeks."

"Weeks," he barks, like he thinks I'm stupid and irresponsible.

I close my eyes briefly, sneering. "No need to yell, I get the fucking point."

"She's hot," he smartly remarks, drawing my attention. "That's got to be it."

Her high cheekbones, long brown hair, and honey eyes I could get lost in, invade my mind.

I snort in an attempt to dismiss his assumption. "Pretty or not, she's a pain in my ass. And I need her to fucking listen to me."

He chuckles down the line, which irritates me further, causing me to snap. "Focus, please."

"Do you want her business or is this to show Dad you can do this?" he probes thoughtfully.

"I have zero desire to run an event business. A failing one, at that," I assert as my frustration builds.

Jeremy hums, as if he's thinking. Exiting the elevator, I walk through the lobby, and I tug at my black vest, smoothing my black jacket, before nodding at my waiting driver and slipping into the backseat. "Buy her flowers."

I raise an eyebrow sceptically. "It's not a fucking date."

"Trust me. It'll work," he insists.

"Based on what?" I challenge, though a small part of me is entertaining the idea.

"I've been around longer..." Jeremy begins, but his voice trails off, hinting at past experiences. *A time before Nova*

I let out an audible sigh, as I give in to the idea. "Flowers. Right."

Pulling my phone away from my ear, I direct my driver to head to a florist before my surprise upcoming meeting with Ms. Recaredo later this afternoon.

Jeremy gives me a list of flower names. I've never heard of them. I thank him for the tip and let my brother get back to his day.

We pull up to the curb outside the florist's... Bloom & Ivy. Noticing my apprehension to get out, my driver offers to buy them. He'd probably buy her a bouquet of roses, giving her the wrong idea. Nope, I need non-romantic flowers, so if I leave it up to other people, not only will it backfire, but she'll eat me alive.

Climbing out, I enter the flower shop. This is my first time. I've never brought flowers for any of my flings, since my focus has always been on building a name for myself.

I'm just as good as my older brothers. I'm the youngest and I feel like I have to prove myself. My parents have never made me feel less than. These are just feelings I struggle with deep inside. Relationships are a distraction. One I can't afford. My focus needs to stay on the reward my dad will give me at the end of this deal.

As I scan the mountain of flowers my brother suggested, I wonder how I'm supposed to choose the right one for her. My gaze settles on a cluster of purple flowers, their uniqueness drawing me in. I even find the name ranunculi to be odd. After staring at them for a long time, the sales assistant comes over to offer me a hand, and all I want to do is leave. I ask for a large bouquet. She asks what for, and usually, I hate unnecessary small talk, but these flowers need to work. So I explain it's to impress a woman, but my tone drips sarcasm, leaving the sales assistant looking at me, bewildered.

Grateful to be leaving the shop, I take in the fresh, cool New York air, but at the same time, the buttery floral smell from the bouquet hits me at full force. They smell surprisingly good. Jemima's thorny. Maybe I should've stuck with roses. But with no more time, I settle back into the car.

Ten minutes later, I run my hand through my hair, ready to come head-to-head with the new owner of Recaredo Events.

Stepping out of the car, I take in the glass building and its surroundings. Broadway is prime real estate for a new business. Setting my shoulders back, I stride in, holding the bouquet as if I do this all the time. I need to win her over.

I arrive at the large doors with frosted glass panels with her business name stuck on the front in bold letters. At least it's not peeling, unlike the paint.

Not bothering to knock, I push the door open with a squeak and follow the soft voices. A familiar voice is mumbling into the phone. It's Molly, her receptionist. I've spoken to her numerous times. She's always apologizing, but she never puts me through to Jemima. She seems to be around my age, with blonde hair that falls in loose waves just past her shoulders. Pushing her tortoiseshell-framed glasses up her nose, she twists her chair to face me. I stand in front of her wearing a lop-sided grin. My signature one will be sure to win her over.

"Good afternoon."

Her eyes drift over my outfit but don't get very far. Her gaze pauses on the enormous bunch of flowers I'm holding.

"Well, good afternoon, Mr...?"

"Harvey Lincoln."

Her eyes almost bulge out of their sockets before glancing over her shoulder in the direction of another doorway. My guess... Jemima's office.

"You don't have an appointment," she murmurs.

My mouth tugs up a little more. "I don't need one, do I?" I look around the quiet, empty office space. "Good thing it's not very busy."

Her eyes drop to the flowers again. "I've never seen flowers like these before."

I nod, holding back a chuckle when her lips part. Maybe Jeremy is right.

"Ranunculi," I answer her silent question.

"Never heard of them."

"I need to speak with Jem."

"She's out," she rebuts quickly.

I know I heard two voices when I walked in.

"Are—" My question dies on my lips when the brunette walks out holding papers and talking. Jemima stops walking the moment her gaze settles on me.

"Hi." I wink like the smartass I am.

"What are you doing here?" she asks.

"We need to talk."

"I'm busy." She holds up her papers.

"I bet." She's probably digging through everything to find a pot of gold. But this isn't *The Wizard of Oz* and I'm no Tin Man.

I'm known as the determined one, yet with this honey-eyed woman, I seem to be a little weak, especially when she wears an outfit like this. My gaze trails from her black pumps, up her long legs covered in a black suit, stopping at the lace trimming her top. Drinking in her exposed neck, then her pink pouty lips, my eyes land on her hard glare.

"Is delivering flowers a lucrative side gig?" she says, teeth catching her lip as her brow furrows.

I chuckle. "No. They're for you."

"Why?"

"Don't women usually say thank you?" I grip the stems harder.

"I don't."

I laugh. I knew I should've picked up a thorny bush. It would've been helpful if Jeremy told me what to say to her because I have no idea what to do next, and I don't want to fuck up this moment.

"I know. But still, take them and put them somewhere."

"You mean a vase."

I don't care if she leaves them with her assistant, who is currently bouncing her eyes between us. I bet she's enjoying the show.

"Can we talk in your office?" I ask, holding the flowers out to her. She hesitates before grabbing the bouquet from me, spinning on her heel, and storming into her office. She doesn't sniff them or admire them. Following her, I watch as she pulls a vase, fills it with water, unwraps the flowers, and sets the stems into the water. She leaves them there without another glance. But before I take a seat, I grab them and place them on her desk.

She frowns. "Why did you do that?"

"You look like you need them to brighten your day."

"What would brighten my day, Mr. Lincoln, is if you'd leave me alone."

I smirk. "You know I can't do that."

She rolls her eyes and folds her arms over her chest. "You can."

I pull out the chair and take a seat, easing back into the worn leather.

"Don't get too comfortable."

"I wouldn't dare." I bite back a grin.

She huffs and mumbles under her breath. It's cute how flushed her cheeks are. I get under her skin. Well, she's not the only one; she gets under my skin too.

"I want to help you pay your debt."

Her eyes narrow. "Why?"

Do I tell her about the deal with my dad?

Her piercing glare would have anyone squirming in their chair. I find it weirdly attractive. Her confidence draws me in. It's at this moment I realize the one thing I haven't done yet is be honest with her. The flowers got me in here. I can't waste this opportunity.

I fix my gaze on hers. "My dad won't release my trust fund unless..."

Fuck, this is humiliating. I scratch the back of my neck.

Her face softens. "Unless what? You get married? Because that's a hard no."

I shake my head. That would be easy...

"You wish."

Her lips purse. "I think this conversation is over."

I've clearly upset her.

It's now or never.

The clock is ticking. I have less than five months left. I've never failed at anything before. I will not lose this opportunity because I'm afraid of being honest. No fucking chance. So I swallow my pride and spill.

"I have six months to help you make your business profitable. Well, five now that you've blown me off for weeks."

Her head lifts. Curiosity settles on her face, and that's all I need to see to keep talking.

"You're a Lincoln, don't you have plenty of money?" Her eyes drop briefly over my designer suit.

"Not for what I want."

Her eyebrow quirks. "What do you want?"

I exhale heavily. "A consulting firm, and I want my trust fund money to create the company."

"Why this company? Can't you find another one?"

"No, my dad wants me to make Recaredo Events successful. He believes it will have more merit if I turn around a business I don't particularly enjoy."

She stays silent, and I think it might be working, so I keep talking.

"My dad said I can't try again for six years if I fail, so I can't let that happen."

"And you think you could help me?"

"Definitely."

"You can't throw your money around here and fix things."

I chuckle darkly. "I know. He wants me to start from square one without throwing cash at the problem."

"And that irritates you."

"You have no idea." I want to explain to her this whole situation irritates me, but she's distracting me by nibbling on her lip.

While she struggles internally, I take this opportunity to ask more business questions.

"How long have your parents owned this?"

I know these answers, of course, as I've researched the business, but I want to show her how serious I am.

"It was originally my grandparents'."

"How did it get into so much debt?"

She peers down at her desk before rolling her shoulders back. "My dad died, and my mom tried to take over. It's a mess."

I nod, sensing that it's bothering her.

"Two eyes are better than one."

"I don't think so…" she mumbles under her breath.

She's still on the fence, so I need to show her I'm willing to help find events she can host to repay the debts.

That's when I have a brilliant idea.

"I'm also here to invite you to attend a networking cocktail event for my company."

She blinks. "Why would I go?" she argues. "You don't need to rub my nose in your successful business."

"Maybe you can form some connections and help your business."

"You're helping me with your money."

"That's untrue. There'll be potential clients. Just come and bring your business cards."

"Your tone isn't convincing me that you want me there."

I suck in a deep breath through my nose. "Fine. Ms. Recaredo, I would like you to attend the event, this Friday, at my office?"

"I'll think about it."

"You're impossible," I mumble. Suddenly, I remember the nickname for the flowers, *buttercup*. I stand there, wanting to leave a mark, just like the way her molten eyes leave an impression on me. I lean toward her, my hands resting on the edge of her desk, bracketing her in. She gasps audibly. My face is only an inch away from hers, and fuck, this might have been a mistake, she smells so sweet. I lick my lips, our gazes locked. I reach down and grab my business card, holding it up to her. She snatches it and slowly leans back, but her chair stops her from going too far.

"If you show up at my event on Friday, I'll take that as a yes, buttercup." I wink, then push off the desk and stride out the door.

CHAPTER 8

JEMIMA

MY MOUTH HANGS OPEN as I stare at the space he just walked out of. I bring my fingertips to my lips, still feeling the warmth of his breath. His scent lingers, pine and fresh as if he's been wandering through the woods.

"What did he want?" Molly practically skips in.

I shake my head, still rattled by his powerful presence, but I swallow my nerves before Danny returns from his lunch break. I would prefer to keep this to myself until I figure out the right thing to do.

"He wants to help me sort this out." I gesture at the scattered papers around the room.

Molly says, "Eek," and claps like a schoolgirl.

I roll my eyes at her reaction. "I can't accept his help."

I can't risk him taking over the company and worse working alongside his cocky self. He cannot be trusted.

"Why?" Walking over, she takes the spot Harvey just left.

I stand up and walk around my desk, gripping the edge as I feel a head rush from standing too quickly.

"Are you okay?"

"Yeah, I just need water."

"Here." She hands me my water bottle. "Maybe eat something too."

Checking the time, I realize it's not lunch yet. "No, I'll work on this baby shower concept then eat."

"He invited you to a party?"

It's a networking event. I shouldn't be surprised she eavesdropped. The door was left open and, of course, she would be curious. I would be too, if a handsome, tall young man came into our office to talk to her.

"I'm not going."

Molly's smile falls. "Why?"

Because if I go that means I accept his help with Recaredo Events.

"I can't have him here telling me what to do."

Trying to take over.

"Is that what he said he was going to do?"

I sigh. "Not in those words. He did bring up the networking side, which I'm interested in, but..."

"Have you thought about just trying it out?"

"No," I mumble, thinking about it.

"You can always tell him to shove it if it's not working. But I think you should consider Chad in this decision."

My heart squeezes, as if she knew the right words to wear me down.

"Fine. But I still can't go to the event."

"Why not?"

"Single mom, remember? I can't ask Pedro and Jade to babysit last minute."

"I'll do it. Hugo would love to have Chad sleep over. Plus, I owe you one."

"Two kids for a whole night is a lot," I say, giving an excuse.

She waves me off. "They go to sleep at seven-thirty. I'll be fine. Stop making excuses."

The corner of my lip lifts. "What will I wear?"

She wiggles her brows at me. "A sexy dress."

I giggle. "Of course."

"What are we giggling about?" Danny asks, as he strolls back in, standing in front of us, his eyes flicking between us.

"Nothing," I say at the same time Molly answers.

"Mr. Lincoln wants to help the business succeed and wants the boss lady here to attend his party with an answer."

I don't bother correcting her wrong recollection. My showing up *is the answer* and he has no idea I'm coming unless I don't show up at all.

I glance at the email exchange with *him* earlier today.

Harvey: 55 Wall Street. 6pm.

To get under his skin, I email a sassy reply back.

Me: Do I get a plus one?

He replies instantly.

Harvey: No.

Me: What if I promise they'll behave?

Harvey: I'm not convinced you'll behave.

Me: Who, me? I'm a model guest.

Harvey: *I'm not so sure about that.*

Me: *I'll show you tonight.*

Harvey: *I can't wait.*

Flirting is a fun distraction, but I don't have time for all this. So as soon as I get close to the address, I message Molly to check in. My stomach twists with nerves, so if Chad needs me, I'll have an excuse to leave.

Jemima: *Is he alright?*

Molly: *He's fine! Stop messaging and go have fun.*

Jemima: *I'm here to work.*

Molly: *Well, do that tomorrow. Tonight have fun. I promise to call if I need you. Otherwise, I'll see you in the morning.*

Stuffing my phone in my purse, I take a moment to gather myself, rubbing my hands together. Not because it's a cold night, but to shake some of my sudden nerves.

The noisy hustle and bustle of workers surrounds me, car horns blare in the distance, and I pause on the sidewalk across the road. I feel a rush of anticipation mixed with trepidation.

I don't know anyone besides Harvey. But here in the hustle of the city, I find myself thinking of the potential work opportunities this party may bring. *I just need a couple of decent events to host and figure out what went wrong, and continues to go wrong, with my company's finances.*

I'm taking control of my life, and it includes tonight. I'll accept his help, but the bottom line is, it's still *my* company. He can't come in and take over. I've lost everything because I let my ex do that. So I'll never make that mistake again.

Crossing the road, I can't help but admire the skyscraper. The city views from such a prestigious location must be incredible.

As I pass security, they nod at me in acknowledgment, and I step into the lobby. The building is sophisticated, with lights highlighting the polished marble floors. Inside, a dark-purple haired woman greets me with a warm smile, asking for my name before directing me upstairs to the event.

I enter the elevator with a few other guests, glad I chose a nicer slim black dress from Molly and straightened my hair, after seeing the couple next to me. They ooze elegance. The woman is in a floor-length emerald-green dress with her hair tied up into a neat bun, showing off her dazzling diamond earrings. Her companion wears a black velvet suit with an emerald-green bow tie, in the same shade as her dress.

When the doors open, I let them lead, mesmerized by their graceful movements, suddenly feeling out of place in my borrowed dress and old shoes. They hold hands, their connection palpable. I don't even remember what it would feel like to do that. I can't help but feel a pang of longing. Butch and I hadn't been out together since before Chad was born. By the end, intimacy was just a distant memory.

Entering a grand ballroom, I take in the soft glow from the large chandelier, the decor is rich fabrics and luxurious furnishings around the space. The linen color is a little too dark here, but it's not my event...

Servers pass me with trays of yummy pastries, the smell wafting through the air, tempting me.

Just as I'm about to grab one, the sound of Harvey's deep, guttural voice interrupts me.

"Hey, partner."

I close my eyes briefly, take a deep breath to compose myself, and turn to face him, ready to snap. "We're not partners."

"Then what are we if we aren't working on your business together?"

"Acquaintances."

I can't help but let my eyes wander over him. His black tuxedo fits him like a glove, accentuating his broad shoulders and tapered waist. I've got to admit, he's dangerously handsome in this outfit.

"Are you sure about that?" His eyebrow is arched, his gaze piercing mine with an intensity that sends a shiver down my spine.

He totally catches me checking him out. I've seen him before, but this time, I'm really taking it all in. I can't help it; Molly's been gushing about how hot he is and made me promise to give her every detail about him tonight.

"Very," I reply.

"Well, come on. Let me introduce you to some people." The twinkle in his eye says that he means business, and with that, I find myself drawn back toward the crowd.

A server with drinks stops us, and I go to grab champagne, but then I remember I'm about to meet potential clients, so I retract my hand. I need to keep my mind sharp.

Harvey leads me with a gentle hand on my lower back toward a woman with short brown hair, who introduces herself, then goes on to explain to me that she has a birthday coming up and she's planning to invite over one hundred people. Of course I'm thrilled to hand over my business card. We arrange to discuss the details next week.

I meet a few more people, each interaction fuelling my determination to succeed. Then, I'm introduced to a man in a sharp black suit who seems oddly familiar. I wonder if we've met before.

"Jemima, this is my brother, Oliver," Harvey introduces.

Now I know why he's so familiar. *My Google research.*

"Nice to meet you," I say with a polite smile.

Another two men join them, all dark-haired, and before I can even take a guess, Harvey introduces them.

"These are my other two brothers, Evan and Jeremy."

"Nice to meet you all," I say to the group.

They all nod and greet me back, their expressions a mix of curiosity and amusement.

"You all look alike," I comment, noticing the striking resemblance among the brothers.

"Our dad's genes are strong," Oliver replies with a chuckle.

"This is the CEO of Recaredo Events," Harvey adds, his gaze flicking around to his brothers before meeting my eyes. "Make sure to grab her business card. You're not throwing another party without her help."

"She's the one you're helping," Jeremy says with a smirk, shooting a knowing glance at Harvey.

"Yes," Harvey warns.

"How did you get her to agree? And Jemima, I thought you'd eat him alive before you did that," he says in a playful tone.

"Jeremy," Harvey snaps, a hint of annoyance in his voice. He winks. "Payback."

I don't know what he's talking about, but I don't want to tell them that the owners of my apartment complex are selling, and I could be out on the streets if I don't find some way to save my parents' business. I shift uncomfortably, hoping my anxiety isn't too obvious.

I meet Harvey's gaze before turning my attention to Jeremy. "Must be his good looks," I say, giving Harvey's chest a light pat, hoping to steer the conversation away from my personal struggles.

They all bark out laughing.

"Good one, Jem," Oliver says.

"I knew you had a thing for me," Harvey says.

I roll my eyes. "Don't flatter yourself. I like men, not boys."

"Ouch." Jeremy winces.

Shit, was I a little too harsh? Because he is good-looking, but he's eight years younger and extremely well-off. He's not on the same life path I am with my kid.

Scanning his face, I watch as a tic in his jaw pulses. His eyes harden, and I fight the urge to stand taller, suddenly self-conscious under his scrutiny.

"I'm not a boy. I'll remind you of that one day," Harvey retorts, a hint of sadness in his tone.

Yep, I officially hurt him. I shift uncomfortably, feeling a pang of guilt for my sharp words.

"I'm sure you have plenty of women who want——" I start.

"His money," Evan interjects. He's been quietly sipping amber liquid from his tumbler.

I'm definitely not a girl interested in a man's money. I'm now in control of my life, including my finances.

"I'm not interested in anything serious. So if they want to be wined and dined for one night, then so what. I'm not harming anyone," Harvey says.

That's true. And what's different about him is his honesty. First about his reasons to help me and now his expectations.

"Anyway, Jemima, I have galleries all over New York that I host many gatherings at. Would you be interested in talking about consistent work?" Oliver asks, his tone shifting to genuine interest.

My heart rate picks up, but I keep my breathing regulated so I'm not showing my feelings on my face or in my voice.

"Definitely," I reply with a confident smile, handing him a card. All the other brothers take one too, their interest piqued.

"I'll call you and set up a meeting," Oliver promises, his eyes gleaming with anticipation.

Harvey wears a knowing smirk, and as much as I want to wipe it off his face, I also want to kiss it.

God, he's so fucking annoying.

"Sure, that sounds great." I try to maintain my composure despite the mixed emotions swirling within me.

I'm starting to feel a little hot, maybe I'm just overwhelmed by all the opportunities and the presence of such attractive men. Or maybe it's a combination. Either way, I want to go to the bathroom and compose myself.

"Excuse me," I say, feeling the need for a moment alone. "Nice meeting you all." I offer a polite smile before turning around.

As I navigate through the crowd in what I think is the right direction, I squint, trying to find the signs for the bathroom. I weave through the crowd of guests.

"Are you alright?" Harvey calls from behind me, his concern palpable.

"Yes," I reply, smiling despite feeling unwell.

"You look—" he starts.

"It's just a little hot," I interrupt quickly.

"Hmm," he mumbles, his gaze lingering on me.

"Why don't you be a good boy, and stay with your brothers," I suggest, attempting to divert his attention.

His hand grabs my waist as his mouth leans toward my ear to whisper, "I'll be your good boy any day." I suppress a shiver as his warm breath tickles the shell of my ear.

He's trying to play with me, and I'm not buying it. He's so fucking smooth, and I'm annoyed that his words make me feel a throb between my legs.

"I'm sure that works on other women, but it won't work on me," I snap back, gathering all the resolve I can.

I don't want to tell him I enjoyed calling him my good boy. Fantasies are both exhilarating and terrifying. Butch was three years older than me; we had an average sex life, and he was a selfish lover. It changed over the years, just like our marriage. I miss the early days of a relationship, when everything was fun.

"What works on you, then?" he asks, his tone lowering, a hint of fire gleaming in his eyes.

Usually, that seductive tone would get me turned on, but instead, I feel clammy. I lean forward, my voice barely above a whisper. "Nothing works on me." And then I'm about to spin on my heels and walk away, but before I can, everything goes black, and I faint, going down like a sack of potatoes.

CHAPTER 9

HARVEY

One minute, we're talking, and the next, she's collapsing.

I catch her in my arms before she hits the ground. Esme rushes up next to me, concern evident in her wide eyes. I tell her to call an ambulance, urgency creeping into my tone.

People surround us, murmuring and gasping, so I hold her tighter, cradling her gently against my chest.

"Oliver," I say quietly as I nod toward the crowd. "Move them." I need some space, and I'll do whatever it takes to protect her in this moment.

Her heat seeps through the fabric of my shirt, and the faintness of her warm breath hits my neck, so at least I know she's breathing.

I move her from the hallway and into a nearby spare room. As I lay her down on her left side, I'm struck by her softened features. Her usual hard lines are nowhere in sight. Loose hair tendrils of her curly brown hair stick to her perspired forehead, so I reach out, grazing my finger-tips to brush them away. I'm now able to see her delicate pale face. It's painted in light makeup, which accentuates her natural beauty.

I shrug out of my jacket and lay it over her. Keeping one hand on her arm, I wait patiently for her to wake.

Esme is back quickly, and I instruct her to go grab some water. As I watch her hurry off, my attention returns to the unconscious woman. The muscles beneath my hand twitch, drawing my focus. I look up at her face and notice her eyelids slightly fluttering.

I shush her softly, hoping to soothe her even in her un-conscious state, and gently encourage her to stay relaxed. Soon, the sound of sirens fills the air, and the ambulance arrives. I step back, allowing the paramedics to take over, my arms crossing across my chest as I watch them work.

"What happened?" my brother Evan whispers, concern etched in his voice.

"She fainted," I reply, filled with worry.

He nods in understanding. "Do you need anything?" he asks, his hand reassuringly squeezing my shoulder.

"Not unless you want to help Esme with seeing this party out."

"Yeah, if you want," he offers, his willingness evident.

"Thanks. I want to take her home."

"Of course you do," he murmurs teasingly, but I couldn't care less about what anyone thinks

He wanders off to assist Esme, and soon the EMT arrive and approach us. She informs me that Jemima's fainting appears to be due to low blood sugar and low blood pressure. My throat tightens as I realize she hasn't had anything to eat or drink since she arrived.

After Jemima wakes up, we move her into a chair where they can start an IV for hydration and ask for juice or soda, plus a sandwich, which Jeremy quickly goes to find. I explain that I have a private doctor who will meet us at home, where they can reassess her. They agree not to take her to the hospital, if her blood pressure and sugar improve after they re-check.

Jeremy returns with the food and drink, and the paramedics encourage her to eat and drink, which she does.

Fifteen minutes later, they check her vitals and sugars again, and they're happy with the results. They finish the IV before tidying up.

Once they leave with Esme, I squat down beside Jemima, gently brushing a stray lock of brown hair from her forehead.

"Are you ready to go home?" I ask softly.

"Mmm," she murmurs tiredly, her response barely audible.

I pull my phone and send a message to my driver, arranging for him to meet us outside. When he texts me to say that he's waiting downstairs, I carefully scoop her up into my arms. A small sound escapes her lips at the movement, causing my heart to beat harder.

"Are you alright?" I ask, hoping she's not going to faint again.

"Mmm." She snuggles in closer to me as I make my way to the elevators. "I still hate you." she whispers weakly.

I chuckle. "Glad to see your mouth still works."

We reach the car, and my driver opens the door, allowing me to sit her in the back seat carefully. I climb in and she lies down to rest her head on my lap before we head off to my penthouse. Along the short journey, I can't help but steal glances at her resting face and then over her body. She's in a sleek black dress, the fabric clinging to her curves in a flattering way. I find myself mesmerized by her.

Ten minutes later, we arrive at my house, where the soft glow of lights welcomes us. Cradling her in my arms, I step out of the car, the cool night air swirling around us. With the help of my driver, I carry her inside.

For a moment, I look around, contemplating leaving her on the plush sofa, but a pang in my gut hates the idea. What about the guest room? My gaze flicks to the doorway that leads there. However, if something were to happen to her, I wouldn't know. That only leaves one place. My bed.

Though I'm hesitant, I know it's the best choice for her comfort and safety. I walk her to the opposite side of the bed to where I usually sleep and lower her down onto the soft mattress.

She curls into a ball and snuggles into the pillow, breathing steadily. Stepping back, I take her in, the gentle rise and fall of her chest a reassuring sight. She looks peaceful.

The loud ring of my phone breaks the silence.

Without hesitation, I reach for it, eager to answer the call. Doctor Scott is waiting outside my door, so I let him in.

After I explain the situation, he agrees that she'll be fine after some rest. The paramedics had already treated her with an IV, and as soon as she wakes up, I'll feed her again. Happy with the course of action, he leaves.

I wander back to my room and text Esme to check that the party is okay without me and to thank her for helping.

She assures me it is and asks how Jemima is. I tell her she's resting, then toss my phone on my side of the bed and decide I need a shower.

Pulling at my tie, I step into the bathroom and leave the door ajar in case she stirs. I remove my shirt and start the shower. The room fills with steam.

I'm nearly delusional with sleepiness from a long week. So I step into the steamy hot shower and wash away tonight's disaster.

Coming out of the bathroom with damp hair, I see she still hasn't moved. I approach her but hesitate, my fingers hovering over her shoes. With a gentle touch, I unbuckle the straps and remove them one at a time. I ignore how soft her skin is and how cute her purple painted nails are and focus on making her comfortable. So I pull the covers up and tuck her in.

With a sigh, I walk around and slip beneath the covers. It doesn't take long until I'm fully knocked out. Maybe it's because the sound of her breathing felt like a lullaby.

There's a hand on my morning wood. My eyes snap open as I look down to find tousled brown hair on my side, her hand between my legs.

I don't move.

What should I do?

My heart is pumping as I feel her strong and long fingers wrapped around me. I don't know if she's dreaming, but fuck, I think she is. Plus, when she wakes up and realizes she did this... Now that's going to be fucking priceless.

She nestles her face into my skin. I'm only in my boxers. When my breath catches at her grip on me, she stills, and I count...3...2...1.

Sitting up in a rush, she drops her hand and spins around to look at me.

"Be careful," I warn, already missing her hand on my cock. "Now, if you want to go back to holding my dick, I'd love it if you moved your hand up and down."

Her face turns pink. A much better color than last night.

"I'm not touching you."

"Sorry, but you already did."

She grunts and grumbles, "You're unbelievable," then pulls the covers off her legs and gets out of my bed.

I slip out of my side in a rush, scared she'll run away.

"Please stay. Have a shower, eat, and I'll drop you off at home."

I must have said something right because she exhales heavily and says, "Fine. Do you have a spare toothbrush?"

"What do you think this is, a pharmacy?"

"No, but you know…"

"You think I'm a manwhore."

"Aren't you?" She raises an eyebrow.

I shake my head, disappointment filling me. "Sorry to disappoint you, but I don't have a spare toothbrush. You're welcome to use mine."

Her face scrunches. "That's gross."

I shrug. "Whatever, buttercup, I'll meet you in the kitchen."

"Wait…" she starts to say, and I turn, curiosity settling in.

"Can I maybe have some clean clothes?"

"I don't have a women's department store here, but you can take my clothes," I offer, moving to my wardrobe and pulling out a t-shirt and some sweatpants. "This is all I have."

She gives me a small smile. I leave the room, allowing her to freshen up in peace. There's water and crackers by the bed, so if she wants them before breakfast, she can have them.

Moments later, I hear the shower. It's strange having an attractive woman in my penthouse showering. She's the first but, surprisingly, I don't hate it. As she's showering, I can't help but imagine her using my soap to wash herself, picturing what her body looks like without her dress.

I'm going to blame it on the fact her hand was on my cock this morning.

A little while later, I'm dishing up bacon, eggs, toast, and potatoes. I eye her up and down as she crosses into the kitchen and almost choke on my tongue. She's in my T-shirt and nothing else, though to be fair, the T-shirt settles at the top of her knees.

I shake my head, trying to focus.

"Hey," I say casually, a faint smile tugging at my lips. "Feeling hungry?"

"Yeah, a little."

"Did you want to sit at the dining table or here?" I gesture to the large marble island with stools where the morning light comes through the blinds.

"Here is fine. I won't hold you up much longer."

"It's fine, really." I lower a plate in front of her, the food neatly arranged, steam rising from the hot plate.

"Thanks. I have to get home anyway."

"The doctor is on his way. Once he's seen you, I can take you home."

She doesn't pick up her silverware, pausing instead. Her fingers brush the edge of the plate but don't lift it. "I don't need a doctor."

"Yes, you do. You fainted last night."

She drops her gaze to the floor and murmurs, "I can't afford one."

"It's my doctor and I'll pay."

I can practically see the steam coming from her ears.

"You can't throw money at everything."

"It helps." I try to lighten the mood, but I see the flicker of frustration in her eyes.

She shakes her head vehemently.

"Please." I soften my tone. "You scared the fuck out of me last night. And..."

"And what?"

"You owe me, you know, for touching me." I give her a playful wink, hoping to ease the tension.

Her eyes widen in horror, and she puts a hand up between us like a stop sign. "We are never to discuss this morning again."

"Why are you embarrassed?"

"About accidentally touching you? I'm not embarrassed. I'm absolutely mortified."

"I didn't think I was that repulsive."

She rubs her face in exasperation, and it softens her sharp words. "I didn't mean it like that."

"Would you like some juice, tea, or coffee?" I ask, trying to move things along.

"I'm starting to think there's something wrong with you."

"Why's that?"

Her eyes narrow, lips pressed together. "Because you're being unusually nice."

"Do you want me to be a jerk? I'm just trying to take your Starbucks order."

She must find it hard to resist because she eventually gives in and asks me for a chai latte. I place the order on my phone and settle on a stool beside her to eat.

After we finish eating, she asks to wait on the sofa for the doctor. I can't shake the feeling that she's not feeling well, but she insists she's just full and in need of a nap.

The doctor arrives, pleased with Jemima's observations, and leaves, after she promises to take better care of herself.

"Ready to head home now?" I ask.

"Yeah, I've got a lot to do, including meeting up with a friend who's probably waiting for me." She sits up, holding her Starbucks, sipping slowly.

"Just work and family stuff. Nothing urgent. It was nice meeting your brothers last night, and thanks for the help with the introductions."

"What helps you, helps me."

"Are you close with your family?" she asks.

I'm surprised by the sudden personal question, but rather than question it, I just answer.

"Yeah, we're pretty close. And you?" I ask.

She hesitates slightly, her fingers stilling for a moment before she meets my gaze. The shift is subtle, but it's enough for me to notice. What's behind the pause? But I don't get time to dwell on it.

"My dad died over a year ago, and my mom's off traveling the world. She doesn't want to be tied down to one place."

I understand what she means, but she didn't quite answer my question.

"But are you close with her?" I ask again.

"Yeah, I suppose so."

She stands from the sofa and gathers her belongings. Returning to the living room, she's ready to leave, so I grab my keys.

Dressed in a matching beige sweat suit, while she's standing in just my shirt.

"Did you want a jacket?" I ask.

"No, I'm fine."

"It's cold out," I persist.

"Harvey, enough. I'm fine." Her voice wobbles slightly, but I don't overthink it. She's probably just tired and shaken up. I'll crank up the heater in the car.

We ride in silence until we reach her apartment block. As I park, I move to unbuckle, but her hand lands on my chest, halting me. My gaze drops to where her hand touches me, igniting a fire beneath my clothes.

"Stay, please. You've done more than enough."

I sigh. "Alright."

She withdraws her hand away, dropping her chin.

"Thanks again... for everything."

"Don't forget to return my shirt."

A faint smile quirks her lips, easing the tension between us. "Never. It's mine now."

"We'll see about that."

But deep down, I know it looks better on her than it ever did on me. As she exits the car, she pauses to say, "I'll see you Monday. Don't be late, pretty boy."

With a smirk, she closes the door, heading up the stairs of her brick apartment building. I find myself exhaling and admiring her for a second before remembering I have a lot of work to do.

CHAPTER 10

JEMIMA

MOLLY'S EYES WIDEN IN disbelief, covering her mouth with her hand when I tell her what happened with Harvey. "You didn't," she says, her voice muffled by her palm. The boys are busy in the other room playing at her place, so they can't hear our conversation.

With a slight chuckle, I raise my teacup to my lips and take a sip before responding. "Embarrassing," I admit, shaking my head. My fingers twitch as I remember how hard and big he was.

Leaning forward, Molly's curiosity gets the best of her. "So, how did you get home?"

I close my eyes momentarily, feeling a wave of awkwardness wash over me. "He dropped me off," I confess, my voice trailing off.

Clearly amused, Molly lets out a low whistle. "Now that's a story," she remarks, eyes sparkling.

I feel my cheeks heat as I cover my eyes with my hands. "Right, it's humiliating," I mutter as a pang of self-consciousness washes over me.

"Did he seem bothered?" Molly asks, her expression filled with concern.

I drop my hands from my face, memories of the morning flooding my mind. "Not at all, which is the problem."

"He's young and hot. I can't blame him for trying." She offers a sympathetic shrug.

"I have a kid, and I'm not interested in dating. I can't trust anyone right now." A hint of vulnerability creeps into my voice.

As Molly stands to take her cup to the sink, she calls over her shoulder. "One day you'll change your mind."

I doubt that.

I offer her a weak smile in response.

"You're one to talk?" I quirk an eyebrow at her, attempting to change the topic to her.

"Well, at least I'm on the dating apps," Molly replies with a chuckle, pointing to her phone.

The thought of being online is my own version of hell.

"How is that going?" I ask, picking up my cup and taking a sip of my tea. Happy to shift the conversation to her.

After she finishes washing her cup, she sits back down at the dining table opposite me.

"I'm sorting through the crap ones," she replies with a wry smile, her eyes twinkling mischievously.

"How bad are they?" I ask, genuinely curious about her experiences.

"You have no idea." Her laughter fills the room.

Call me curious or naive, but I need to see what she's talking about, but there's no way I'll be setting up my own profile just to find out. "Show me," I urge.

She swipes open her phone and passes it to me, and I can't help but to lean in to read the message bubble that sits on the screen.

Remember me? Oh, that's right I've only met you in my dreams.

I lift my eyes to her gaze.

"So cheesy," I reply with a soft chuckle, handing the phone back to her.

"There's more. Let me show you the one I got last night." Molly eagerly scrolls through her messages to find the one she's referring to.

When she turns the phone screen to me, I read the message out loud.

Is your name Google? Because you've got everything I've been searching for.

I scrunch my face in disbelief. "Why are men so cringy?" I wonder aloud.

"No idea," she replies with a shrug, a playful grin tugging at her lips, "but with shit like that, they'll be single forever."

I finish my tea and take it to the sink. "True. Well, thanks for having Chad last night. I better get home."

She rises from the table, and together we walk to the living room where the boys are playing. "Take it easy and call me if you need anything."

"Will do. Otherwise, I'll see you Monday," I say, offering a small wave as I head toward the door with Chad.

"I'm dreading Monday now," I tell her with a sigh, already feeling the sense of dread for the upcoming week.

"Why?"

"Because Harvey will start on Monday, and after touching him, I would rather hide at home."

She snorts. "That made my day."

"I'm glad one of us finds it funny," I murmur.

"Come on," she says. "You have to find it a bit funny."

I do, but I'm not telling her.

I leave with Chad and head home. We haven't even been home for ten minutes when my doorbell rings.

Who is that?

I move to open the door. My mouth falls open as Harvey stands there, wearing a wolfish grin, dressed in blue jeans and an olive-green long-sleeve top, clutching bags of... groceries.

Just as I'm about to ask him what he's doing here, Chad squeezes beside my thigh.

Shit.

Harvey's eyes widen into the size of saucers, staring at Chad. The look on his face makes me laugh. He's spooked.

Has he never seen a kid before?

He juggles the bags clumsily, so he can extend a hand out to Chad.

I frown. What on earth is he doing?

"Mommy, what's he doing?"

"I have no idea," I say.

"I'm offering to shake his hand," Harvey says.

Chad is hesitant. Ever since his dad went to jail, he's been protective of me. I've never uttered a bad word against my ex, but kids are smart. They sense things.

Without thinking, I slide my hand into his and shake it. The instant our skin touches, electricity shoots through my hand and up my arm, causing me to pull my hand away. I don't know what that was. Is my body somehow sensitive to him now that I have touched... other parts?

I pull my hand from Harvey's grip, feeling a tingle linger as I curl my fingers around Chad's smaller hand. My gaze stays on Harvey, wondering why I stupidly enjoyed it.

I need to have a serious talk to my body and get it on the same side as my head, which will never let a man back into my life. *Our* life.

"Who is he?" Chad's innocent voice cuts through the tension, his wide eyes fixed on Harvey.

"Harvey. A work... friend. What brings you here?" I ask, in a soft voice for Chad's sake, though I'm battling the urge to bite out the remarks that sit on the tip of my tongue. I never intended for anyone other than Danny and Molly to meet Chad. Harvey and my personal life aren't supposed to mix.

So why is he here?

Harvey glances at me, concern flickering in his eyes. "Checking on you. You fainted and after the doctor——"

I shake my head at his words, already anticipating Chad's.

"What doctor, Mommy?"

"I'm fine, honey. Could you go play with your toys while I talk to Harvey?"

"Will he play basketball with me?"

"I don't th——" I begin, but Harvey cuts me off with a reassuring, "Yeah. I'd love to."

Chad's eyes lights up. His squishy face melts me and makes it so hard to say no. I shoot a pointed glare at Harvey, silently communicating a well-rounded, *fuck you*.

"Come inside, and then we'll walk to the neighborhood courts," I say.

As Harvey steps past, that familiar pine smell hits me like a truck. Did he cover every part of him in that scent so I would drown in it? As if I haven't had memories of his chiselled stomach and his smell.

I scratch my temple, observing Harvey make himself at home at the kitchen island. Closing the door, I take in the clutter of toys scattered across every room of the apartment, cursing inwardly at the mess.

He lowers the bags and scans his surroundings. I move to the first bag and start unpacking. The quicker we play basketball the quicker he can leave. His rich ass has to be judging me hard. His penthouse versus my peeling walls and leaking faucet.

I unpack the water bottles, as he pulls out the snacks, a variety of fruit, bars, and breads. When he opens the fridge and comments that I have nothing in an accusing tone, it hurts. It's as if he's judging me as a mother and my ability to care for Chad. It causes me to sneer, masking the sting of his judgment. "I haven't had time to shop. I was planning to go later, but then you showed up."

It's a lie, but I don't want him to know just how bad things are.

I think my small frame and fainting are enough of a sign, but I want him to know I look after Chad. He's always well-fed; I'd rather starve than not have enough for him. I don't want to be reported to the authorities because he thinks I'm not feeding my son. I am, and that's why my parents' business is so important. I need it to get me out of this hole I've found myself in.

We continue unpacking in silence, and out of the corner of my eye, I take glimpses of Harvey moving effortlessly around my tiny kitchen.

"You don't have to help. Would you like to sit and have a drink?"

"No, I'm done anyway," he says, his gaze wandering around the apartment.

"I just need to change. Take a seat, I won't be long."

I make my way to the bedroom, pausing at the doorway to steal a glance at Harvey sitting on the sofa. Out of both sofas, he chose the spot where I sleep. He looks too big on the small sofa in my tiny living room. Chad rushes off to get his shoes on. I avoid looking at the bed in the center of the room.

I go to the closet in search of something comfortable yet clean and pull out a sweater and sneakers. Running my hands through my hair, I check my appearance out in the full-length mirror I have in the corner of my room.

Why do I bother? He's not interested in a woman my age, with permanent lines on her face and tired bags under her eyes. With a heavy sigh, I tear my gaze away from the mirror.

Stepping out of my bedroom, my mouth parts to speak, but the words die on my tongue. Chad is in front of him, talking animatedly about something. My heart beats loudly in my ear as a mix of anxiety and frustration swirl within me. I need to get Harvey out of here.

"Are we ready?" I announce, re-entering the room.

Chad nods fast, and Harvey twists to face me before rising from the sofa. I don't miss his gaze briefly running over my frame, probably revolted at my baggy clothes. The goal here isn't for him to find me attractive; it's actually the opposite. I want him to leave me alone. My head feels like it's spinning when he's too close, blurring the trust lines, and I don't like that. I need to regain control by pushing him away.

A couple yells at each other from the apartment upstairs, and Harvey looks at me, but I just ignore him and walk toward the stairs.

As we make our way to the sidewalk, the cool breeze wraps around me, but the way the sunshine penetrates through my clothes onto my skin is a relief. I feel the cold deep in my bones all the time.

We walk in silence for five minutes until we reach the public courts.

When we arrive, one court is taken by a group of teenagers, so we head toward the empty court, and I take a seat on the weathered bench, watching as Harvey and Chad prepare to play. Chad takes charge and bosses Harvey around explaining the rules of the game with confidence.

He's definitely like his momma. I can't help but smile at the sight. He makes it all worth it. No matter how tired or fucking sad I am, he makes the days so much brighter.

Harvey doesn't argue with him, which is funny because he always talks back to me.

As the game begins, I find myself enjoying the effortless movements between the two. The sounds of their laughter, the ball bouncing on the concrete, and their sneakers on the court erase the noise of the rowdy teenagers.

Harvey's shirt has a dark patch on his lower back. He's wearing jeans, and I'm sure it's uncomfortable, but I guess he didn't expect to come over and do this.

He didn't expect Chad.

I've never discussed him or my life as a single mom.

Harvey runs over and I expect something to be wrong. But he rips his long sleeve shirt off and tosses it at my face. I swat it away to my lap. But the sight of his sweat-glistened skin and the smell of his aftershave cause my brain to short circuit, and I'm instantly consumed by him once again. And I'm pretty sure he can tell when he throws me a charming smile and says, "Hold this."

"I'm not your maid, Lincoln," I fire back.

"Now don't be dirty with me." He winks as he jogs off toward Chad.

I roll my eyes, but the corner of my lip lifts.

His back is to me and it's glorious. The guy is cut, and with every dribble or shot of the ball, his muscles contract, causing heat to pool between my thighs.

When Chad gets the ball, Harvey turns, and his solid chest and abs are fully visible to me. And I say *abs* because the guy has a six-pack. It's never been something I care much about. My ex-husband's dad bod was hot to me, but I admit Harvey's perspiring body is undeniably attractive.

I wish I had my sunglasses to hide behind, because every time I run my gaze over his body, I get caught. Like, does the guy have some weird telepathic power where he can sense when I'm checking him out? It's like a desire switch has been turned on inside me and I can't turn it off.

A few minutes later, a bead of sweat trickles from his neck down to his chest. His chest hair is short like he trims it or maybe shaves it.

I can't be caught staring again, so I can't inspect it properly, but if I could have one touch...

No. Stop.

My heart pounds harder, my breaths becoming ragged as I struggle to maintain control. I shuffle uncomfortably on the bench, irritated at how my body reacts despite everything. The boys are busy playing, but all I can focus on is how my skin feels too hot, how I can't stop thinking about him. It's frustrating, especially since I want nothing to do with guys, especially not ones like Harvey Lincoln.

Chad scores. And when Harvey grabs the ball, he says, "The next person to score has to buy the winner a treat," grinning mischievously.

I don't like where this is going because it feels like he knows he'll win, and he gets to buy us more food, spending his money like he was born to do.

"You're going to lose." Chad gives Harvey the cutest sour look. He tries to pull the ball out of Harvey's hand, and I watch as Harvey doesn't let him have it. Yeah, he really doesn't have kid etiquette. Most people would give the kid the ball, but Harvey doesn't. He smiles and shoots the ball through the net with ease.

"You suck," Chad announces, to which Harvey chuckles and jogs to him, ruffling his hair.

"Come on, don't be like that," he replies, again lacking the talk-to-kid rule. "It was a good game. Ready to celebrate?" Harvey asks.

Chad huffs. "Fine."

The boys walk side by side over to me, and the vision has my heart racing.

This reminds me of what a positive male influence could do for him... Something I can't provide, no matter how much I wish I could.

"No treat," I say, trying to gain some control of the situation.

"Why not?" Chad asks, frowning, his eyes pleading for a reward.

"Because I said so." I feel a pang of guilt for saying no.

"How about your mom has to shoot and score for me to lose?"

I die inside because I'm so bad at sports.

"I can't," I murmur, embarrassed.

"Why?" Harvey asks.

"She's not good," Chad says matter-of-factly, unintentionally adding to my embarrassment.

"She can't be that bad," Harvey says, his tone playful yet challenging.

"Wanna make a bet?" I look at the basket that doesn't look too high and hope for a miracle. I've tried once before, and I wasn't too far off. If it means I get rid of Harvey today, then I'll try.

His eyes shine with excitement. "Yeah."

"You can't buy us anything if I get it in," I announce.

"You're confident you can, even after what your son said?" Harvey asks with evident amusement.

Determination floods my veins as I toss his shirt in his face, momentarily obscuring his vision before he laughs and frees himself. I grab the ball and march over to the court, silently pleading for it to go in.

Come on, please make this day end.

I try to calm my shaky hands. Remembering my dad's tips on how to shoot, *stand with your feet shoulder width apart.*

But before I can, Harvey steps up behind me, his presence steady and warm. "Okay, feet shoulder-width apart," he says gently, placing a hand on my shoulder to guide me. "Focus on the shot. Don't rush it."

The heat of his touch lingers as he moves his hand to my wrist, adjusting it ever so slightly. "Now bend your knees a little more. Nice and smooth."

His fingers graze mine for just a second as he steps back.

With a deep breath and a steady hand, I adjust my feet, and then I throw it. The ball sails through the air, and my hope shatters when it hits the ring and bounces back toward us. *Shit.*

"Looks like you lose," Harvey's voice whispers darkly in my ear, his tone laced with glee. He's loving every minute of this.

I squeeze my eyes shut. Blowing out a breath, I spin on my heel to face them, forcing a smile to hide my disappointment.

"I've got to admit, I thought you'd be worse," he says with a hint of honesty.

"Yeah, Mom, with practice you could be better," Chad adds innocently.

I stare at my six-year-old, like, *why are you throwing words I say to you back at me?*

"I'll have to practice with you," I say.

"And Harvey? He would be a good teacher. He's really good," Chad exclaims, oblivious to my discomfort.

Gritting my teeth, I flick my gaze to Harvey. His eyebrow lifts. "I'm really good."

I don't want to spend more time with Harvey, well, any more than necessary. Work will be torturous enough, but Chad really enjoys having Harvey around. I can see how much he likes it, and it makes things more complicated for me.

"I won, which means I can buy the treats," Harvey says, his tone light, and victorious.

"I'm thirsty," Chad says.

"I forgot your water, sorry. We should just go home," I suggest.

And we could send Harvey on his way.

"I'll buy one at the corner store," Harvey says.

"Yeah, Mom. The shops have water," Chad interjects.

I sigh with defeat. Harvey puts his shirt back on, and I can finally concentrate again.

As Harvey makes his way out, I follow the boys, and we leave the courts.

We end up at Sugar Cafe. When I'm inside, I stop to read the menu. Harvey announces he'll order himself a milkshake, and he turns to me, his gaze penetrating, giving me a look that sends a shiver down my spine. "What will you have?"

"Nothing, I'm fine," I reply, my discomfort palpable.

He stares at me, his gaze unwavering, but instead of calling me out, he bends down to Chad and whispers, "What does Mom like?"

"Chocolate."

Harvey straightens, wearing a wicked smirk that sends a flush creeping up my neck.

I mouth, "Traitor."

His grin widens, and I feel my lips twitch, so I turn to call over my shoulder, "I'll find seats. Chad, come on."

"I'll help Harvey," Chad says with enthusiasm.

What?

I guess he found his new favorite person.

My bottom lip drops, and I stare at Chad, who is looking up at Harvey like he's his new idol.

I shake my head and walk off to grab a table.

A few minutes later, Harvey comes back with two chocolate milkshakes and a cotton candy one for Chad. He also has a white paper bag.

"What's in the bag?" I ask Chad when he sits down.

"Cookies," he beams.

"You're going to hear about it when he gets a stomach ache," I mumble to Harvey.

Harvey pokes my side playfully, and I flinch at the unexpected touch. "I got you one too. I figured you needed some cheering up."

"And a cookie is going to do that?"

"Of course. Sugar makes everyone happy," Harvey replies with a grin.

"You don't look like you know what that is," I murmur under my breath, and I sound jealous of him. And it's because I am. I'd like to have a nicer body, but minimal money means lack of food and exercise. I can't afford the gym, nor do I have the time. When am I expected to go? I bet he goes early in the morning or after work. I don't have the luxury to do that; I have Chad to worry about.

I'd love to have his money, to make this a weekly thing for Chad, so he could grow up with the best memories of me. And it's not just Harvey's money that I'm envious of, but his age and intelligence. At his age, he seems to have life figured out in ways that took me decades to. I'm forty-two and feel like I've wasted so much time. I stayed with my husband because I loved him, but I gave him all my power, and now that I think about it, I should've learned how to manage my bills, money, and life. I'm starting over and I feel stupid.

"Nice that you take notice of me," he says before wrapping his lips around the straw. And, of course, he looks so hot doing that too.

"I didn't mean that," I retort, even though his body doesn't look like he eats much sugar. I felt the muscles, not just the one between his thighs.

We drink our shakes in silence. I'm surprised it's not as awkward as I thought it would be. Chad has welcomed

Harvey with open arms, and that worries me. He's not going to be in Chad's life. The job will be done, and we will both move on. He'll forget about us. And I can't blame him, but I need to protect us from the potential heartbreak.

Once we finish our shakes, Chad holds the bag of untouched cookies, saving them for later.

We slowly walk home, and I let Chad soak up the last few minutes of his outing with Harvey.

When we arrive at the steps of the apartment complex, Chad speaks up.

"I wish I had someone like you to play with all the time," he says, longing evident in his voice. It makes my chest ache.

And before I can respond, Harvey interjects with an offer, "I can. Just tell your mom to call me."

I shoot him daggers. *Asshole.* Using my kid to call him is a low blow.

"We might be busy," I say.

"Doing what?" Harvey asks, but the grin he's wearing shows he knows I'm trying to avoid him.

"Working."

"You don't work all the time," he challenges.

I know Chad is hanging on to every word. So I sigh. I can't let my own feelings get in the way of Chad's happiness no matter how I feel about Harvey. "I'll call you when he asks."

"Good. Now, thanks Chad for a good day," Harvey says.

"Do you want to come in and play the Switch or Legos?" Chad offers.

Alarm bells ring in my ear. I've had enough of him with us for today. I'm twisted up from him, and I just need a second alone to breathe.

"I can't today, maybe next time," Harvey says.

He probably has a girlfriend to visit.

"Where are you going?" Chad asks.

"Chad, that's enough," I say.

Harvey smiles at Chad. "It's fine. I'm going to my grams' house. I have dinner with her on Sundays."

"You do?" Chad asks with a hint of awe in his voice, and it's similar to how I'm feeling.

Harvey simply nods.

"Mine is away," Chad says, sounding sad.

He nods as silence envelops us.

If I'm honest, I find it kind of cute that he hangs out with his grams on a Sunday night. Not what I expected of a rich, hot thirty-four-year-old guy.

"Well, we better let you go," I add.

"Thanks, and I'll see you tomorrow," Harvey says, waving.

"How could I forget," I breathe out, but a small smile tugs at the corners of my lips.

He smirks knowingly. "Bye, Ms. Recaredo."

"Her name's Jemima," Chad replies.

"I like her name," he tells Chad, throwing me a wink.

We watch as Harvey turns and walks away. I then usher Chad upstairs, listening to him talk about how much fun today was and all about Harvey's basketball tips. As soon as I open the apartment door, Chad walks to his room to play. I close the door and lean back on it, closing my eyes for a second to regain my composure.

After a minute, I peel myself away and walk to the sofa with a full stomach. The milkshake is making me need to lie down.

As I settle back on the sofa, Harvey's scent lies heavy on the worn fabric. The day spent with him catching glimpses of his skin and then memories of his hot touch replays in my brain. But that's not even the worst part; it's how he interacted with Chad. I hadn't realized until today just how much he enjoyed having a male around. Would it be all that bad to let him hang out and play hoops every once in a while? The heaviness in my gut says, *but what happens when he leaves?* Because he will.

CHAPTER 11

HARVEY

Glancing over my shoulder, I take in the little boy walking up the steps into that hellhole of an apartment.

The place is old and falling apart. It's not what I had as a child his age. When I was little, I had the best of everything, including a house in the safest area. Chad doesn't seem bothered by it, though. I wait in case Jemima turns back around, but when they both disappear from my vision, I head to my car.

Chad goes against everything I thought kids brought into one's life. My friend Xavier has a child. He was on track to make partner at his firm when he had a baby on the way. His partner said they'd "figure it out together," but somehow, it all landed on him. He missed deadlines, skipped networking events, and suddenly he's the guy who's "not reliable."

We invite him out, but he's always too exhausted. I never want that for myself while I'm trying to set myself up. In five or ten years? Sure, but now? No.

But then why do I care where they live?

Why do I care about her?

I find her beautiful in that effortless way. She doesn't care to put on makeup or dress up in order to impress anyone. But the natural flush of her cheeks on her pale face makes me crave for her to touch me again.

Maybe that's the problem. She touched my dick and now I can't stop myself from wanting her to do it again.

At first, I didn't know how to talk to Chad. I haven't interacted with children much. My brothers don't have kids. All my close friends are childless too—except Xavier, and we're not as close as we used to be—meaning my experience is minimal. But Chad was honest and fun. It was nice shooting hoops with him, and having his mom squirming made it that much sweeter.

The time went by so fast today when the three of us were hanging out. I'd steal the occasional glance at Jemima, who at times shared her softer side.

She'd hate it if I pointed that out.

Chad has the same honey-colored eyes as his mom, but his hair color is much lighter. That he must get from his dad.

I'm aware of her ex-husband's recent arrest because one of my staff members brought it to my attention when I was originally going to acquire Jemima's business. But we haven't spoken about it.

Is she done with him? He's in jail, but it doesn't mean she's over him. Again, I don't know why I care; I don't need to know anything that's going on in her life. She has a kid, and that's one thing I'm not ready for.

I'll learn the business, make it profitable, and then get the money from my father and move on. But I don't want to hurt Chad like that, especially after everything he's been through with his father. During the basketball game, he mentioned he played with his dad before he went away. The question "do you know where?" sat on the tip of my tongue, but it didn't feel right to ask him. I'll have to ask her.

He didn't seem upset when talking about his dad.

I think about my parents and my silver spoon life versus what he's got. Yet, he doesn't know what he's missing. He's truly a happy kid. And that has to come from Jemima. She's a wonderful mother, trying to do her best in life. She's trying to protect her family, and I can't blame her. I just wish she didn't see me as the enemy. I want her to see me as more than someone with money.

Driving to Grams', I wear a stupid grin that refuses to leave my face. The moment I step into her limestone house, she asks what I'm so happy about.

"I'm happy to see you."

"Don't fib, Harvey." She giggles, gracefully making her way with her walker toward her kitchen, and I eagerly follow.

"How do you know?" I ask, my grin widening.

"I've watched you grow up, dear." She starts gathering ingredients for the cake she's about to make.

Her mention of my upbringing causes me to ask something that's been playing on my mind since I left Jemima's.

"Do you think I'm different because I grew up in a more privileged lifestyle?"

She pauses her task to face me, giving me her full attention.

"Not at all, Harvey. From what I've seen, you've always had a strong sense of determination——"

"People call me cocky," I interrupt, a tinge of defensiveness in my voice.

"Don't say that word," she says firmly but kindly. "You grow up how you grow up; that's not a choice you get. It's what you choose to do with the rest of your life, but even more than that, it's how you treat people. Do you treat them like you're better than them because you have money, and they don't?"

"No," I say, the words coming out stronger than I expected.

"Exactly." She smiles and returns to pour the batter into the tin. "You're a brilliant man. Money or not, you were born to be successful because you work hard. And you've got great parents who pushed you to see your potential."

I was lucky to have two great parents. Helping Chad's mom save the business will help him and that's where my focus needs to stay.

"Thanks, Grams."

"How are you feeling?" I ask as I glance at her pale complexion.

"I wish people would stop fussing over me. I'm not going anywhere any time soon."

My lips twitch at her smart comeback. This interaction warms my heart and reminds me of the easy banter I have with Jemima.

"I just want to make sure you're taking care of yourself."

"Your dad's here every day watching over me. I can't scratch myself without him worrying about me. All I'll be remembered for is having cancer."

Is that what she actually thinks?

My heart sinks at her admission. "Grams, you'll be remembered for being the most fearless woman anyone has ever met."

"Don't flatter me, you look silly doing it."

I laugh.

She steps over and cups her hand to my cheek, her fingers cool against my face. I swallow the question, *Do you need the heater turned up or a thicker cardigan?*

She drops her hand away from my cheeks, and as I see her veiny, frail hands, it hits me how we don't know how much time we'll have with her.

When she carries the tin to the oven, the chocolate mix makes my mouth water. I've always had a thing for chocolate, and it brings back the moment when Chad told me Jemima also likes chocolate. A secret I'm sure she didn't want me to know.

Eyeing the empty bowl, I dip my finger in, and I scoop up some batter. Grams smacks the back of my hand and warns me, "Harvey."

I chuckle around my finger as the sweetness of the raw batter hits my tongue.

"Your baking is too good to resist."

"You've always had a sweet tooth."

I laugh as a memory floods my mind. "I was always the first to steal the bowl and run around the house with Oliver chasing me."

"Or Jeremy trying to trick you so he could grab it first. But you always figured it out and you never lost."

"I never did."

Truthfully, I've never lost anything. Determination and intelligence are my power tools.

I help her clean up the kitchen and make her tea, before joining her on her plush sofa. When her eyelids droop, I can tell she needs to rest, so I stand.

Her eyes widen at my movement. "Where are you go-ing?"

"Rest, Grams." I kiss her paper-thin temple. "I'll be here when you wake up," I whisper.

She smiles, not bothering to argue.

At least one woman in my life isn't arguing with me.

CHAPTER 12

HARVEY

I HANG UP THE phone with my private investigator who's looking into Danny. Carrying a tray with four cups of steaming coffee, I walk into the office, careful not to spill a drop. Molly's head lifts and a warm smile greets me.

"Welcome, Mr. Lincoln."

"Harvey, please," I say with a grin.

Approaching her, I extend a latte. "I wasn't certain about everyone's order, so I opted for chai lattes. I promise to come better prepared tomorrow."

"Chai is perfect," she says, rising from her seat.

As the aroma of freshly brewed coffee fills the air, a tall, blond-haired man emerges from an office to the left, his confident stride announcing his presence.

"Hi, I'm Danny, the Project Manager here," he introduces himself, holding a hand out for me to shake. Giving me a peacock vibe, as if he's trying to tell me without saying it that he's *the man* around here.

"Harvey Lincoln." I slip my hand in his and give it a quick yet firm shake before offering him a latte from the tray.

He shakes his head. "I don't drink chai."

"No worries." My gaze then shifts to Molly. "Is she in yet?"

"Boss lady has been here for an hour already."

My eyebrow lifts. "Boss lady." I laugh. "Nice."

"She hates it when I call her that," Molly says.

"I heard that," Jemima calls out.

Molly rolls her lips, and I beam. I love how she won't come out here and greet me. I have to go to her.

Turning, I spot her in her office clothes. Confident, ruthless Jemima is back. I can't help but feel a little disappointed. This one doesn't give me many passes.

"Good morning," I greet, holding out the tray with three chai lattes.

Her eyes lift to mine, then the coffee. "You don't need to do that."

"Lighten up, buttercup, it's just coffee."

"Stop calling me buttercup."

"How about boss lady?" I sit in the chair opposite her. Molly's phone rings in the background.

Grabbing a cup, I slide it to her, watching her teeth grind together.

"Neither. Ms. Recaredo."

"Oh, the formal term. Got it." I wink.

I swear I can see steam leaving her ears. Taking a sip of the sweet drink, I watch her over the cup, noticing the determination in her eyes.

Whatever we shared yesterday is gone.

"What are you working on?" I ask, scanning the cluttered desk before me. There are papers thrown about in disarray.

She exhales as she looks over her messy desk.

"The real question is what am I not working on..." she mumbles, her voice trailing off.

"How can you see anything with this mess?" I gesture toward the chaos.

"They're in piles," she retorts, as if it's obvious.

I could show her how to file, but it would be a waste of time today. We have too much to tackle. "Give me one task, and I'll do that while you do a different one," I offer, eager to get involved.

She rubs her forehead and then scans her "piles."

"What do you think you're good at?" she asks.

I pinch my lips together to stifle a laugh. "Give me your hardest," I say, ready to take whatever challenge she gives me.

Her eyes widen, but she shakes her head.

I sip my chai and wait. There's a faint shadow under her eyes that wasn't there yesterday, and I can't help but notice how tired she looks. The sight opens up a pit in my gut; I shouldn't be worrying about this woman.

"The upcoming events are better for Danny," she finally decides.

"Hand me his pile. I'll give it to him." I rise from my chair and hold out my hand.

Her shoulders drop in relief, as she hadn't thought about it, and I carry the pile to his office with purpose. As I enter, I catch him browsing social media, and I can't help but raise an eyebrow. "Working hard, I see."

He clicks out of the page and sits back in his chair.

"Clearly, you need more to do." My tone is laced with impatience.

"You know I'm Jemima's family friend."

"I understand, but she needs to turn this business around; otherwise, you won't have a job."

I lower the pile of papers onto the desk.

"These are upcoming events. Please organize them," I instruct, trying to maintain a professional attitude, despite my growing anger toward him.

Biting my tongue, I resist the urge to confront him. There's something about him that rubs me the wrong way. He scratches his skin nervously, and I decide to walk out leaving him with the task.

As I exit the room, Molly gives me a grateful smile, and mouths *thank you*.

So it's not just me who doesn't like him.

Entering Jemima's office again, I retake my chair, ready to tackle the next task. "Now what am I doing?"

"Old events," she replies, sliding a stack of papers across the desk toward me.

"And you're working on?"

"Finances."

"Great. Where do you want me to work?"

I glance around the office space. The clutter leaves limited room for both of us to spread out and work.

"I have other offices from previous employees. I just haven't cleared them out yet."

She rises and gestures for me to follow.

Grabbing my chai and the piles of paper, I follow her. She gives me a guided tour, and I try but fail to concentrate on her words, as my attention drifts to the way her hips and ass sway in her pants.

But when we arrive back at her office, she brings my focus back because she wants an answer.

Which office will I be working out of? I point to the spare office beside hers.

"This one is perfect."

She shakes her head. "Of course you'd choose the one next to me."

"Driving you wild is my new hobby," I tease, unable to resist the opportunity to play with her.

She shakes her head. "I hope you know it's not in a good way."

"How's Chad?"

She chews on her lip, deliberating her response before finally admitting with a sigh, "Still talking about you."

"And you hate that."

"So much," she murmurs.

I chuckle at that. "Well, I better get to work, or the boss lady will have my head. We need to turn this business around, and there's no time like the present."

She rolls her eyes in response. Turning away, she wanders back into her office, not giving me a chance to reply.

But I smirk, betting she drinks the chai I brought her.

Sucking in a breath, I prepare myself to get my hands dirty. I know she lacks the qualifications to handle the situation on her own, so I'm ready to apply my knowledge and skills. Offering strategic advice, streamlining operations, and finding ways to make the business more profitable to help.

A few hours later, a soft knock sounds at the door.

I peer up to find Jemima standing in the doorway, nibbling her lip.

"Hard at work, again?" she asks, her voice a little wobbly. Her gaze drops to my chest before she meets my eyes. She's not looking at the papers in horizontal piles across the floor. She's looking at my partially exposed chest. In the process of sorting the files, my tie was thrown onto the floor, the top buttons of my shirt were undone, and my shirt sleeves were pushed up. Inside, I'm smirking at her obvious admiration.

"There's a lot of work to sift through," I say, gesturing toward it.

There are legal and financial documents here, along with a list of former clients we could reach out to and see if she might work with them again.

"No shit," she says, grinning.

"I love it when you talk like that," I reply, my grin matching hers.

She releases a frustrated sigh. "I shouldn't have bothered," she murmurs, then promptly turns to leave.

Her words pique my interest. "Was there something I can do for you?"

She subtly tenses before answering. "Lunch. Just seeing if you want a break?"

In a cute, awkward way that seems so unlike her, she shuffles on her feet.

"Well, when you put it like that, how can I say no?" I reply with a faint grin.

"Molly is coming too."

"Danny?" I wonder what our colleague is doing.

It might be a good chance to bond as a small company and discuss upcoming events or how everyone is doing on their assigned tasks. I'm curious to see how Danny is doing with his work. There's a niggling suspicion in my gut that tells me something is off with him, but I don't have concrete evidence to back me.

"No, he's gone out to meet a potential client."

That cold feeling still sits in the bottom of my stomach.

"Can I ask how you know him and why you kept him?" I ask, hoping to understand his role in the company.

"Do you have a problem with him?" she asks with an accusing tone.

"No. I'm trying to understand every aspect of the business."

She knows I'm here to learn and help it turn around, so she needs me to be honest with her about everything.

"He's a family friend."

There's a trace of vulnerability in her words.

She trusts him.

"How long has he worked here?"

"Molly and Danny worked with my dad. Danny was one of my dad's first hires."

A connection to her family, specifically her father, will blind her in business. So I need to be gentle. Doesn't mean if I find anything, I won't do what I have to do.

I have to make this work, so I walk away with my trust fund. My friend Wyatt is drawing up a business plan for the consulting firm. I want to be ready to go in a few months.

"And Molly?"

"She's just a co-worker and friend. Why?" she says, her voice firm, but there's no bite to it. She folds her arms across her chest and glances away, as if the question doesn't quite land the way I intended.

"I'm just asking." I shrug, trying to keep it light. "Why do you always think I'm attacking you?"

Her eyes flick back to me, and the sharpness fades in them a little. "You're always putting me on the spot."

"I'm not judging, I swear." My tone is teasing now, hoping to ease the tension.

She hesitates, then half-smiles. "You always try to play it cool, but I know what you're up to, Mr. Lincoln."

"Do you?" I smirk. "Well, then you'd know I was going to ask if you wanted to step out for lunch today instead of being cooped up in the break room."

Her brow furrows at my suggestion, but there's no anger in her eyes. "What's wrong with the break room?" she asks, but the softening of her stance gives me hope.

"Nothing, if fluorescent lights and no fresh air are your thing," I reply with a grin.

She exhales, looking around, like she's deciding whether to make a sarcastic remark. But instead, she shakes her head. "You're impossible, you know that?"

"You mean impossible to resist?" I smirk.

She laughs softly, and I swear I see her grip tighten on the files in her hands. "Keep dreaming, Lincoln. Meet you in the break room." Spinning on her heels, she treks away.

I exhale a breath and wipe a hand over my face.

I finish up the final paper, file it, before rising, not bothering to do up my buttons, put my tie back on or roll down my sleeves. If anything, I undo an extra button, which is usually not my thing, but neither is a forty-two-year-old single mom. *There's just something about her...*

So I stride out to drive Ms. Recaredo crazy. Or at least count how many times she checks me out. I can hear whispers from the break room, and as soon as I step inside, the girls stop talking, their eyes on me.

CHAPTER 13

JEMIMA

"MAN, HE'S HOT," MOLLY whispers to me before taking a bite of her noodles. Not the cheap packet ones that I buy, but the yummy ones with thick, soft noodles and real pieces of meat and vegetables. I wish I could afford to buy the good stuff, but the weight of all our bills is weighing down on me.

I peer down at my basic sandwich, which has been my go-to for the last few weeks when I've needed to find something nutritious but also inexpensive.

His heavy footsteps come closer, I keep my eyes cast downward because I'm unable to look anywhere else but at that damn sculpted chest. As soon as he stood in the doorway, I could tell he had lost another button.

Did he do that on purpose?

I shake my head. *Don't be ridiculous.*

We are opposites, and the biggest problem is, I don't trust him.

His firm body, pine scent, and blue eyes that could lure me in, are all things that I don't need to focus on.

"Where's your lunch?" Molly asks.

It brings my gaze up; he's pulling out a chair across from us.

Sitting at the basic white table, he answers, "I ordered it."

"What's your order," Molly asks.

I take a big bite of my sandwich, pretending that I don't care about his answer when, really, I want to live vicariously through him.

"It's actually pre-made meals from my friend's company. I've ordered a week's worth."

"So you can't cook?" I ask.

"Of course I can. I can even bake," he replies with a cocky grin.

Molly gasps, but it's almost a moan. I hit her leg under the table.

Is she serious?

"And what do you bake?" I ask, wanting to catch him in his lie, even though I'm imagining him in an apron with nothing underneath.

He leans his elbows on the table as his gaze flicks between Molly's and mine.

"I watch my Grams bake, and I lick the bowl."

I snort, but I end up coughing and my food gets stuck.

"You alright?" he asks, frowning.

I nod vehemently. Trying not to look at his worry-filled eyes, I take a sip of water, washing it away.

"So you can't bake but you can cook?" Molly asks.

"I can bake."

"Bullshit," I retort.

His eyebrows lift to his forehead as he clasps his hands together. My eyes follow the way the shirt gapes open and his chest contracts. He's firm everywhere... and a flush rushes through me.

"Let's have a baking competition," Molly exclaims.

"I don't have time for this," I argue with her.

"You can't bake." Harvey chuckles.

His teasing makes my teeth grind as I get up to get a napkin. "I can. Fine, Molly, let's have this dumb bake-off."

I curse myself, unable to believe I'm agreeing to this.

"So what are we all baking? To make it fair, everyone has to do the same thing," Molly interjects, calming the fire burning between us.

"Who'll be the judge?" Harvey asks as I walk back to my chair. My eyes cast over his more relaxed posture. I don't miss his forearms; the vein popping, and I tear my gaze away when I reach my seat.

Molly purses her lips. "I should and you both have to put it on the same plate, so I have no idea whose is whose."

"Good idea," I murmur with a smirk. She's my friend, surely, she will know which one I baked and choose it. This will be a piece of cake!

Literally.

"Cake."

They both look at me.

"We're making a vanilla sponge cake, and it's due Monday," I announce, folding my arms across my chest.

"Easy," Harvey says as he sits back to pull his phone out of his pocket, the light on his screen lighting up his face.

"What does the winner get?" I ask, my tone light, but with an edge of curiosity.

"I'll choose," Molly says with a mischievous twinkle dancing in her eyes that I don't like.

"Bring on the baking. I can't wait to win," Harvey says as he winks at me, which sends a shudder of annoyance straight down my spine.

"How will we know you baked it?" I ask, raising an eyebrow as I lean forward.

"You don't trust me?" he asks through a tight mouth and a challenging gaze.

Is he kidding?

"No. You will need to call your grams when you bring it in," I say matter-of-factly.

"Are you serious?" His chair screeches across the floor as he shifts.

"Do I look like I'm kidding?" I hold his gaze steady, daring him to argue.

He shakes his head, muttering under his breath, "Whatever. But then we will need to call Chad when you bring yours in."

"Why are you so pissy?" I ask, my tone sharper than I intended.

"I thought you'd trust me," he fires back.

At least he didn't lie and say, *Nothing.*

But I barely know him, so I laugh. "After one hangout with my son?"

His jaw clenches, and he remains silent. The air between us thickens with unspoken words.

"Sorry, but it takes a lot more than that. I've been burned one too many times." The words tumble out before I can think better of it.

Shit! Why did I have to say that? My stomach twists as I realize what I've just revealed. Opening myself up and being vulnerable wasn't part of the plan. Not here with him, not now.

Silence fills the room, and I get up to throw out my dirty napkin and grab a new bottle of water.

"Food's here," he announces, pushing out his chair, and without waiting for a response, he strides toward the door, his hands sliding into his pockets as he goes.

Molly's eyes burn a hole in my head.

"What?" I whisper-shout.

She arches an eyebrow, her lips curving into a knowing smile. "Don't *what* me," she keeps her voice just as low. "You know exactly what I'm thinking."

"I don't," I reply, a little too quickly.

She rolls her eyes and murmurs, "You two keep eye-balling each other. You think you're subtle, well, you're a walking billboard. With fucking neon lights."

I scoff. "Yes, he's nice to look at. But he's annoying."

"Nice to look at? Jem, stop being scared. Have some fun."

"I am having fun," I scoff.

"No, have some fun with him," she adds.

"Why don't you go for him?" I say, and as soon as the words leave my mouth, my stomach bottoms out. I shouldn't have said that. What if she does go for him? Unwelcome feelings of jealousy creep in and I hate it. It's not who I am.

"He's not looking at me. His eyes don't..." she says, dropping her voice to a whisper when his heavy steps indicate his impending return, "leave...you."

He enters the room with a brown paper bag, moves to the fridge, and pulls out take-out-sized boxes. His broad back and ass are hard to miss. I rub my hand through my hair as I reluctantly tear my gaze from him.

No, Jem. Not him. Hell... no.

But my mind wanders to Molly's words.

His eyes don't leave you.

I must zone out because I didn't see him return to the table or hear Molly speak.

"Jem," Molly calls in the distance. But it's the touch on my thigh that snaps me back to reality. Gasping at the warmth of the large, firm hand gently squeezing me, I blink rapidly.

The hand on my thigh belongs to the same person I've been having the wickedest fantasies about.

What's gotten into me? I need to snap out of this, and fast. But he's making it impossible by keeping his hand on my thigh.

I realize she's not far away; she's sitting directly across from me. "Sorry," I murmur. "What did you say?"

"Where did you go?" Harvey asks, a wolfish grin making me suddenly worry he can read my mind.

I straighten my back as my gaze meets Molly's.

"We were talking about our hobbies. It's your turn," she says.

"Hobbies," I repeat.

"Yeah," Harvey says with an expectant look.

"Um, I don't really have any because I spend all my time with Chad."

"What do you two do?" he asks. His hand retracts, and though I want to protest, I start talking to avoid any further physical contact. I'm so deprived of touch that I'm craving it from the person I shouldn't.

"We watch movies. Mainly Marvel or Disney ones." Once I start, I can't stop. "My life changed when I had Chad. There wasn't any free time to do what I used to do."

"And what did you used to do?" he pries.

"Dance classes, reading, travelling." I sigh. When was the last time I did any of that?

I gave up dance classes when I fell pregnant... seven years ago.

Reading? That was mostly during holidays or long weekends, but the last time I read was last year.

Traveling? The last vacation was my honeymoon in Bali. Before that, I used to travel with friends every few years. I was so carefree back then. Now, I don't even recognize that person. She's so different from the stressed-out one I've become.

To steer the conversation away from why I don't do those things anymore, I add, "Now I work or hang out with Chad."

"He beat me and Hugo at Chutes and Ladders the other night," Molly chimes in.

No surprise there. We play together often because it's a game I played with my dad and now with Chad. "Yeah, he's competitive," I mutter.

"I wonder where he gets that from?" Harvey teases.

"I'm not competitive," I argue, with a raised eyebrow.

Molly and Harvey look at me like I'm joking.

"What?" I say, feeling offended.

"You can't be serious," Harvey says.

"I am serious." I cross my arms over my chest.

"It's not a bad thing. He'll be successful," Harvey says.

"Just like his momma," Molly adds, throwing me a wink.

"Not yet," I murmur.

"We will be. I'm not wasting my time here for it not to pay off," Harvey adds confidently.

My mouth falls open as I stare at him for a moment. *Wasting his time...*

Clenching my hands into fists at my sides, my nails stab into my palms, grounding me. "No one's holding you here."

He winces. "I'm sorry, that came out wrong."

"Just a bit insensitive," Molly adds, scrunching up her nose.

"I just meant I wouldn't be here if I didn't see potential. My office is running without me," Harvey says.

"What's your job?" Molly asks.

"I own Lincoln Acquisitions and soon to be Consultations," he answers.

Molly whistles. "Dayum."

"With all of us working together, we have a very good chance," Harvey adds.

"Agree," Molly says.

I remain quiet, returning to my sandwich. This is why I refuse to have him help me personally. I'll accept his help here, in this office, because that makes his presence temporary.

Even though I was close to giving him the finances, I decided against it. After what my ex-husband did, I vowed to never let another man handle my finances. I'll learn it myself. Sharing the work has been such a relief, and honestly, I wish I had thought of it so much sooner.

I finish my sandwich as Molly hands over a coffee she made me. Harvey grabs something from the fridge and brings it to the table.

He takes out a lemon meringue pie.

"Did you make this?" Molly exclaims, taking the words right out of my mouth.

"No. My grams did," he says, looking directly at me.

"Doesn't mean you wouldn't have her make the cake to win," I say.

"I wouldn't."

My stomach grumbles at the sight. I haven't had a homemade pie since my mom used to bake when I was little. Once my parents took over the business, it consumed them.

He cuts six pieces.

"You cut too many pieces."

"One for Chad and one for Hugo."

I freeze momentarily. I can't refuse just because I don't like handouts. Food is one area where I'm struggling, and I know he's aware of that. Yet his gesture doesn't seem like an afterthought or out of sympathy. It's more caring, which sends a tremor through me.

He's more dangerous than I thought. He's hitting me where I'm weak.

I've got to be stronger.

Harvey sets the pie down, and we waste no time eating it... or should I say, inhaling it.

"This is so good," I say between bites.

"Yeah, Grams makes the best pies," Harvey replies, his voice sounding low and heavy.

I look up and notice his expression changes to something... darker. "Everything, okay?"

He hesitates, then sighs. "She has breast cancer."

The words hang in the air, and I pause, the fork halfway to my mouth. "Harvey... I'm so sorry."

"Thanks, it's been really hard to see her go through treatment." He takes a breath. "She hates how everyone's treating her like she's sick or fragile. She's stubborn. Won't let anyone help her, insists on doing everything herself."

We share a look before one of us smirks. "I wonder where you get that from."

Harvey laughs, and for a moment, it feels like everything is normal.

When we finally return to work, the mood shifts. Danny has been out for most of the day, and there's a pile of things waiting to be done. Molly comes in not too much later, saying she needs to leave early because Hugo is sick. Then

Danny texts me, saying he's heading home after distributing a few of our cards to potential clients. I text him back, telling him I'll see him tomorrow.

Now it's just me and Harvey.

My phone rings with an unknown number. "Recaredo Events, Jemima speaking."

"Hi Jemima, it's Oliver Lincoln."

I sit up in my office chair, sifting through papers on my desk to find a pen.

"Oh, hi. How can I help you?"

"I'm wondering if you could host a gallery birthday?"

"Sure. What date?"

He chuckles, his tone a bit lighter than his brother's.

Why am I thinking of Harvey's laugh right now?

"Here's the issue: before we met, I had another company running my events, but the design is off."

"What's not working?" I ask, scribbling down notes.

"It's immature. Gold and black, like a 90s prom. I want something elegant—"

"Masculine?" I ask.

"Yes. Not too dark, though."

"Got it. When's the birthday?"

"Saturday night."

I gasp. "This Saturday?"

My pen freezes, and I look across the room, wondering how I can manage this while restructuring.

"Yeah. I'm sorry. I wasn't expecting us to work together until my next project, but I need my events to represent me. So, I fired them."

I can do this. This is a big opportunity.

Please tell me it's not a big event.

"And how many guests are you expecting?"

"Only 50 to 100. It's a small celebration for the gallery's birthday."

I tap my pen on my desk, trying to think quickly.

"What's your availability look like tomorrow?" I ask, knowing it might be quicker to design a brief, and run it past him. Creating a detailed document that covers the key elements of the event. Which includes the event's objectives, target audience, budget, timeline, location, logistical details, and any other specific requirements. The brief will serve as a guide for me and my team to ensure everything runs smoothly and according to plan. It will also allow Oliver to be well prepared for the night.

I rub my forehead as I look at my calendar.

"Does ten a.m. work for you?"

"Could we make it eleven to give me enough time in the morning to draft an event brief."

"I don't expect you to do that."

"I know, but it'll make it easier for you to envision, and then tell me what you like and don't like."

"Makes sense. See you at eleven. I'll text you the address, and we can meet there." A thought rushes to me. "Do you have pictures of the gallery?"

He chuckles lightly. "Plenty."

"Send me those when you have a second." I share my work email with him.

"Thanks, Jemima. I'm sorry to throw this on you so suddenly."

"No problem," I reply, ignoring the way my heart races at how much I actually need this. "I'm happy to help."

I don't mention how big this opportunity is for me. After hanging up, I wander over to Harvey's office. Ignoring the buzz in my body as I take in his focused expression, I raise my hand to knock, but he notices me before I can.

"Hey," he says, sounding as tired as I feel.

"Hey. Have you heard from your brother Oliver today?"

His eyebrows knit together, and he grabs his phone to check. "No. Why?"

"He just called. He fired his event planner and needs help with his gallery party."

His face softens. "That's good. When's the event?"

"Here's the problem... It's Saturday."

His eyes bulge slightly. "This Saturday?"

I nod. "I scheduled a meeting with him tomorrow to present a design."

"Can I come?"

Do I tell him I assumed he would? But that feels like I'm letting him too deeply into my business, and I need him to understand it's mine.

I need to seem unfazed. "Yes, if you want." I shrug. "It's at eleven."

"What do you need me to do?"

I hesitate, a bit lost. I'm not used to receiving help. Molly would, but she's got a lot of work on her plate, and I want her to focus on running the office and keeping it organized. My goal since we started this new plan with Harvey is to keep on top of paperwork, invoices, and finances.

"Could you compile a list of potential suppliers so we can start calling them in the morning?"

His lip quirks, an annoyingly sexy yet adorable grin, as if he knows delegating is hard for me, but he's glad I did. This still doesn't mean I trust him.

"I'm going to get started on the design concept. When I have notes typed up, I'll email them to you."

As I return to my office, I'm feeling a welcome sense of familiarity. With a new motivation, I leave my messy office as it is for now. I can focus on organizing the finances after this event is sorted out.

I spend the next few hours working on the concept. I haven't heard from Harvey, so I guess he's as busy as I am. His dedication is alluring. I try not to read too much into it. My ex-husband was never a career-driven man. He was a warehouse auditor who showed up every day, but without enthusiasm. He always had something to complain about. It was draining to be around someone so negative. Now it makes sense why he got tangled up with drugs—he wanted quick money.

Rubbing my temples, I feel fatigue setting in and decide it's time to go home. Harvey shouldn't be working this late. It's my company; he doesn't need to do more than necessary.

So why is he?

I'm so tired I'm getting delirious. As I shut down my computer, the smell of soy sauce, garlic, ginger, and spices hits me. Chinese food. Chad is having dinner with Jade and Pedro tonight, so I'll probably end up eating toast. I'm about to clean my cups from my desk and take them to the kitchen when Harvey appears, and my breath catches.

"Hungry?" He holds up a bag filled with food.

My mouth waters and stomach rumbles. "I can't. Chad..."

But I don't move to turn him away, so he takes it as an invitation and sits in the chair opposite my desk. He opens the bag and pulls out containers of rice, barbecue pork, satay chicken, and a stack of skewers dripping in sauce. There are also drinks and dessert. It's enough food to last a whole week, and I wouldn't put it past him to over order on purpose to keep the fridge stocked all week.

"Do you have someone helping you take care of him?"

I'm too tired to redirect his question, and I guess sharing an honest conversation once in a while will make working with him easier.

"Molly, or the apartment owners, Jade and Pedro." My voice wobbles. "I've valued their willingness to help, but I know that time is coming to an end."

He looks at me inquisitively.

"They've decided to sell to developers, and I want this business to succeed so I can buy my own place."

"You don't want to rent?" His eyes search mine, trying to read between the lines.

I glance away as heat fills my cheeks. "Not the places I can afford."

"I could help you if you get stuck," he offers softly.

I shake my head. "I couldn't afford the places you'd suggest."

His brow furrows for a second, but then he straightens, his expression firm. "We're going to make this business successful, so you won't have to worry about money."

His confidence catches me off guard, and I can't help but challenge him. "How do you know?"

"I know a lot." He gives me a sympathetic smile.

"What's your story, Harvey?" I sigh.

He tilts his head. "What do you mean?"

"You're wealthy, yet you work a lot. No girlfriend..."

"I see you're trying to get me to open up," he says, an amused smile tugging at the corners of his lips.

"You know so much about me..." I fold my arms across my chest.

"I don't know everything," he says, tilting his head sightly.

I lift an eyebrow. "What would you like to know?"

He leans in, his voice lowering a touch, his eyes gleaming with mischief. "So much."

"Like?"

"Tell me about Chad's father."

The temperature in the room seems to drop. He's asking me a personal question...

I'll answer it, but I will ask him one too.

I shake my head. "You'll look down on me."

"I don't and won't look down on you," he argues, his gaze intense.

His stare makes me uneasy, so I exhale and decide to be honest. He could easily find out anyway, since he has the resources. Yet he's asking me and that feels different. He's choosing to trust me, even when I haven't given him much to work with. Maybe he deserves the truth.

I glance at him, then drop my eyes to the floor as I twist the hem of my sleeve as I let him into my past.

"We met at work. He was my boss. I was young and made some dumb decisions."

"Why do you say that?"

I uncross my arms. "My parents warned me he was bad news, but I didn't listen."

"We all need to learn things on our own. Mistakes make you human."

I exhale, glad he's not pushing for more.

Leaning forward, I ask, "Tell me something about you. Something you wouldn't normally tell anyone."

"I want the consultation firm to prove to myself that I'm not just another young, rich member of the Lincoln family. That I'm successful on my own."

"But you said you still need your trust fund, which is from your family," I ask, trying to understand.

He sits back. "Ouch, no need to rub it in."

"Sorry. I didn't think before I said that."

"No, I like that you don't bend and that you challenge me," he says in a hushed tone.

A lump forms in my throat, but I swallow it down and ignore it. "You are successful. And you're not at all like I thought you'd be."

His eyebrow lifts. "Which was?"

"Do you really want to know?" I ask.

He eats a piece of chicken and some noodles. "I told you; I appreciate your honesty."

"Young, mean, selfish, and an asshole. Though I'm still debating the 'asshole' part." I laugh, and when he joins in, mine turns into a full belly laugh. For a second, I forget everything, the tension, my worries, the walls I've built around myself. It feels good to let go for a minute. I haven't laughed in a long time. I haven't spent time with a cute guy in even longer. This feels scary and way too easy.

He's a charming fucking trap. Too good to be true... *They all are.*

He swallows, as if he's struggling with something. So when he speaks, it's coming from a vulnerable place. "I think I come across that way because I want to be taken seriously. Being called the 'cute, rich young, Lincoln,' never made me feel worthy."

"So now you work hard."

He continues eating the noodles, which smell amazing.

"Make a name for myself that's separate from my parents."

"Are you angry at them?"

"No, it wasn't intentional. They always wanted to push us to reach our potential."

A warm smile spreads across my face as I understand what he means. Before I became a mother, I had no idea what that truly meant. Now, with Chad, all I want is for him to follow his dreams. Right now, he wants to be a basketball player, and I'd love to have the money to get him into a better club where he can follow his passion. That innocent hope without fear is so special.

"I understand."

"Meeting Chad was scarier than meeting someone's parent."

I laugh again, the sound coming out more freely this time. "He's six."

"I haven't been around kids," he adds, running his hand through his hair, as his eyes flick to the floor.

"So none of your brothers have kids?"

"No," he replies, glancing up at me, his face unreadable. "I don't have experience with them, and I wasn't expecting him, so I freaked out."

"I remember how you tried to shake his hand," I say, before falling into a new fit of laughter.

He immediately shoots me a mock glare, his brow furrowing. "Hey!"

Trying to stop the giggles, I wave my hand in apology. "I know, I'm sorry. I shouldn't be laughing at you."

"No, it's mean," he grumbles, but there's a twinkle in his eye. He's not really mad.

"Oh, did I hurt your feelings?" I tease, a grin tugging on my lips.

"No," he says quickly. "I'm actually tough. Nothing fazes me." There's that cocky grin.

"That's a good thing. Life is tough, and having thick skin helps. I dread the day Chad comes home telling me something bad happened to him."

"Chad's incredible, and that's a testament to you. If he has half of your resiliency, he'll be okay," he says, settling back into his chair, his hands relaxing on the armrests.

"Thanks." I smile as my body temperature rises from his compliment.

"We're learning something new about each other today," he adds.

Earlier, I only saw his body as a problem. But now, as we talk, he genuinely seems interested in getting to know Chad. For a moment, I indulge in pretending. He's so good at making me feel seen and heard. Whether or not it's for his own gain, tonight's been a surprisingly pleasant experience.

"We are," I murmur.

Tension rises in the air, and our eyes lock in a strange connection. Why did I tell him so much? I feel exposed because he knows some of my hard truths in life. He knows things that he could use against me, which has the power to break me.

I move to the kitchen sink to help clean up before heading home. As I turn to grab a towel to dry my hands, I find myself inches away from him, staring into his intense blue eyes. They pierce me, and instead of shrinking away, I feel my body giving in. His gaze drops to my lips as he leans closer, briefly licking his own. That simple move sends an ache between my legs, and I hitch a breath that nearly makes me cry. *It's been so long. Just once, I want to forget about everything and feel good.*

No matter the consequences or that I once thought he was the devil for always disputing me, I want him. If he's looking at this tired mom in her forties like he wants her, then why the fuck am I fighting it? Let him kiss me.

As he leans down, I close my eyes, but a rattling sound at the office door snaps my eyes open, and I automatically step back.

I turn toward the sound, my heart beating in my throat, and see the cleaner.

"Oh, sorry." she says, clearly realizing she interrupted us.

But it's enough to wake me up.

"It's okay, we're finished for the day," I mumble.

The cleaner is used to seeing me here, but not him. Not a guy and girl alone, looking at each other like we were.

"Goodnight," I say as I brush past Harvey, heading to my office to get my bag, ready to make a quick exit to the safety of my car. Just as I'm about to leave, Harvey steps into the doorway, holding a container with a knowing smirk. "Don't forget Chad's pie."

"Thanks."

He leans forward and whispers in my ear, his breath warm on my neck, sending a shiver down my spine. "Next time, buttercup, we won't be interrupted."

Freaking hell. It was a good thing she came in.

I don't glance back at him; I just finish tidying up and go greet the cleaner, asking how her family is doing.

We often share a cup of tea while I work, chatting about her teenage kids and family. She knows about my husband's arrest and my efforts to save this business, but she always asks about Chad.

She gives me a funny look tonight, and I brace myself. Another person looking at Harvey with a glimmer in their eyes. I shake my head at her in a silent no. But she just smiles, clearly not believing me.

"See you tomorrow, Harvey."

Heat rushes to my cheeks as I walk by him, and I don't look back until I'm outside. I welcome the cool air on my skin. He's getting under my skin. The small pieces I'm learning about him, and the way he cares for my son, make him hard to resist. But I have to. He's not ready for kids, and I'm not ready to trust a man again.

I can't let him kiss me.

No matter how much I want to.

CHAPTER 14

HARVEY

THE NEXT DAY, I'M in my office, wrestling with the printer. I've already fed the same stack of paper through three times, and it's still flashing that infuriating 'paper jam' message. My fingers are smudged with toner, and no matter how many trays I slide out or panels I open, I can't figure out where it's stuck. It's pissing me off. Why can't I figure out something so basic?

"Molly!" I call out. "Can you come in here for a sec?"

She's at my door in seconds, one eyebrow raised, amusement tugging at the corner of her mouth. "Printer win this round?"

"Don't start," I mutter, stepping aside to let her work her magic. She kneels down, pops open a panel I'd checked twice already, and with a flick of her fingers, pulls out a crumpled sheet of paper. She holds it up. "This what you're looking for?" she teases as she shakes the paper.

"Yes. Thanks," I mutter.

Flashing a smirk, she walks away, and I just stand there, giving the printer a hard look like it's about to be replaced.

I shake it off and turn my attention back to the invoices on my desk. Several transactions on these invoices don't add up, and they're dated before Jemima's time. I need to sort through the final few papers, but I've got one of my guys investigating, as it looks like embezzlement. I don't want to worry Jemima; she seems so fucking fragile. Last night, I just wanted to kiss her and make her forget all her troubles.

This morning, I'm pretty sure she's avoiding me. She hasn't told Molly, because if Molly knew, she'd be looking at me differently, as she wears her expressions openly. Jemima, on the other hand, isn't so easy to read. But when I almost kissed her, her facade dropped, and her eyes shimmered with pure lust and longing.

It's nine o'clock, and Jemima is late. So I send her a text.

Harvey: *Are you avoiding me?*

Jemima: *No. I'm not a child.*

I smirk as I type back.

I tuck my phone away as I enter the bathroom, but then I see Danny fumbling. His shirt sleeves are rolled up past his elbows, and he drops something. I spot it before he can hide it... A needle.

Drugs? Is he fucking kidding?

"What are you doing?" I demand.

"This isn't mine; I'm cleaning up," he says defensively.

"Funny, I saw the cleaner last night, and she didn't look like a druggie."

"And I do?" Danny raises his voice.

His agitation is evidence of guilt.

"Yeah, actually, you do." I shift my gaze to his arms.

He quickly throws away the needle and adjusts his shirt sleeves.

"You think you can come in here, throw money around, and take over," he snaps.

His accusation and rapid breathing tell me he's struggling with addiction, and his jittery body language and sheen of sweat on his forehead don't help either.

"Jealousy is a bad trait," I counter.

Danny snorts. "I'm not jealous of you."

"You'd have money if you didn't blow it on drugs."

"I don't do drugs."

"Denial won't help you."

He stares at me, the wheels turning in his head before his head and voice drop. "Don't tell Jemima," he pleads.

"Prove to me you're worth keeping around, then. If it were up to me, you'd be gone."

"I've been here for ten years."

"And probably using the entire fucking time, hiding behind the 'family friend' card."

"What are you going to do?" Danny's voice wobbles as he realizes the implications.

I rub my jaw, thinking, my eyes narrowing as I consider my response. "I don't know yet."

He straightens up, determination etched in his face. "I'll work harder than before, and I'll stop using."

I shake my head slightly, feeling frustration rising. "Don't lie. You won't give up shit, but at least take your job seriously for Jemima's sake. She only sees the good in you."

Piece of shit. This is going to devastate her. Another person letting her down.

He leaves, and I lean on the sink, needing a second to think. Telling Jemima about Danny's secret will crush her. I need to protect her. I need to get rid of him without her knowing. I need to shield her from the truth. "Fuck!" I slam my hands on the sink.

Pulling out my phone, I call my private investigator, who informs me it was Danny who made the account errors and embezzled money. He found discrepancies between physical cash count and recorded amounts, creating fake vendors with unusual details, unusual check numbers and error in bank account numbers. He will send me an email with the proof.

I fucking knew something was up with him.

Marching into my office, I scan the email and then the papers I found with the questionable transactions. The sloppy bastard left his trail all through it. It's so fucking obvious now.

The first thing I do is hide the papers. Carefully, I tuck them away, and then transfer some of my money back into the business account in various amounts, referencing them with invoice numbers so she can track them if she asks.

With this, and some new jobs, she'll soon be back on her feet. She could finally afford to rent in the good neighborhood.

Danny knows about Chad. Realization hits me hard as I connect the dots; the last name on one of these transactions match with her ex-husbands. As Molly takes a call, I slip into Danny's office and close the door behind me.

"You were friends with her filthy fucking ex, weren't you?" I hiss.

His head snaps up from his phone, where he was lost in yet another social media platform, scrolling. *Of course, he wasn't working.*

The expression on my face must be lethal because he's shrinking back in his chair, nodding like a frightened child, misty-eyed as he starts to pack his shit. My hands curl into fists, the urge to hit him strong, but my father always taught us that fists weren't the answer. I've never been this tempted. *Not until him.*

"I need you to leave and never come back."

"I can't."

I step closer, aiming for his weak spot. "How much do you want?"

I'm willing to pay him whatever it takes to make him disappear. If I call the cops, it'll lead to a drawn-out court case, and Jemima will have to go through that for months, not to mention the legal fees. Plus, if it blows up in the media, it could damage her reputation. Even though she's innocent, the scrutiny would drag her name through the mud. She's just starting to get back on her feet, and I won't let anything tarnish that.

I'm willing to pay him whatever it takes to get rid of him.

"I... I don't know."

I pull out my phone and show him a number. Ten thousand dollars. His eyes widen.

"Yes, that will work." He nods vehemently.

I transfer the money to his account as he rattles off the details.

"You'll leave while she and I are out at a meeting at eleven. Don't tell Molly. Just take your shit and go."

He remains motionless, but I don't wait. I need to leave his office before Jemima turns up for work. I also need time to calm down, so she won't suspect anything.

Pausing at the door, I turn back for a final word. "If I find you here when I get back, I'll take all the evidence I have on you to the police."

"I'll be gone before you return."

Adrenaline rushes through my veins as I open the door, leave his office, and march back to mine. Needing a distraction, I bury myself in the final few piles of work now that the major issue is dealt with. I don't know how much time has passed, but I hear the sound of shoes clicking and female voices approaching. I'm still irritated but not as much as before. I turn to my emails, working through them, and once I catch up, I get up to find her.

Despite knowing she's avoiding me—even if she denies it—I'm feeling much lighter knowing I'm about to see her.

She's in the break room, talking to Molly. I wander in and make myself a coffee from the new machine I had ordered. She hasn't commented on it yet, but I don't think she'll complain since it benefits her too.

"Mornin'," I greet them.

Molly beams a cheerful "good morning," while Jemima avoids my gaze, mumbling, "morning" into her coffee cup.

"Did Chad like the pie?" I ask.

"Yeah, he did. Thanks," she murmurs again.

She's being awkward, and it seems Molly's noticed too, as her head tilts as she glances between us.

"Do we need to discuss anything before we head out?" I ask.

Just then, Danny enters the room. His eyes widen, and he looks ready to bolt until Jemima speaks.

"Hey, Danny. I got a new job this morning. Did you want to come?"

My whole body tenses as I glare at him. He gets the message and replies with a tight smile. "No, I have work to finish up here."

"Alright. What are you working on?" Jemima asks.

He looks around, panicked. *Fucking hell, keep it together, you moron.*

"Is it a new job?" I offer.

"No, closing one," he rushes out in a panic.

"Awesome," Jemima says.

Before she can ask more questions that lead to him stumbling through more lies, I cut in.

"Do you want a drink?" I try to sound pleasant so the girls wouldn't pick up on anything, but my jaw is unintentionally tight.

"No, I'm good," Danny mutters, almost running out of the room.

Molly leaves with her coffee, so I don't ask her anything. Jemima beams. "This week is turning around for us."

"Maybe I'm not so bad," I whisper, leaning closer.

She shudders at my nearness, but quickly retorts, "You wish."

I chuckle and finish making my coffee as she leaves, and I call after her. "I'll see you in half an hour so we can leave?"

"Unfortunately," she murmurs.

CHAPTER 15

JEMIMA

AFTER BEING UP LATE last night, brainstorming ideas for Oliver, I got to work late this morning. Now I'm spending the last half hour finalizing the design concepts for Oliver Lincoln. After some googling to figure out how to sketch and formalize it, I'm pretty pleased with how it turned out. I won't lie, Harvey's presence and his impeccable organizational skills have inspired me to improve, or at least give it a shot. He's impressively successful for someone his age, so if he has a method, I want to follow it. Not that I'd admit that to him.

"Ready?" I ask, knocking on his door, and notice how clean the floor is. He's already completed the tasks I assigned him. I'm halfway through the finances, while Danny has been absent lately. It worries me, but mostly it annoys me. He should be helping with the business, not leaving it for Harvey to sort out. Danny was great in the beginning, but now, getting more than an hour's work out of him is a struggle.

Harvey looks up from his keyboard. "Hang on, just sending an email."

I wait, trying not to check him out. But it's useless, with his clean, masculine scent playing tricks on my brain. His well-fitted navy suit, crisp white shirt, and yellow tie create a striking mix that makes my skin prickle.

A few minutes later, he finishes and strides toward me. "I'll drive."

"Fine." I don't have it in me to argue. Besides, he knows the way to Oliver's office, and I'm in no hurry for him to see my car. It's a mess, littered with crumbs from Chad and old coffee cups from me. I'll get around to cleaning it... eventually.

As we pass Molly, I tell her, "We'll be back later."

"Take your time!" she calls out, waving us off.

In the parking lot, I follow his lead, though it's not hard to spot his car. I remember the color from over a month ago when he was leaning up against it waiting to talk to me.

The matte black Lamborghini stands out, and up close, I recognize the badge from one of Chad's toy cars.

A boy's toy, certainly not family friendly.

He opens the passenger door for me, and I slide into the luxurious leather seat. This isn't a family car. There's no way Chad's car seat would fit in here, but I can't help imagining his excitement if he saw this car. Honestly, I'm impressed myself. I mentally slap myself for the thought.

When Harvey starts the car, country music blares through the speakers. He dives for the volume and turns it down.

My lips curl into a smile. "I wouldn't have pegged you as a country music fan."

He leans back into his seat and starts to drive. "What did you expect?"

I tilt my head slightly, a playful smile tugging at the corner of my lips. "Techno, maybe trance."

He chuckles as he backs out of the parking spot smoothly.

"Why country?" I raise an eyebrow.

He shrugs. "My grandma always played it at her place."

"So, you grew up with it," I say, my tone softening as I lean back in the seat.

"Yeah. What about you? What kind of music do you like?" His eyes glance over at me for a moment before focusing on the road.

I can't help the giggle that slips out of me. "Guess."

"Jazz?" he suggests with a teasing grin.

I frown, shaking my head. "No."

"Choir music," he adds, the corners of his mouth curling up.

I roll my eyes, crossing my arms. "Stop messing around. Take a real guess."

"I am," he says with a smirk, not looking at me as he focuses on driving.

"Country."

I shake my head, smiling. "Nope. I enjoy it, but I'm a 90s girl at heart."

He raises an eyebrow, peering at me. "You must have some interesting stories."

I smirk. "My lips are sealed."

His eyes glow with mischief as he chuckles. "We'll see about that. I'll get them out of you sooner or later."

I stay silent, my senses heightened in such a small space. His scent grows stronger, my heart beats louder in my ears, and the car's smooth yet powerful ride is an experience I won't get again so I simply sit back and enjoy the purr of it.

Staring out the window, an easy smile forms on my lips as we pass familiar streets. We soon arrive at another parking lot. Before I unbuckle, Harvey's hand lands on my knee, squeezing it firmly.

"Are you okay?"

I turn to him, ignoring the twitch in my thigh where his hand rests. "Yeah, why?"

"You're quiet."

I can't deny it, but I won't tell him I was thinking about Chad being in his car. I don't want him offering him a ride. Keeping them apart is better for all of us. No one will end up hurt that way. "I'm just nervous."

"You? Nervous?" He sounds genuinely surprised, his eyes briefly flicking to me before returning to the front.

"Yeah, is it that shocking?" A slight laugh escapes me, though it's more out of nerves than humor.

"You usually seem unfazed by everything."

I take a deep breath, trying to calm the butterflies in my stomach. "I need Oliver to like this."

He stares at me, this time with a look of understanding. "You really want this job."

I meet his gaze, my heart beating a little faster, and nod. "Yes, I do."

"Are you confident you've done your best?"

I don't hesitate as the word comes out easily. "Yes."

His hand moves higher, squeezing just above my knee. "Then you'll be fine."

He's right, and his words calm me. What I've put together meets all Oliver's requirements. There's nothing to be worried about.

"Thanks."

His hand slips from my leg as he climbs out of the car, coming around to open my door again. This gentlemanly behavior is making my head spin.

"Who taught you that?" I ask. It's another reason he's a good male figure for Chad.

"I watched my father do it for my mom."

Whenever he talks about his family, it hits me in the heart. It's not hard to connect with him. It's easier to keep him at a distance when he's not sharing personal stories with me, especially since not every family is as dysfunctional as the one I've created for Chad. I never intended it, but it kills me that he doesn't get the family he deserves.

"Your dad sounds like a good man." I smirk, a brief, amused expression flickering across my face, but I shake it off. Forcing myself back into business mode, I clear my throat, straightening up. "Now show me where Oliver's office is."

"Let's go, boss lady."

He leads me into a limestone building with arched windows. Inside, it's painted gray with a frosted glass roof and light wood flooring that brightens the space. The arrangement of the art is elegant, not too crowded or sparse.

We wander to the offices in the back and hear Oliver's voice as we approach.

Entering Oliver's spacious office, I notice the sofas, paintings, and large desk.

He waves us in, and I take a seat on the sofa, setting up my file on the coffee table while Oliver finishes his call. Harvey leans in close to my ear, and I bite the inside of my cheek to suppress a shiver from his proximity.

"What would you like to drink?" Harvey asks.

"I don't—"

"You do," he says, cutting me off, his face inches from mine. To get him to back off, I say, "Gin."

He nods and steps away. I breathe easier and concentrate on setting up my proposal. I can't help overhearing Oliver's tense voice.

"Why is it taking this long to find him? Impossible. Keep digging until you do."

I sit in silence, shocked at hearing Oliver raise his voice. My face remains blank to maintain my professionalism, but inside I'm wondering what that was about.

Harvey returns with a glass tumbler, and I take a sip before setting it down as Oliver joins us.

"Thanks," Oliver mutters as Harvey hands him a drink, taking a seat across from me, his eyes on my setup.

He whistles, looking over the documents I put together. "Nice. I thought only my brothers were this anal."

I laugh, meeting Oliver's gaze. He has a similar look to Harvey, but his eyes carry more mystery. Harvey, on the other hand, is cocky yet annoyingly charming. I never thought I'd be attracted to someone like him.

Harvey sits beside me, but I ignore the warmth that naturally radiates from him, focusing on my job.

"Glad to see you're doing better, Jem. You gave us a scare the other night" Oliver says.

"Thanks and I appreciate you giving me this opportunity." I try to ignore that he's talking about my fainting spell and stick to business.

"So, show me your concept."

Oliver shuffles forward in his chair. His enthusiasm calms me down for the first time in twenty-four hours.

I start with the timeline, colors, lighting, music, layout, food and drink list, and security plans.

"This is impressive." Oliver whistles once more.

"Is there anything you don't like?" I ask as butterflies swarm my stomach. *Is he being polite to appease me?*

"No, it's exactly what I wanted," Oliver replies.

Reading his soft expression, I nod, hoping he's being truthful. "I need the guest list and any other details you have."

Oliver smiles boyishly. "Sure, I'll email them over."

"Can I walk through and take some photos and measurements?" I ask.

Oliver raises an eyebrow at my full glass of gin and tonic. "Let's have a drink first. You work too much, like my brothers. Your energy is making me nervous."

A giggle bubbles out of me. "I'm not that organized."

"Not like these freaks." Oliver inclines his head toward Harvey.

I laugh harder, glancing at Harvey, who doesn't seem fazed. If anything, he looks warmly at his brother.

"She's not," Harvey says bluntly, but not unkindly.

I'm not offended. Harvey says it like it is, and it helps me relax into the chair and sip my drink. I give myself a moment to enjoy my hard work.

After another sip, I put my drink down, wanting to stay sharp. I'm lucky if I can handle two drinks these days. The boys finish their drinks, and we head back the way we came. Oliver talks about the building's history and art.

"Sorry about my call earlier. There's an artist I'm trying to find," he says bitterly.

His earlier call comes to mind. "They don't want to be found?"

"Clearly not. But I will. I want to feature them in my new gallery."

"Which gallery is that?" I ask.

"I haven't acquired it yet," Oliver admits.

"The owners want to sell but won't sell to him," Harvey explains quietly.

I frown. "Why?"

We reach the main entrance of the gallery, where a large body sculpture takes up the main view. We stand in a circle in front of it.

His face rumples with an annoyed expression. "They think I'm not mature enough."

"Isn't Harvey the youngest?" I ask, my eyes flicking between them.

Harvey tilts his head toward me, his jaw working in a tight circle. "Hey. I'm proving I'm a lot more than just a little brother."

I shake my head. "I'm just trying to understand the issue."

"Yes, I'm the second youngest," Oliver says. "But like Harvey, I'm single. The gallery owners want to sell it to a new version of themselves."

Questions keep gnawing at me. "Which is?"

A shadow comes over his face. "A happily married young couple who's passionate about art," Oliver explains.

Harvey's eyebrows shoot up. "But you're not even dating."

Oliver flashes a sad smirk. "I'm well aware."

I roll my lips at the tension. It's cute brotherly banter, but at the same time, I get a twinge of pain when I'm reminded Chad will never have a sibling, and how I missed out on having one myself. I had planned a big family with my ex-husband, but things changed after Chad. Plus, conceiving Chad wasn't easy, and now I've given up hope.

"Do we need to leave the sculpture here?" I ask, trying to shift the focus.

Oliver sighs as he looks at the large piece. "No, I can move it. Why?"

I point to the pieces around it. "If we place it off-center, it'll still stand out, but the other pieces will be visible too."

He makes a satisfied noise in the back of his throat. "I'll have it moved." His eyes return to me.

"Will you be here on Friday?" I ask.

"Yeah, but if not, I can give you a key."

I blink in surprise at his casual offer. The ease with which he's willing to hand over the keys reminds me of a time when trust was more freely given and received. God, I miss those days. Now, I'm burdened by past betrayals, constantly second-guessing people's intentions. It's a heavy way to live. I crave the lightness I once had, before trust became a risk.

"I just need to let the suppliers in," I explain.

"My plan is to be here, in and out all day, unless something urgent comes up," he replies.

I nod. "That should be plenty of time, but I'll confirm on Friday," I say. "I'll take some measurements and photos now, then I'll be out of your hair."

"Take your time. Harvey and I will wait here," Oliver says.

I begin to move around the gallery, taking in the space with a critical eye. As I work, I catch sight of Harvey out of the corner of my eye. He's watching me with a mischievous look that sends my heart pitter-pattering against my ribcage. His presence is a constant distraction, making it hard to focus.

"All done?" he asks as I finish my last note.

I nod subtly, then shift my gaze back to Oliver's.

"Thanks for your time. I'll be in touch soon."

"Nice seeing you again, Jem," Oliver replies, shaking Harvey's hand before they embrace briefly in a brotherly hug. I can't help imagining them as little boys, full of energy and trouble.

Harvey and I walk back to his car, and he surprises me by heading to my side and holding the door open for me again. There's a comforting ease between us, a natural flow that makes it easy to let go and allow him to take the lead. It's a rare feeling for me, and I can't help but savor it.

In the car, I start organizing the delivery schedule for the event on Saturday on my phone. This time, it's not because I have to, but because I'm genuinely excited about the event. Oliver's approval has sparked a new confidence in me; it flicks a switch of happiness in me. A new passion for work... for life. This feels like a new beginning.

"Take a break." Harvey's voice pulls my head up from my planning.

"I want to get this done as soon as possible," I insist, my voice laced with urgency.

His forehead creases with worry. "I'll help when we get to the office."

A sigh escapes my lips as I let his offer sink in. Surprisingly, I don't mind sharing the workload with him. "I know, but I'd like to get started now."

"You're excited, aren't you?" he says with a soft laugh.

I chuckle in return, the sound light and unforced. "Is it that obvious?"

"Yes." He grins. "You're smiling, and your eyes are so bright."

"Okay, enough with the compliments. You'll make me sick," I tease.

"I like seeing you like this, happy," he says with a chuckle. "It makes you nicer to me."

I make a shushing sound, trying to reassure him. "I'm nice and I smile."

A flicker of a smile passes his lips. "Only with people you trust."

His blunt honesty stuns me. I'm at a loss for words, caught off guard by how accurately he sees through me.

Just as he's about to say more, the car's monitor flashes with an incoming call. The display shows, Esme. And a sweet, young voice fills the car.

"Esme."

"Hi, Mr. Lincoln. There are some papers I need you to sign," the voice says. I can't help but wonder how many women he works with and if any feel the way I do about him.

Stories about rich guys and their personal assistants flash through my mind. I know it's none of my business, but curiosity eats at me.

"Send them to my email. I'll sign them in about ten minutes," he responds.

"I also need you to come in and get your new suit altered," she adds.

He needs someone to organize his life, I think with a touch of irritation.

"Put it in my calendar, and I'll come in," he says, then ends the call.

Biting my tongue, I can't help but blurt out. "Is that your mom?"

The jealous tone that seeps into my voice even surprises me. I know it's not his mom, but I'm rattled by how easily he shakes me up. He seems too good to be true, and I just want to catch him in a lie.

"No, that's my personal assistant," he replies, glancing at me with a hint of amusement.

I tilt my head to look at his profile. "And you can't organize your own suits?"

The muscle in his jaw tightens slightly. "I can, but delegating tasks like that allows me to focus on important projects."

I've read about how successful people delegate minor tasks to stay productive. Why did I let it bother me? Why did I say anything at all? *Because I'm jealous.*

Harvey's calm explanation only makes my earlier outburst feel more ridiculous. He's just being practical, and I need to remind myself that there's nothing wrong with that.

CHAPTER 16

HARVEY

AFTER A LONG STAKEHOLDER meeting, I retreat to my office, which feels strangely cold. I can't quite pinpoint why it feels different? It's not that the office is shit. In fact, it's a dream workspace for most people. Compared to Jemima's, my office is luxurious, dark gray walls, a plush gray rug, glass-top tables, and splashes of dark purple in the artwork and cushions. Normally, it exudes a cozy, inviting atmosphere. But tonight, as I gaze out at the city lights, it doesn't feel right. It's not that I miss Jemima's cluttered offices, but something is off.

The sharp ring of my desk phone interrupts my thoughts. I hesitate, considering ignoring it, but with a heavy sigh, I stride over and pick it up.

"Esme," I answer.

"Hi, Mr. Lincoln, the tailor is here for your suit. Are you ready?" Esme asks.

"Yes," I respond, then hang up.

The suit, a new dark green velvet outfit with black lapels, a white shirt, and a black bow tie, is perfect for Oliver's gallery celebration. When my assistant brings in the tailor, I ask her to reschedule my monthly hairdresser appointment to Saturday. I want to look sharp.

After the tailor leaves, I wrap up the strategic review of the day, making final adjustments to my plans. A quick call to my managers ensures everything is in place before I head off home for poker night. I'm relieved it's at my place tonight, because juggling work and Jemima's responsibilities is exhausting. Soon, I'll step back and only need weekly meetings with her to discuss new risks, strategies, and operational assessments.

There's something fulfilling about witnessing Jemima's passion for the business. Despite not starting it herself, she's learning as she goes, her disorganized and chaotic approach adding to her charm. Though I'm tempted to guide her my way, I don't want to take away the uniqueness she brings as she masters things like the design brief, reminding me why my father wanted me to learn this. Watching hard work turn something around and help it thrive is something special.

I get home with ten minutes to spare before the boys arrive.

My staff has prepared a selection of food. The poker room is dimly lit in the basement, with exposed brown brick, and a glass wall separating the wine cellar and bar. I pour myself a glass of wine and take a seat at the large oval poker table, which matches the purple theme of my office. As voices sound upstairs, I add some country music to fill the room, and then greet Lukas, Gabino, Richard, Jeremy, Evan, and Oliver.

Cards are shuffled, dealt, and the game begins.

Our conversation shifts to work, and Oliver brings up his upcoming party, ensuring we all remember. *As if any of us could forget.*

"I met Jemima properly today," Oliver announces. "You should see how hot she looks when she's talking about art," he adds, causing me to tense.

My jaw is rigid at his obvious admiration, and I can't help but feel protective. "She's a woman, give her some respect."

"Technically, she's a mom," Oliver retorts, raising an eyebrow.

"What?" Jeremy asks, leaning forward as if he's never heard about her being a single mother. Though she isn't my usual type, she's different. Mature, confident, feisty, but also an incredible mother. Something I never thought I'd care about.

"Yeah, single mom to a six-year-old," I confirm, annoyed that we are discussing her personal life.

"Are you serious about her?" Evan's voice cuts through the chatter, silencing the room. When our older brother speaks, we listen.

There's something in the way he cares about me that makes me be honest with him. He might actually have some genuine advice unlike my annoying brother Oliver. "I can't be serious with someone whose business I'm rebuilding," I say, placing a bet. "My money won't work to lure her in."

Plus, it doesn't help that she's not interested in me... The usual tricks for women don't work with her.

"So, where's the ex?" Evan asks, and I feel the hairs on my neck stand up as I think about him and Danny. Their friendship, and the hurt they have caused Jemima.

I run a hand through my hair making it flop over my eye.

"Maybe dye your hair and she'll find you attractive."

"Fuck off, dickhead," I shout to Oliver.

I've caught her eyes lingering on me multiple times, so there must be something she likes.

"Where's the ex?" Evan cuts in, reminding me I haven't answered him.

"In jail."

"What for?" Evan probes, while the others eat chips or sip their drinks in silence.

"Drugs," I reply, letting the word hang heavy in the air like a bad smell.

"Fuck," Gabino murmurs.

Nodding, I continue, "She's got a lot of debt from him. I'm helping her turn the business around, but I discovered one of her family friends was embezzling."

"Shit," Evan mutters.

"You call the cops?" Richard asks.

"No, I paid him off," I explain.

"Fuck," Evan spits, clearly disapproving my decision, but it's already done.

"Have you told Jemima?" Oliver asks, rubbing the back of his neck.

I shake my head, determined to keep the progress Jemima and I have made. She's finally letting her guard down, and the last thing I want is for her to shut me out again. "No, I don't plan to. She's happy right now; no need to upset her."

"I would," Jeremy chimes in.

"I don't give a fuck what you'd do. You don't know her like I do," I snap without thinking.

"Jeez, calm down." Jeremy laughs. "Just making a suggestion."

"Everyone needs more drinks," I say, trying to regain my composure.

Why is Jemima such a touchy subject for me?

"I can't," Lukas says. "Emmy hasn't been sleeping, so I've been taking the night shift."

Normally, kids disrupting someone's life would annoy me, but I find myself sticking up for Lukas.

"This is why I won't have kids any time soon," Oliver remarks, his back turned to the group as he pours more drinks.

"They're not that bad," I counter.

"Oh, look out, incoming stepfather," Oliver teases, glancing over his shoulder with a grin.

My gaze shoots across to Oliver, and I glare at his smug face. "Shut the fuck up."

No one is being a stepfather. Just because my views on children have changed doesn't mean my goals have.

"What am I missing?" Jeremy asks, his gaze darting between us.

I won't allow Oliver to get in first, so I say, "Nothing. Oliver's making shit up again."

"Am fucking not," Oliver retorts.

"Calm down, you two," Evan's icy tone cools the room. "Fucking children."

"If something changes between you two, you'll tell us, right?" Richard asks.

"Of course," I say, taking the chance to change the subject. "But have you had any luck with getting the neighboring building?" I ask Richard. He's a successful real estate developer.

"No, they still won't sell for that price," he replies.

I rub my forehead with my free hand, considering my options. "Offer more."

"How much?"

"Whatever it takes to get it."

I lean back into my chair, grateful that my dad will be handing over my trust fund in five months. Every penny will go toward getting that neighboring building.

CHAPTER 17

JEMIMA

I'M DETERMINED TO FINALIZE the schedule and complete outstanding orders for Saturday. As I approach Molly's desk, I can't help but notice the deep wrinkle between her eyebrows, and her head bent low. Even the sound of my heels clicking on the floor doesn't make her look up. *What is holding her attention?*

I pause in front of her desk. "Molly."

She raises her head. "Oh, hi."

My eyes flick to the paper in her hands. "Are you okay?"

She holds out the paper toward me. "Here... This was on my desk this morning."

I turn it over and read the simple message.

I'm sorry, but I can't do this anymore. I quit. Danny.

I feel a sinking sensation inside my heart. My stomach. Maybe both...

Molly tries to lift the mood. "I think it's a good thing. His sales have been down, and maybe this is an opportunity to bring in someone with better skills."

But I don't feel like it's a good thing. This isn't just anyone; it's someone who was important to my dad. It feels like I let my father down. Was I too distracted by Harvey to notice Danny felt neglected or threatened?

But he knew Harvey wasn't staying. I struggle to remember the conversations I had with Danny weeks ago. I can't remember my exact words.

"You found the note just sitting on your desk?" I ask.

She points to her keyboard. "Just sitting here."

"I'll call him and see if he's okay," I say, walking to my desk and pulling my phone from my bag.

I ring him, but he doesn't answer. I call three more times before I send a text.

Me: *Please call me.*

I've never managed people, especially friends, so I head to Harvey's office for advice. But as I approach, I realize he hasn't arrived yet. Feeling defeated, I return to my office to figure out how to handle this situation until I can afford to hire a HR person.

I don't have any experience in this business, so I'm solely relying on instinct, research, and advice. Each decision feels like a gamble, and I'm starting to second-guess myself. I pour over articles, watching tutorials, and even call a few local planners who are willing to talk to me.

Finding no helpful answers, I pull up my list and begin organizing the food choices for the gallery. My focus is entirely on the tasks at hand, the rhythm of following my list and ticking each task off is helping me organize my thoughts.

After a while, a firm knock sounds at the door. Startled, I look up and breathe a sigh of relief as I see Harvey standing there.

"Hey," I greet him with a small grin.

"Morning," he replies, a concerned look crossing his face as he furrows his brow. "Are you okay?"

As he walks in, I shake my head slightly, feeling the weight of my worries. "Actually, I wanted to talk to you about something."

"This sounds serious," he says, his tone shifting to match his expression.

I try to muster a light-hearted response, but can't manage it. "As much as I want to joke around, it's serious."

He pulls out the chair opposite me and sits down, his eyes steady and patient.

"Danny left me this note," I explain, my voice a bit unsteady as I hand the note over to him. Our hands touch, sending electricity up my arm, but I ignore it. Yet, before letting go, I notice his jaw tighten, and his grip on the paper becomes visibly firm.

"How do you feel about it?" he asks, his voice low and controlled, his eyes searching mine.

"Confused," I admit. "I've tried calling and texting him, but he hasn't called me back."

"I get it, it's hard to have personal connections to your employees."

"Yeah," I murmur, scratching my head as I think. "But now I have to handle his workload on top of everything else."

"Focus on finishing the financials first." I keep my voice steady, controlled. "Once you're done with that, you can worry about his work."

"But I need to follow up on his leads," I protest. The pressure of not following up on bookings or securing new work weighs on me.

"I'll take care of that," he offers. "I've already finished my tasks anyway."

"Show-off." I snort, though a smile tugs at my lips.

"Hardly," he responds, with a casual air, crossing one ankle over his knee. The movement draws my attention to his outfit, a sharp navy suit that fits him perfectly. I quickly drop my gaze to my desk, embarrassed by my brief distraction.

"You took the hardest task and gave us the easiest ones," he says softly. He's right, and I can't help but chuckle.

"Guilty," I confess, the laughter fading but leaving me lighter than I've felt all morning.

"I can't decide whether you deserve a punishment or a reward for that," he says, a playful rasp in his voice, his eyes dark and fiery.

My heart skips a beat as I meet his blistering gaze with my own, swallowing roughly. "Definitely a reward."

As I walk the steps to the gallery, dressed in my black sweats and sneakers, I feel a rush of excitement and nerves. I knew formal wear wouldn't be practical. I carry my bags up to the door and text Oliver to let him know I'm outside. We had agreed that I'd arrive fifteen minutes before the deliveries to ensure everything else was in order.

Oliver opens the door and greets me with a calm, collected smile. "Hey, Jem."

"Hi, are you all set?" I ask, trying to hide my nervousness. I can't help but notice his crisp black suit and bow tie, his normally unruly brown hair now slicked back. He appears unfazed. But I guess, this is his world. Unlike me, I'm still finding my footing with Recaredo Events. This is my first big official event since I took over the business.

"I hope you've got your outfit in that bag, because I thought you were joining the party after the setup."

"Yeah, I just wanted to be comfortable while I ran around." I smile, stepping inside.

The gallery is quiet, except for soft background music that leaves an air of sophistication.

I begin instructing the deliveries, and before long, I'm finished. Walking outside, I check the set-up for the final time. It's a modern space with soft warm lighting, valet parking, and a red carpet leading to the entrance, lined with beautiful floral arrangements and sculptures. Inside, neatly dressed attendants hold trays of champagne, setting the tone for the evening. I shift a few lights to better highlight some pieces and make sure there's enough space for guests to appreciate the art. Each piece has a plaque detailing the artist's background.

There is a live artist setting up in the corner, adding to the intimate experience, with lighting that highlights the area without overwhelming it. The live jazz band is already set up and warming up. There's a DJ for later, which was Oliver's request to keep the energy up for those who wish to dance long into the night.

The black-tie theme is tied into every detail, including beautifully packaged gift bags containing handmade art pieces and small prints. Molly put together all the goodie bags, including tying ribbon and handwriting every tag. I start setting them up, ensuring each one is perfect. After checking on the catering staff and servers, I give them a rundown of the schedule and expectations.

With everyone in position, the first guests arrive, dressed in tuxedos and evening gowns. I watch from the sidelines as they each take a glass of champagne and head straight to the photo booth, where the pictures will be in keepsake frames provided in their gift bags.

Auctions and raffles for exclusive pieces are on the agenda, but the main focus is on the celebration of the gallery, rather than a typical auction. Guests will enjoy signature cocktails, fine wines, champagne, or the bartenders are ready to create a custom drink based on guest preferences.

Servers come out with trays of gourmet canapés, delicacies, sushi, meats and cheeses. There's no formal dinner, just constant food so people can mingle while they enjoy the art.

Happy with how it's starting, I move to the office Oliver let me leave my belongings in and slip into a strapless royal blue dress with a chunky bluestone necklace. The dress is snug, but it's also ten years old. I wore it once to a wedding and it's the only elegant gown I own. Since becoming a single parent, I've lost weight so I'd assumed the dress would feel tighter, maybe even too small. But, to my surprise, it fits just right, and for a moment, I feel a strange mix of relief and disbelief. In the bathroom, I check my make-up and there is nothing to fix other than adding red lipstick. I'm surprised to find I still look half decent despite running around. My hair is swept into a bun, and I twirl to check every angle of me. I take a big breath and exhale, ready to go mingle.

Moving around the room, I say my hellos and stand to the side. I'm waiting for someone I know. But there is only going to be Harvey. With a sigh, I spot Oliver and quickly check in to make sure he's happy and there's nothing else I can do. He tells me to switch off and grabs me a wine from a passing server, insisting I drink and relax. Once he's off, I drift through the room, trying to let myself unwind.

Oliver taps on the microphone to deliver his speech. The room falls silent, ready to soak up the host's words.

"Good evening, everyone. First off, I'd like to thank each one of you for coming tonight. You all look spectacular.

"We have a great band and DJ, so you can enjoy the incredible collection of art and dance to the music. I want to thank all the artists for giving us their pieces. You guys are creative and talented and inspire a lot of us.

"Also, if you haven't been in the photo booth, please make sure you do. The gift bags include a special frame designed for your pictures.

"Before I let you go, let's raise our glass to a night filled with incredible art, good food and drinks, and of course great company. Cheers and enjoy tonight."

We all clap and women flock to him and his brothers, except I can't see Harvey.

"I don't get the draw for the Lincolns," a blonde woman beside me says. I don't know when she came, but I can't help but reply with a smile, "You and me both."

"Maybe it's the shit talking they do," she says, winking.

I stifle a giggle.

She extends a handout to me; I can't help but notice she's not wearing jewelry and she doesn't have her nails done. I slip my hand into hers for a brief shake. "I'm Jem."

"It's nice to meet you. I'm Karley," she says with a warm smile.

"Are you here alone?" I ask, keeping the conversation casual.

"Yes, but I'll be out soon," she replies, her eyes flicking around the room.

"Are you here to buy art?" I ask further, genuinely curious about her.

"Browsing. You?" she responds, her tone light.

"I'm the event planner," I offer a small, professional smile.

"Really?" she exclaims, her face lighting up, and it fills me with a sense of pride.

"Then you know the Lincolns."

"She does," Harvey's gravelly voice interrupts from behind us. Karley twists to face him, taking a step back before heading off, but not before giving him a curious look.

He meets her gaze with a quick nod, as if this exchange is routine.

I turn to Harvey, my breath catching at the sight of him. "Your hair."

His eyes glimmer with amusement. "Do you like it?"

The blonde highlights aren't usually my thing, but there's nothing about him that's typical, so I let how I feel about looking at him spill from my lips.

"Yeah, I guess," I say, my voice soft, not fully trusting myself to say more.

He frowns. "What do you mean by that?"

"Are you going through a teenage rebellion stage?"

His lips curl. "No, I wanted a change."

"It's different."

"Good or bad?"

"Good." So fucking good, I stupidly imagine my hands curling in it as I kiss his smug lips.

I wish I wasn't hosting so I could drink more and dull the turmoil of my feelings with alcohol. But instead, I get to feel every rush, pulse, and ache between my thighs.

My eyes drift lazily over his suit and bow tie, the dark green making his eyes pop. I lower my chin, trying to collect myself.

"What are you thinking about?"

His right hand catches my attention, giving me the distraction I need. "Your ring. Is it new?"

He spins the square silver ring on his index finger. "No, my grandpa gave it to my dad."

"Who passed it down to you," I finish for him.

"I think it was meant for my dad, but honestly…" He leans forward, bringing his lips close to my ear. Keeping my eye on the ring, I notice the Lincoln name engraved on top. "It didn't fit his finger."

His confession makes me laugh. I wasn't expecting it. But my laughter is cut short when he inhales deeply.

"You smell incredible."

My eyebrows shoot up in disbelief. "Did you just sniff me?"

He pulls his face away from my neck, and I'm grateful, though he wears a proud, wolfish grin. "I thought licking you might be too far."

"Way too far," I say, shaking my head. "And weird."

"Oh, it wouldn't have been weird, trust me."

His finger, adorned with the ring, skims my arm from shoulder down to wrist, a slow, velvety touch.

Needing to make conversation before my body takes over, I ask, "You never asked your dad why he gave it to you?"

He shakes his head, his eyes briefly distant. "No. I just love having something from the family."

Trying to read his body language, I pause, looking for something more than the words he's saying. There's a hesitation in his voice, but it's buried under layers of calm.

"You really feel like an outsider, don't you?" He inhales sharply, and we stare intensely at each other. I don't think he'll speak until he whispers so only, I can hear it. "Always."

His hand reaches my wrist, and something snaps. He's messing with my head again. I need to focus. "Let's go find people to rub shoulders with."

His lips twist knowingly. "Good thinking."

CHAPTER 18

HARVEY

"She's done a great job." Oliver smirks.

"She has." My eyes scan the crowd. The room is full of people admiring the paintings and sculptures, and a large group dances to the band.

"Why the fuck is she talking to Liam?" Oliver's voice turns icy.

I straighten and follow his gaze across the room. Liam is blocking Jemima, but I can see the edge of a blue strapless dress peeking out from behind him. The dress fits her perfectly, clinging to her every shape and catching the light in a way that makes her look beautiful. It's a simple shade of blue, but it makes her skin glow. Her hair is pulled back into a neat bun, showing off her slender neck, and I can't help but want to kiss it. When I notice his hand is on the spot I touched earlier, I freeze, trying to read her face.

I can't tell if she's uncomfortable, but Oliver's competition, Liam, is known for being ruthless. He won't stop until he gets what he wants, including people.

"No fucking idea," I growl, striding over to them.

Jemima's eyes widen as she spots me. I edge myself between them, forcing Liam to drop his hand. My blood boils at seeing him touch her.

"Liam," I mumble in greeting.

"Harvey, long time no see." Liam smirks.

"It hasn't been that long, has it?"

"We always catch up at Oliver's events. Maybe next time we could talk over lunch."

"Sure, call Esme, and she can make room in my calendar," I add, knowing that I won't approve that schedule.

"Maybe Jemima would like to join us? She tells me she planned all of this for Oliver."

"She's amazing," I say, shifting my gaze to Jemima. There's warmth in her eyes as she gives me a small, soft smile.

My hand moves to her back, feeling a tremor run through her. "Let's go get you a well-deserved drink."

"Sure," she says with a small smile.

"I offered," Liam says, a hint of annoyance in his voice.

"Sorry, I changed my mind," she says, her tone polite but businesslike. She's keeping it professional, even though it's clear she's not keen on Liam.

"I'll call you about my gallery events," he says, still pressing.

She glances quickly at me before turning back to him, offering a tight but genuine smile. "Of course, I look forward to hearing from you."

As she walks away, my hand drops from her lower back, but I follow close behind, giving Liam a quick nod as I say goodbye. Once we're out of earshot, she slows her pace so I can catch up. "Is he a friend of yours?"

"No. He's Oliver's competitor," I say, shaking my head slightly.

"Makes sense."

My brow furrows. "What happened?"

"He found me fixing the flowers that had been damaged and started asking a lot of questions about Oliver and the gallery."

We arrive at the bar, and I order two glasses of wine, handing her one.

"He wants to run Oliver out of business," I say, my voice low as I take a sip of mine.

"Then I won't work with him," she replies firmly, her eyes narrowing.

I shake my head. "Do what you need to do for your business. Oliver can handle him."

"I'd rather work with Oliver than him," she says with a shrug, her gaze drifting to the floor for a moment.

"You like Oliver, then," I murmur as a knowing smile tugs at the corners of my mouth.

"Number one fan," she responds, her tone light.

A server interrupts, wanting to talk to Jemima. I'm surprised when she turns and says, "I've got to go and check on things."

She gives me her wine, and I stand there, holding two full glasses.

"Son, I'd say they're both yours, but judging by the red lip mark on one, I'd guess you're holding it for a lady?"

My dad stands there, holding his champagne flute, his posture stiff as he watches me. His eyebrows are pinched in concern, and there's a slight tension in his shoulders, like he's bracing for something.

"Did you just arrive?" I ask, scanning the room for my mom and brothers, the words slipping out as I keep my focus on the crowd.

"Yeah. They're talking to Oliver." His eyes shift to the distance briefly before returning to me, his voice lowering a bit. "I saw you alone and wanted to check in on how you're doing at Recaredo Events?"

"It's good."

I take a breath, trying to stay calm. Tonight is not the time to tell him that one of her long-term employees has a drug addiction. He was embezzling money, and that's why it hasn't been profitable.

She's got enough to deal with without wondering how Danny's desk magically cleared out. People like him don't leave quietly... well, unless someone gives them a reason to. This is better for her. Cleaner. She deserves to focus on what's in front of her, not the mess behind it. If that means I carry the weight of it alone, fine. Some things she doesn't need to know.

His eyes move around the room, taking in the event. "She's done a sensational job. I've never seen live art, a photo booth, or a red carpet at an event like this."

I glance at him, my voice tinged with admiration. "Can you believe she pulled it off in just a few days?"

His eyebrows raise in surprise. "And she's never worked in event planning before?" Dad asks, his tone laced with disbelief.

"No, she worked at Macy's before her position was laid off."

He nods thoughtfully as his lips curl into a small smile. "She's detailed and organized."

Her paperwork pops into my mind. Her office... I shake the thought away, focusing back on my dad.

"What's the plan when you leave? Will you hire more staff?"

The thought of leaving makes my chest tighten, but I keep my voice steady. "It's just her and the receptionist."

His gaze sharpens, a flicker of concern in his eyes. "And you."

"She has great casual staff, but if she picks up more work, she'll need to hire more. We need to move forward with that over the next few weeks."

I feel a sense of pride as I think about Jemima. She's so talented, naturally too. I want someone who can take the load of the day-to-day tasks off her so she can concentrate on running and growing the business.

"And how's your business? Is it managing without you?"

I pause with a slight shrug. "I've gone back to the office for a few meetings. I book them for late afternoons or early mornings so I can work around Jemima's schedule."

His lips twist into a proud smile, and I feel a rush of satisfaction. It's what I've been craving. *Recognition.*

"And how's the consultation firm looking? Have you started planning?"

I take a breath, firm in my decision. "The inheritance is going toward buying the building next door."

His eyes narrow slightly, a warning in his voice. "I hope you don't spend too much."

"I've reviewed the comps in the area with the realtor and it's a solid investment."

He pauses for a moment, then asks, "Are you learning much from being with Jemima?"

How lucky I am, and how grateful I am to have a supportive family and friends.

"Definitely. Starting from below zero is tough."

"You know you can't keep helping her with your connections. Part of the journey is her learning to hustle and scout her own work."

A muscle in my jaw ticks. "I know. I just introduced her to Oliver. She did the rest. I haven't intervened."

Jeremy, Mom, and Evan come over.

"Where's Grams?" I ask, worried she's declined, and no one's told me.

"It's too late of a night for her," Dad says.

"And she'd be on her feet all night," Mom adds as she kisses my cheek hello.

I breathe a sigh of relief. She's okay. I'll see her for Sunday dinner anyway. We're having chili.

"And probably too loud," I add as the band suddenly gets louder.

"Too fucking loud," Evan grumbles, moving away.

"Hey, grumpy. Grab me a drink while you're there," Jeremy adds smartly.

Evan glares at him. If looks could kill, Jeremy would be instantly dead.

Jeremy laughs, and I shake my head.

I stand to the side of the bar, sipping my drink, watching people dance to the DJ. The band just finished, and the mood shifts immediately as the dance music starts. Accent lights are sprinkled across the ceiling, which only adds to the ambiance. Her attention to detail is incredible.

My gaze meets Jemima's dark eyes, perfectly set on a heart-shaped face. She's watching the dancers from the edge, two outsiders looking in, wishing... I set my glass down on the bar and stride toward her, holding out my hand.

"What are you doing?" she whispers, her eyes narrowing slightly in confusion.

"Offering to dance with you," I reply with a flirty grin and step closer.

"I can't," she says shakily, turning away. I follow her across the room to a corner, where a painting of a large pink peony against a dark purple background hangs. She stands facing it, admiring the piece.

"It would be nice to be anonymous." She finally breaks the silence.

"Why?" I can't imagine her hidden; *she* stands out in every room to me.

"An easier life," she says quietly, her eyes briefly dropping to the floor. I study her, noticing the subtle shift in her expression, the vulnerability she's trying to mask.

"Nothing good in life comes easy." My voice is firm as I meet her gaze.

"That's what I'm holding on to," she replies, her tone steady but with a hint of determination, her eyes not leaving mine.

"Take Oliver, for instance. He's determined to find the artist of these paintings. It would be easier to give up and focus on artists who want to be found."

"But there's something so captivating about this."

"Exactly, which is why he won't give up, no matter the challenges or dead ends he runs into."

I turn to face her, my hair flopping over my eyes. She gently pushes it back.

My hands twitch beside me as if they want to reach out to her, but I hold them back.

"You could've trimmed your hair."

"I did."

"So you like the piece that goes in your eye?"

I smirk, loving her sarcasm. "I love it even more when you touch it."

Stepping closer, she asks, "Like this?" Her fingers graze my scalp, sending shivers through me. She gives a slight tug on my hair before she lets it go, and it drives me wild.

"Exactly like that," I rasp. "Don't stop."

"And he begs."

Willing to do anything for her touch, a grin pulls at my lips. Now that she's more open to flirting with me, I'm hopeful to where this may lead. "I'd give you anything just to have your hands on me again, Jemima."

Her eyes widen, lashes fluttering as she struggles to maintain composure. I decide not to call her out on it, not wanting to scare her away.

My eyes drop to her lips, parted and panting. When she runs her tongue over her bottom lip, I groan.

"We shouldn't," she says, gently pushing me back. "I'm working."

Her warning should remind me of my goal, but it's only a kiss. "I know, but I want you," I murmur, my hands finding her waist as I pull her back toward me.

Her eyes close as if she's in pain.

I close the distance between us, cupping her face with both hands. As I lean in, she tilts her head back, her lips just a whisper away from mine. Her breath warms my skin, and when our mouths finally meet, the touch is electric.

"I seem to be the king of walking in at the worst times," Oliver announces.

Sucking in a breath, she steps back and moves around me. I close my eyes, trying to cool my body and temper.

"You're not interrupting anything," she says, clearing her throat.

I wring my hands, keeping silent.

Turning around, I see Oliver's amused face. "Seems I did."

"That was my most successful party ever," Oliver gushes.

Jemima laughs. "Don't suck up to me, Oliver."

"I'm not."

"Is there anything she could improve on?" I ask, knowing she needs constructive criticism to grow.

Oliver pulls out his phone and shows us the screen. We lean in together, and my nostrils flare as I inhale her perfume, my body instantly igniting with recognition and need. Messages of congratulations, praise for the band and DJ, comments about the photo booth fun, and the art. Literally everything. There are even requests for her contact details. I pull back and notice her eyes are misty.

Seeing how much this means to her hits me hard. But I don't want her to get false hope. Businesses aren't always sunshine and rainbows. I need to be practical and not get lost in how captivating her eyes are under the dim lights, or how the strands of hair that has fallen makes me want to reach out and touch them.

"There has to be something negative," I say.

"Liam sent me a text saying you were getting too involved," Oliver responds, his tone slightly apprehensive, caught off guard that I would say something like that. He studies me, trying to gauge his reaction.

My body stiffens. "Are you fucking kidding me?"

"Nah, look." Oliver taps his phone until I'm reading a message saying my involvement could ruin her business.

"He's a jerk. Don't worry about him," Oliver says.

"You could have messaged him back and told him to fuck off," I reply angrily.

"Don't let him get to you."

"I can't help it."

He's already deep inside my head, messing with me. I'm not usually the jealous type. Well, I wasn't, but with him hitting on Jemima, it's brought out a side of me I've never seen and don't know how to handle.

Oliver walks away to see the DJ off.

"Let's pack up so we can all get out of here," I say.

"You don't have to. I'm sure you have somewhere to be on a Saturday night."

"You seem to think a lot about my life," I say with a teasing grin.

"I was your age once." Leaning back slightly, her arms cross as she watches me, a knowing look in her eyes.

"And what did you do?" I'm unsure I want to hear the answer, but curiosity gets the better of me.

"I was out with my friends or with my ex."

"I'm out with my friends. Unless we aren't friends?" I raise an eyebrow, half-joking, half-testing.

"We are," she says with a small smile as her posture relaxes just a little.

"We even shared a drink." I nudge her lightly, grinning.

Her expression softens as she shakes her head. "You know this is not the same thing as going out and clubbing."

"So you would club at my age? I would've liked to have seen you then."

"I was fun." She says it with a playful wink, but there's something almost wistful in her eyes.

"You are fun." I smile genuinely.

She sighs deeply, looking away momentarily, a shadow of something crossing her face before she meets my eyes again.

"I don't feel like my life is fun anymore."

"You're not what I thought you'd be like," I say, studying her closely.

"No?" she asks, tilting her head, her eyes searching mine.

"No. You're way more fun to be around. I actually enjoy your company," I add, a little softer, hoping she can tell I mean it.

"I'll hold you to that when we're back at work on Monday," she replies with a smile, but I can tell there's more to her words.

Why does Monday seem so far away? "I look forward to it."

She bumps my shoulder. "Come on, let's tidy up and get out of here. I'm tired."

"Okay, now the old lady comes out."

I squat down, and she squeals. "What are you doing?"

"Give me your shoes."

"What, no! Are you into feet or something?"

"No, silly. I'm trying to make you more comfortable," I say, a laugh escaping as she watches me lift her foot, adjusting it gently.

"You know I can take my own shoes off," she mutters, but she lets me remove one, her hand settling on my back. I reach for the other foot, tapping on it so she lifts it. "I know you can. Figured it's time someone looked after you."

"This isn't a Cinderella story."

"I'm aware. Cinderella wasn't a hot single mom."

She snorts, shoving me as I stand up. We lock eyes for a moment, and something sparks between us, but she quickly shakes her head and walks off. I'm holding her shoes.

"Does this mean I keep your shoes?"

"No, I need them." She spins back and quickly snaps them from my grasp with a giggle. Grabbing her hip, I bring her close to me. She gasps, her eyes meeting mine.

My voice low, my eyes slowly moving up and down her body, taking in every detail with a quiet appreciation. "You look incredible tonight."

I watch her throat work on a rough swallow. "You're not having sex with me, Harvey."

"I never said I was."

"Then what are you doing?"

"Telling you how beautiful you are. That's what Prince Charming does at a ball."

A whoosh of air leaves her mouth as she pushes back and walks away, carrying her shoes. "This story has Cinderella walking away holding her own shoes."

CHAPTER 19

JEMIMA

I PICK UP CHAD from Molly's after letting him sleep in. The sun is warm as we drive home. Once we get inside the apartment, I tackle the housework with new energy. Then we head to the local shops, indulging in some freshly baked bread to celebrate last night's success.

Back home, Chad and I decide to build a fort. We drape blankets over chairs and inside we spread out his Legos to build an entire village. We laugh and talk as we play. This is my favorite time of the week, simply being with Chad and playing with him. The joy on his face as he builds is infectious. I realize how much I've missed moments like this, just being here with him, without the weight of work or worries clouding our time together. For so long, I've been caught up in making ends meet, but now, I can finally relax and just be a mom.

After lunch, Chad suggests we go play some basketball, but I have an idea.

"Where are we going?" he asks from the back seat of the car, his eyes wide with curiosity.

"You'll see soon," I reply, a smile playing on my lips.

His favorite music fills the car, and the upbeat tunes have him dancing in his seat. But barely five minutes later, he asks, "How much longer?"

"We're almost there," I reassure him, my excitement mirroring his.

I pull up outside a pristine basketball court in one of my dream suburbs, where the surrounding apartments are sleek and modern.

"This is so cool, bro," Chad exclaims, running toward the court.

"I'm your mom, not your bro," I remind him with a laugh.

He races across the court, and I decide to join him in a game instead of sitting on the bench. The sun shines brightly down on us, and as we play, I realize it's not as easy as it looks. Sweat beads on my forehead, and I'm grateful for the shorts I have underneath my sweatpants. Since my weight loss, I usually don't show off my legs because I'm self-conscious of how thin they are. Stress and minimal food have taken a toll on my body, my curves disappearing.

I grab a big drink of water, glancing over at Chad to check on him. Next to him, I recognize the glistening chest, squared jaw, and piercing blue eyes.

Harvey.

He throws me one of those wicked smiles that makes my knees weak. His eyes drop over me, lingering just long enough to make my skin tingle. I stiffen, wishing I'd thought to throw on my sweatpants. His eyes trail back up, meeting mine again, and instead of the repulsiveness I feared, there's intense heat.

I make my way hastily to Chad, standing behind him, using him as a shield.

"Mom, look! It's Harvey."

"I see," I murmur, my stomach twisting in ways I can't quite decipher.

Harvey smirks as his eyes dance. "It's me."

I roll my eyes, but I can't stop the corner of my mouth from twitching. He sees it and laughs.

"What are you doing?" I ask, trying to sound casual.

"Running, but I figured that was obvious." He gestures to his sneakers, running shorts, and the earbuds hanging out of his ears.

He's such a smartass, but his cocky grin makes it hard to keep a straight face.

"Do you want to play?" Chad holds out his ball toward Harvey.

"Hey, I've been good, haven't I?" I say, pretending to be offended.

"Mom, you're trying, but Harvey's better," Chad says innocently.

"Ow," Harvey chuckles under his breath. "I really want to play now," he teases. "Especially since your mom sucks."

Chad bursts into giggles. The sound is so pure that it makes me laugh too.

"You suck!" Chad shouts between fits of laughter.

I cross my arms and narrow my eyes at them both, pretending to be annoyed. "You two are mean."

"Sorry, Mom," Chad says, still laughing.

"She just needs practice," Harvey says as he steps closer. He ruffles Chad's hair, and his hand grazes my arm as he pulls away. The soft touch is light, but it sends a spark through me.

"Your hair looks like mine," Chad says, reaching up to smooth his own.

"Do you like it?" Harvey asks as he crouches to Chad's level.

"Yeah! We're twins now," Chad beams.

I roll my lips together, not wanting to correct him. Let him have this moment.

"We aren't, but I like your hair," Harvey says.

Harvey's watch chimes, breaking the moment.

"I have to meet someone." He glances at his watch.

"Well, better not keep her waiting." I start to retract my steps and tug Chad gently.

"*He's* at our meeting point," Harvey corrects me, holding my gaze.

"You better go. I'll see you tomorrow," I reply, trying to hide the embarrassment creeping up my neck, feeling a heat in my cheeks that I'm sure he notices.

He nods. "Are you ready for the bake-off?"

"It'll be an easy win. I'd be worried if I were you."

"Molly's got my back." He winks, and it hits me harder than I want to admit.

I raise an eyebrow and whisper, so Chad doesn't hear. "You better not be seducing her."

His grin widens. "Is that what you think I do?"

"People do anything to get ahead," I tease, crossing my arms.

"I don't. I win fair and square." He smirks, then adds, "But I can always use some backup."

I can't help but laugh. "Well, good luck with that. I'll show you what I've got tomorrow."

Cutting our moment short, his watch sounds again.

"We'll let you go," I say, grateful for the interruption.

"See you next time." He high-fives Chad, and then meets my eyes one last time, softer now, but no less intense. "See you tomorrow, Betty Crocker."

The name brings back memories of my dad. His favorite flavor was red velvet. Mom used to make the Betty Crocker cake mix for his birthday every year.

I watch Harvey jog away, unable to look away as his back flexes with each step.

He turns his head, and I feel a blush rise to my cheeks. Quickly, I spin around and usher Chad to the car. "Let's go."

"Oh, but Mom," he whines.

"Next time, don't tell me I suck, and I'll play with you longer," I tell him playfully, raising an eyebrow as I smirk.

"Harvey said you suck."

"Thanks for the reminder," I mumble under my breath. Looking at where Harvey left, I shake my head, wondering why he's getting to me. This new friendship with a man is unsettling.

I send Danny another text to tell him I hope he's okay and to call me when he's ready. But I still haven't heard back.

When we pull up to the apartment, I see Jade. She comes rushing over to me, her face full of curiosity. "Hi——"

"We went to this other basketball court today," Chad announces, interrupting her.

"Did you?" she asks brightly. "Where?" Her eyes move to me.

"90th street," I say.

"You're a lucky boy." Jade smiles at Chad, who bounces his ball some more. I wonder where he gets the energy from. I'm ready to lie down on the sofa and nap.

"I wanted to catch you because I got a letter meant for you. The postman must have mixed it up."

I take the letter and don't miss the top left corner address. The prison. Jade gives me a sad smile. She knows.

"Did you need some company, love?" she offers.

"No, I'm okay."

"Are you sure?"

"Yeah, I can do it," I say, knowing I'm not okay, but I can't break down in front of Chad. I need to keep it together, at least for him.

"If you need me to come over for a cup of tea or to take the little man, just call me."

"Thanks, Jade," I say, gently squeezing her arm. I hope she can hear how grateful I am. People like her remind me of the good in this world.

As we climb the stairs, Chad chatters away. I hum when needed, but otherwise, my head doesn't know what to do. My thoughts are all messed up from the letter that's burning a hole in my hand. Do I open it now or wait until Chad's gone to sleep?

I go for the latter.

I cut up some fruit for him, but the unknown contents of the letter eat at me. Unable to wait anymore, I tear it open and read.

Jem,

How are you? Sorry it took me so long to write to you. While I've been in here, I've had a lot of time to reflect. My choices were selfish, and I miss our times together. I've been

*working out and reading. I've also been going to counselling
to work on my inner self. I regret my choices.
Let Chad know I wish I was there to shoot some hoops with
him.
It's not my intention to seek your forgiveness, but rather I
hope you find peace and happiness. I'm changing for the
better.
Love, Butch.*

Working on himself? Glad he has time while I just picked up the pieces and carried on, fixing the mess he left me in. And what times is he referring to? The early ones as a family of three? Well, those times didn't last. I want to ask when he started using, but then I'd have to reply, and I don't want to acknowledge him. I hate him. I hate the life he robbed me of. I didn't want this.

What's the point of writing to me? Does he expect me to praise him or congratulate him on his improvement?

I can't do that. I've filed for divorce. I want to start over.

I look around our apartment, the lighting capturing the worn-out sofa that still has indentations where he used to sit, his presence lingering like a ghost. I can almost see him sitting there, eyes glued to the TV, the loud sounds of horse racing filling the room. The sight overwhelms me. God, I hate it here. There are too many memories, each one a painful reminder. The walls feel like they're closing in on me, and I crave a new place, somewhere to start fresh.

I grip the cold paper tightly, its edges digging into my palm. I can't bring myself to throw it out, because Chad deserves the truth when he's old enough to ask. I put the letter away, out of sight but not out of my mind. I never chose anything other than my family, and even now, I put Chad first. My needs, wants and desires always come second.

Turning to the kitchen, I decide to bake, hoping that will distract me. Harvey's cocky grin at the park earlier flashes in my mind, egging me on. Chad joins me, and his little hands stir the batter. He giggles as he licks the spatula and bowl, batter smearing on his cheeks.

I slide the cake into the oven, and Chad runs back to his toys, the sound of him playing filling the room. But my mind drifts back to the letter. Do I respond? The question eats at me.

My phone buzzes on the counter, and I wipe my hands and check the screen, seeing Harvey's name.

Me: *I'll look into it.*

After I hit send, a pang of guilt twists in my gut. I wasn't as nice as I could've been, but my frustrations and self-inflicted pressures, like refusing to ask for help because it feels like admitting failure, only to add to the sense that I'm feeling inadequate as a mother right now. I remind myself it's not on purpose and that Harvey means well, but it doesn't simmer down the turmoil inside me. Chad's talented and deserves the opportunity, so I'll look into it. As long as it works around school and it isn't too far, I can get him the scholarship and, most importantly; if Chad wants it, then I can't say no. Life hasn't been fair to him and seeing him shine in an environment that can support him would be a joy. And God knows, I need that.

The smell of cake fills the apartment. I forgot about the time and get the cake out, just in time. It's a bit more golden than it should be, but it'll do.

"Is it ready?" Chad calls out.

I hand him a small cake I baked in a ramekin, just for him.

"Here you go."

He digs straight in. There wasn't enough batter for me, but I'll have some of this tomorrow after I've decorated it. And it will be so much sweeter when I'm announced as the winner, because it's more than just a baking contest. It's proof that I can do something right, that I can juggle it all and still come out on top. Winning would mean I'm more than just a mom struggling to keep it together. If I lose? I don't even want to think about it. Because if I can't pull this off, what else am I failing at? No. I need this.

CHAPTER 20

JEMIMA

MORNING TEATIME ARRIVES, AND I nervously slide my cake into the middle of the table next to Harvey's. The boxes hide our cakes so we can't compare. Two vanilla sponges. One winner.

I stand back, rubbing my hands together. Molly enters, her eyes flicking between the two cakes. "Are we ready?"

Harvey lounges in his chair, exuding confidence. "I've got this in the bag," he mumbles.

Molly lifts the lids, and my jaw hits the floor. "You didn't bake that," I blurt out, pointing at his cake. It's a masterpiece with two layers of light golden-colored cakes with a perfect jelly and cream ratio, topped with a sugar dusting and dressed in the same purple flowers he brought me.

Beside sits mine, a three-layered sponge that looks more golden, with strawberries neatly arranged on top.

Molly steps in. "Let's do the taste test."

"First, call your grandma on video. I want to make sure she didn't bake this," I demand, my frustration boiling over.

Molly tries to calm me. "I don't think that's necessary."

I plead with her. "There's no way he made that."

Harvey raises an eyebrow. "I followed a recipe. There were no rules against that, were there?"

"No," I admit through gritted teeth.

He pulls his phone out and dials, and a deep male voice answers, "Harvey."

"Hey Dad, is Grams there?"

"Yeah, why?"

"I need to talk to her."

The next minute an older woman's voice sounds. "Harvey?"

"Hi, Grams," he says, smiling as I hear her voice crack through the phone.

"What are you doing?"

"I'm at work, but I baked a cake using your recipe for the vanilla sponge," he replies.

"Oh, you did?"

Harvey glances at me, then to the screen, her eyebrow lifting in mild surprise.

"Did you want to see it?" he asks, holding the phone closer, eager to show her.

"Yes."

He turns the phone camera to the cake, and she beams, "Great job. Did you make two?"

"No, the other one was made by my co-worker."

"They both look great. Which is yours?"

He points to his. "I like the ranunculi on top. I've never thought to use them."

"Thanks, Grams. I better go. I just wanted to show you."

He really did make this cake...

"Well done, Harvey. I'm proud of you," she gushes. A pang of longing hits me.

I need to call my mom later.

Harvey's face softens, a slight blush creeping in.

My anger fades. He's not only intelligent and thoughtful but also genuinely kind to his family, blurring the lines of my frustration.

Molly cuts the cakes, and we all taste both. I try mine first. It's lovely and fluffy but a tad drier than usual. Then I taste his and release a tight breath. It's perfect—light, moist and delicious. I don't dare look at him, knowing he's wearing a shit-eating grin. He would've tasted mine and known it was a little overcooked.

Molly finishes her tasting, nodding thoughtfully as she looks between the cakes. "You both did a great job," she starts.

"Who's the winner?" I ask, already knowing the answer.

She gives me a sympathetic look and turns to Harvey. "Yours wins."

"Fuck yeah!" He fist-pumps the air, a wide grin spreading across his face. As the phone rings, Molly rushes out to answer it.

I roll my eyes. "Calm down. It's only a friendly cake competition."

He steps closer, still grinning. "You wouldn't be saying that if you won. Better luck next time, buttercup." He's in my personal space, his finger lightly grazing my lip. My breath catches, and I freeze as he rubs his thumb over my bottom lip, and then slowly sucks it into his mouth, his eyes never leaving mine.

I'm speechless, standing there with my mouth hanging open.

"Aren't you going to congratulate me?" he teases.

Oh, he's really trying to fuck with me. I force myself to respond, my voice coming out breathy. "Congratulations."

A spark lights up his eyes, and one side of his lip curls into that dangerous smile I can't seem to ignore. "That wasn't so hard, was it?"

I shake my head, trying to focus on something other than him. "I've got to go finish the baby shower preparations before my meetings with the mom-to-be."

"Do you need me?" He steps back into work mode, which I'm grateful for.

"No, it's a small one. I've got it."

"What do you want me to do, then?" There's a tinge of disappointment in his tone.

I think about what new events he can handle without touching the finances. "Maybe you can call Oliver and get the next event's date and location."

"Done. Then if it's okay with you, I'll get started on new software."

I nod. "Go for it."

I walk out of the breakroom as Harvey calls out, "Molly, what's my prize for winning?"

A sense of dread washes over me. I hope his reward works in my favor.

"I need time to think about it," Molly says back. "Let's all meet up when Jem gets back from the meeting."

I leave the room, taking my plate of cake with me. After an hour, I return from my meeting and head to Harvey's office, but he's not there. I find Molly instead. "What's the reward?"

"I haven't decided."

"Molly," I warn.

"Fine, I've decided, but I'm not telling you."

"I'm your boss."

"Don't——" Molly starts.

"What are we talking about?" Harvey strolls in and stands beside me.

I keep quiet and let Molly speak. "She wants to know if I've decided on your prize yet."

"She does? So do I," he says, leaning on the desk, his eyes gleaming with playful curiosity as he watches us, the corner of his mouth tugging into a faint grin.

Molly's face brightens as she sits up in her chair.

"You two have to have dinner together," she says, folding her arms with a knowing grin, chin tilted just slightly higher like she's hit the jackpot.

Her eyes dart between Harvey and me with glee.

"I can't——" I begin to deny as I feel my body flushing.

"I'll have Chad for the night," Molly cuts me off. She knows I'll do anything to get out of this.

"Then I'll organize the dinner," I say, hoping for a low-key meal where I don't have to dress up and we'll be done in two hours. I don't want him to read too much into this.

I can have dinner with a friend.

"I won. Which means I'll organize," Harvey deadpans.

I quickly retort, "But then you're doing all the work, and isn't that the loser's job?"

He shakes his head, his tone making it final. "It's my job. As a man, don't take it away from me."

"Fine," I say, lifting my hands in surrender. "What time do I need to be ready?"

"Six."

I give Molly a death stare, like she owes me. Clearly thinking this is the best thing ever, she just smiles.

I walk off to my office and try to concentrate on work. But as I pull up the spreadsheet I've created, my mind wanders. I'm already thinking about what I'll wear, what we'll talk about, and if he will end the night with a kiss.

I'm putting on my beige coat, the anticipation growing with every second as I expect him to arrive any minute. My hands tremble slightly as I choose my favorite light-wash skinny jeans, pairing them with a thin cream high-neck sweater and gray pumps. Not knowing where we're going, and with limited time, I decided to go with a casual yet chic look. After dropping Chad off at Molly's after work, I rushed home for a quick everything shower.

As I wait, my mind races back to my twenties—the last time I felt butterflies this intense. The nausea and urge to bail are overwhelming, but a knock at the door pulls me back to the present. I take a deep breath, trying to calm the feeling of the tightness in my chest.

"Hi," I greet him, opening the door. Relief washes over me as I take in his appearance, more casual than usual. He's wearing a black sweater and black pants with a simple belt. His hair is its usual end-of-day mess, so he must have rushed too, juggling work and organizing this date.

"You look beautiful."

My cheeks heat, and I drop my gaze to the floor. "Thanks," I mumble, tucking a strand of hair behind my ear.

"Are you ready to go?"

"Yeah." I close the door behind me, his presence close, invading my space, and it messes with me. Locking the door, I step outside, expecting his sports car, but instead finding a limousine waiting. As much as I want this to feel like a casual night out as peers, I can't help but appreciate all the little date-night touches.

"I've never been in a limo before."

"Glad I could pop your cherry," he says with a chuckle.

I shake my head but laugh. It's tough trying to maintain a strictly professional relationship, especially when he's in a playful mood.

A gray-haired man in his fifties, dressed in a crisp suit, opens the door. I smile and climb into the limousine, sinking into the beige leather seats. They're soft and luxurious, everything I thought it would be. Yet I can't shake the feeling that I shouldn't be here. Life has this sick way of pulling the rug out from under me just when I start to feel happy. Letting me fall hard on my ass.

He climbs in beside me, putting a hand on my thigh, and I clasp my hands in my lap, trying to steady them. The drive is short, and we soon arrive in Soho. He gets out first, offering his hand to help me. "How was the ride?"

"Really nice."

"It'll take us back later."

I can't help but wonder how much later.

"Let's go." Harvey ushers me inside, and we take the elevator to the rooftop. It's just us and a few servers here. This place is quiet, except for some soft music playing through the speakers. Where is everyone else?

"Are you sure it's open?"

He chuckles, his hand skimming my lower back. "I booked the place for just us. I wanted you to be comfortable."

A snort-like sound comes from my throat. "I prefer to blend in."

"You couldn't even if you tried."

"I guess my cheap clothes stand out," I mumble, looking down at my outfit.

He moves so fast my breath catches, placing his hand on my chin and angling my face to his. "No. Stop. That's not what I meant. Stop talking down about yourself. I wish you could see the smart, sweet, and beautiful woman I see." His eyes burn into mine with such intensity I feel like I might catch on fire.

The rawness in his words is palpable, and my heart beats faster in response.

"I didn't say I wasn't smart. I'd say I am, since I've been trying to stay away from you."

"You can't outrun me," he says, stroking my cheek. "When I want something, I'm persistent until I get it."

"You're annoyingly persistent, and most times I just wished you'd shut up." I smirk.

"There are other ways to shut me up." His voice dips low as he leans forward.

"Mr. Lincoln," a male voice interrupts.

I glance past his shoulder to see a server wearing an apron and flushed cheeks from interrupting us. We haven't even sat down to have a drink and he's already trying to kiss me... and I don't know if I will be strong enough to fight this.

When it's just us, and he's sweet, it's hard to keep my walls up. He's been slowly chipping away at them, proving to me he's kind and intelligent. I see beyond his money now. Part of me believes he genuinely wants me. And because of that tonight, I plan to have fun.

"Yes?" Harvey says in a clipped tone, annoyed by the interruption. I bite my lip to hide a smile trying to escape my lips.

"Come this way. Your private table is ready."

I stifle a laugh at the way the server emphasizes "private." Something I should be worried about because being alone with Harvey is dangerous.

We follow the server, and I can't tear my eyes away from the panoramic views of New York. It's stunning and something I'll remember forever. The black-and-white seats of the booths, candles lit up in the middle of every table, and fairy lights hanging throughout create a romantic setting.

We sit, and the server comes by to take our drink orders. "What kind of food do they serve here?"

"Mexican."

I grin as I glance at the menu. "I love tacos."

"So I take it you're happy now that I organized this?"

I tap my chin, pretending to think. "I'm surprised. It's this relaxing... and yet beautiful," I admit, letting my eyes linger on him.

"What did you expect?"

I shrug. "Fancy, but not the uncomfortable kind."

He raises an eyebrow. "You thought I'd be bougie?"

I nod, meeting his gaze with a teasing smile. "Yeah."

"I can be if you want, but it's not really my thing. And I guessed from the few times I've seen you that you like to let your hair down after work."

"You mean my lazy attire." I laugh.

"If you have lazy attire, so do I," he replies with a smirk.

"I've never seen it," I challenge with a raised eyebrow.

"I'll make sure to show you," he promises, leaning slightly closer, his grin teasing.

I don't think he could look bad if he tried.

"But I'm not mad now that I lost. Your cake was better."

"Yours just needed to come out a few minutes earlier, and you might have won."

My gaze drops, and I feel the weight of a secret pressing down on me. I want to tell someone about the letter. He sits patiently, waiting for me to speak. The server brings our drinks and chips and salsa, then leaves.

"I got a letter from my ex... I ended up forgetting about the cake," I confess.

The muscle in his jaw pulses, but he remains silent, giving me space to continue.

I sip my drink, savoring the strong tequila, before leaning back. "It's the first time he's reached out since he went to jail."

Harvey straightens.

"What's worse is that I had no idea he was using. He was the father of my child, and I trusted him. I thought he'd always look after me and his son," I say, laughing, but it lacks humor.

"What was in the letter?" he asks, then quickly adds. "You don't have to answer if you don't want to."

I hesitate for a moment, then find myself speaking. "He said he's been working on himself." I pause, staring into Harvey's eyes. "What is it about you that gets me saying things I wouldn't share with anyone else?"

He gives me a warm, crooked smirk. "Maybe it's because I'm an open book. I say it how it is."

I nod, feeling lighter as I rest my hands on the table. "A take-it-or-leave-it attitude. I love it. I wish Chad could be that way."

"He's still young. He'll get there, especially with you guiding him."

"Thanks," I say. "I'm not responding to the letter, but I don't want to throw it away in case Chad asks."

Harvey nods, putting his hand on top of mine, understanding my predicament. "He didn't deserve you and Chad. When Chad's old enough to ask, I'd be honest."

"He's just made me so angry. He took all our money and got us into so much debt. I owe over three months of rent." My eyes widen, and I cover my mouth at my outburst. He makes me feel comfortable that words just spill.

"Do you need——"

I drop my hand and shake my head. "Don't even think about it. I want to pay back without owing you. You're making it difficult..." I trail off, catching myself. I'm not going to date him.

"I'd say I'm sorry he betrayed you, but I'm not. I'm glad I can show you not all men treat women that way and that I can treat you the way you deserve."

My cheeks burn, and I glance away, my fingers fidgeting with my glass. "Harvey," I murmur, my voice barely above a whisper. "Why?"

"What do you mean, 'why'? Why what?"

"Why would you agree to spend dinner with me as the prize? Any other woman would love to be here."

"Except you," he adds with a playful smirk.

"I'm enjoying myself. It's just hard to understand what you want from me."

"There's no hidden agenda." His lips curve into a casual smile, but there's an intensity in his eyes that makes my stomach flutter. "I'm attracted to you, and I think you're attracted to me. We're adults; why can't we just have some fun?"

"I can have fun."

"You said you used to be fun."

He's right. "I did."

"Well, let yourself have fun with me. I promise not to let you down."

The usual alarm bells that would ring through my body to say; *I don't believe him,* aren't there. It's silent. Only desire floods my body.

Feeling my old self returning, I say, "Let's have fun."

He flashes me a wicked grin and waves down the server, ordering us a round of spicy margaritas.

"Have you heard from Danny?" he asks.

"No, he disappeared without a trace. I even contacted his friends, but no one knows where he went. I'll need to hire a replacement before you leave because I can't do this alone."

"No, but you also can't be expected to be doing all the little tasks. You need to be managing," he insists.

"Am I ready for a team?"

"Yes, you are. You're so good at it. The baby shower this weekend will be amazing, and you already have Oliver's connections since you kicked ass at his event. No one has seen an event like it, and now they will want to be bigger and better, especially Liam."

My stomach rolls at the mention of his name. "There's something off about him."

"Liam wants to sleep with you," Harvey says, his voice flat in a way that sends a chill down my spine.

I scrunch up my face, repulsion evident in my expression. "He's never getting that."

Harvey's lips curl into a knowing smile. "Good girl."

As I reach for my new drink, my hand knocks the table, and the glass tips over, its contents spilling onto my sweater. The cold liquid seeps through the fabric, making me shudder.

Harvey laughs, a warm sound that contracts with the chill.

"You can't take me anywhere nice."

"I wish you aimed higher and not worn a bra," he teases, his eyes dancing with amusement.

"Who says I am?" A playful smirk tugs at my lips.

His eyes widen, and I see them drop to my chest, where the wet fabric clings to my skin, outlining my curves. "Fuck. Are you kidding me?" Disbelief edges his tone.

His gaze locks with mine, filled with raw unspoken need.

I hide my smile behind my glass, softly shaking my head.

"Fucking hell," he mutters, adjusting himself, clearly affected. "Please, this place is ours, and they can't see you. Only I can."

For a moment, I imagine what it would be like if it was just the two of us, alone in a room, free from interruptions. If I gave in to this charged electricity, what would he do? How would he make me feel?

Loving the power I hold right now; I decide to push the boundaries. "Be a good boy and behave, and let's see what happens later. I might give you a goodnight kiss."

"I want more than a kiss," he says, his voice a deep, husky growl, eyes dark with intent.

My mind imagines being brave enough and sitting on the table and telling him to crawl over and eat something else... *Eat me.*

"You'll be lucky to get that. Don't push, or I'll give you nothing," I warn, though my pulse races at the thought of more.

"I bet you're all talk." He leans in, looking at me like he could devour me. "I bet if I had you pinned underneath me, you'd be putty in my hands."

Warmth blooms in my lower stomach at his words. "I guess we'll never know, will we?"

CHAPTER 21

HARVEY

WHERE ARE WE HEADED with seeds?" Jemima asks as we leave the health store next to the restaurant. Her voice pulls me from the streets to the mesmerizing sight of her heart-shaped face. The warm light from the streetlights casts a soft glow on her features, giving her an almost delicate look.

"You'll find out." I didn't want our time to end yet, so I came up with an idea to make the date last longer.

"What if I don't like it?" she replies, her teeth skimming her bottom lip in a way that makes my heart skip a beat.

"You will. I don't need people thinking I don't look after the women I date," I say, my attempt at humor falling flat as her eyes meet mine with a hint of hurt.

Her gaze sharpens, and I immediately regret my choice of words. I haven't dated anyone since we started working together, and the thought of being with someone else now seems ridiculous. She's different—genuine, unpretentious, and refreshingly real.

"I won't tell anyone."

"Thanks," I say lightly, trying to fix the moment.

As our steps fall in sync and her arm brushes mine, a comfortable silence envelops us.

"Are you heading into the office tomorrow?" she asks, watching her eyes drift toward the city lights as they cast reflections in her eyes, making her look even more captivating.

"Yeah, I have my quarterly meeting."

"Where do you get your confidence from?" she asks, genuinely curious. Her approach has always fascinated me.

"I'm just good at faking it," I admit.

"Fake it till you make it... So cliche," she says with a vulnerable laugh, her eyes sparkling. It's a rare glimpse into her, and I cherish it.

I nod. "It's true, though. We pretend we do care until it becomes ingrained in us."

"You're strong. It won't be hard to keep it up," I say, my voice filled with quiet conviction.

"Just keep being a bitch to you and I'll be fine?" she teases.

I bump her shoulder. "We both know you secretly like me. But it's okay. I love watching you pretend you don't."

Her mouth parts slightly, and I shake my head in a playful way. When she closes her mouth, a small smile plays on her lips.

"Have you finished the financials?" I ask, changing the subject as we stop walking when we reach Central Park. She won't let me touch the numbers. I still haven't told her I stumbled upon those papers by accident.

"Not yet," she sighs, the weight of the workload evident in her tone.

"When you're finished, we need to have meetings about operations, customer service, sales, and financial reviews."

"It's so much," she murmurs, her shoulders sagging.

I open the small bag of seeds and hold it toward her, and she silently takes it. "It won't be if you stick to running the business. We'll hire good employees to handle the day-to-day stuff."

"I'm scared of hiring people," she confesses, her voice barely above a whisper.

She means people who might leave, disappoint, or hurt her.

I stop our walk, turning to face her. My hand skims up her arm, and goosebumps rise in the wake of my touch. "That's what I'm here for," I say softly. "I'll show you how to ask the right questions and to help you choose."

She purses her lips, her eyes filled with uncertainty. "Yeah, it's getting too much for me and Molly to handle it all."

"Exactly. Your business is growing every day. Expanding will make you become more successful."

She exhales deeply. "I know, but I don't think I can handle any more change."

"Our brains resist change because it's trying to keep us safe."

"I like safe," she says, smiling softly. I know why she craves it after everything her shit ex put her through.

"I've never talked about work on a date before," I confess, wanting to keep the conversation light.

"No?" she asks, her expression cautious.

We finish feeding the birds and naturally resume our walk through the park. "They always talked about their nail appointments, how much money I make, where I was taking them next, or how they spent two hours doing cardio."

"Two hours?" she gasps, her eyes wide as she looks up at me, leaning back. "I do nothing. Unless you count walking to parks and courts with Chad."

"You don't need to do anything," I say, my eyes dropping longingly over her body. "You're perfect as you are."

"I want to. I'm..." she starts, her gaze dropping to the floor before lifting it back to mine, "too weak."

I shake my head, words spilling out before I can stop them. "I think you look great. I mean——" My hand jerks to the back of my neck, and I rub it, heat crawling up my face. "Fuck, that's not what I meant. Not that it's bad or——" I groan, dragging a hand over my face. "I just...

You're beautiful. Always." My gaze flicks to her, searching for a reaction, and I swear my heart skips when she smiles.

"I know what you mean. Calm down."

"Good. I thought I just insulted you."

"I can't look in the mirror as I get dressed. Avoiding mirrors is my specialty."

I stare at her, my jaw twitching. Is she fucking serious?

"Are you fucking with me?"

She laughs, grabs the closest streetlight, and walks slowly around it. Not looking at me but up at the stars above us. My eyes never leave her. She's so fucking beautiful. "You should look in a mirror every day. You're missing out."

Shaking her head, she pauses her twirl momentarily. "On what? The bags under my eyes, the lines in my forehead, or the grays in my hair?"

I'm flabbergasted. She's making me speechless. I don't understand when all I see is her long, shiny brown hair, soft skin I'm dying to touch, and eyes that tell me everything she's thinking.

She resumes her walk, but I step forward, stopping her abruptly, capturing her face in my hands, and bringing my mouth close to hers. My body is heavy from tequila and lust. "You and I see things very differently," I grit out. "You're incredibly beautiful...natural, yes. But fuck, it's perfect for me."

She sucks in a sharp breath, surprised by my words. I'm about to kiss her when her phone chimes.

Tearing her gaze away, she steps back from me to open her bag, quickly answering the call. "Molly."

Crap, this can't be good.

"Chad's upset. I've tried to settle him. I'm sorry." I can hear Molly over the line.

"I'll be there as soon as possible." Jemima's voice has a frantic edge to it. It's a reminder of how different her life is. It's not a simple date or hookup.

I straighten. "Let's go. We'll drop you off at Molly's."

She nods. "Thanks. I'm——"

I shake my head and grab her waist, bringing her closer to me. "Don't apologize. He's the priority."

"Always."

We stare at each other for a second, knowing how close we were to kissing moments before, but Chad needs her, so I take her hand and walk her to the waiting limo.

"What's Molly's address?" I ask.

She rattles it off, and I tell the driver.

She's texting frantically on her phone. I don't know what to do, but I hate seeing her this stressed out. I grab her and drag her closer to me. She stiffens, but then settles as I wrap my arm around her back. Tucking her phone away, she lays her head in the crook of my neck. Holding her like this feels so right. Her warm body in my arms, her scent filling my nose, and her touching me back sends a mess of turmoil through me.

I don't want this to end, but as the car pulls up to another brick apartment complex similar to hers, she lifts her head. I'm breathing heavily, holding myself back from begging to follow her in. I always want to fix other people's problems, but this is so out of my depth. I know nothing about children; I'm like a fish out of water.

When she peels herself away, I slip out of the car and hold the door open. Her hand settles in mine, and she peers up at me from under her fluttering lashes.

"Thanks for tonight."

"Was I as bad of a boy as you thought?" I tease with a playful grin.

"Worse," she replies with a sly smile, her eyes glinting.

I choke out a laugh. The sound comes out unexpectedly breathless. "I'll have to step up my game next time."

"Harv——"

I shake my head, not wanting to hear the words, "there won't be another time," leave her lips.

We stand there, inches apart, as my hand circles her waist. The night air is crisp now, but neither of us is cold.

With my other hand, I grab the back of her head and bring her mouth to mine. She sinks into the kiss, giving me a hungry side of her. Her hand grips my back, and I growl into her mouth. Her lips are soft, and when she parts them, I don't hold back. I slip my tongue into her mouth to touch hers. When she moans, it sends me into a frenzy. My hands grip her waist and head harder, and every whimper is captured by my lips. Her hands roam my back, scratching me with her nails, and I wish there weren't any clothes between us. She feels amazing. I can't get enough.

When we both pull away, trying to catch our breaths, we hold each other's gazes in wonder. Did she feel like her heart was going to burst out of her chest? Because I thought mine was.

Our hands remain together, neither of us ready to leave just yet.

This time, she rises onto her tiptoes and leaves me with a soft yet bruising kiss. When she stands back, her hands pull away from my body, and I stuff mine back into my pockets to resist temptation. I stare at her pretty swollen lips, enjoying the evidence of our kiss.

"I better go," she says, her voice edged with reluctance.

"Can I come up?" I smirk, knowing I'm pushing my luck, but her eyes are sparkling under the streetlights. "Harvey. Do you think that's a good idea?"

"Molly or you would've told him I was with you. Maybe I can help?"

"I don't know..." Her words fail her when I step close, so our lips are close again.

"Let me be here for you. You're not alone in this."

She rolls her eyes, and her lips lift as she turns and heads up the stairs and I follow.

Molly greets us and I don't miss the arch in her brow at Jemima. I swallow a laugh. Entering the small apartment filled with bright colors and dinner on the table. But I don't inspect for too long because a scream that almost pierces my ear drums draws my attention.

Jemima is holding Chad on the gray sofa and running her hands through his hair. She hushes him, but it's like he gets louder. I'm frozen with Molly on the other side of Chad, trying to give him a washcloth, but he smacks it away.

"Harvey?" he calls, and my body moves on instinct.

"Hey, Chad. What's wrong?"

"My head hurts."

"How do you want us to fix it?" I move closer to him.

He holds his head. "I don't know."

"I already gave him Tylenol," Molly says, standing back giving me room.

"He probably needs to get home and go to sleep. It's way past his bedtime," Jemima says, her eyes fixed on Chad.

"I'll drive you," I say, picking up the bag.

Chad rises and steps forward, and before I can process what's happening, his arms wrap around me. I freeze, staring down at the top of his head, my brain scrambling to catch up. My hand hovers awkwardly for a second before it lands on his back, moving in slow, uncertain circles.

"No, I've got it. You stay here. Molly can help me."

A heavy sigh leaves Jemima. "Let me pack up your things first."

Molly nods, and I get ready to pack the bag, but Chad screams again gripping me tighter.

"Hey, what's wrong?" Jemima asks softly.

"I want Harvey."

The empty bag in my hand feels like it weighs a ton. I look at Molly, who shrugs.

My gaze moves to Chad, who's begging me with his eyes, and then I look to see Jemima's matching ones. She just wants him to be happy.

I walk over and hold out the bag to her, and she rises and takes it, whispering, "Thanks. I won't be long."

Sitting on the sofa, I'm unsure what to do next. But Chad decides for me. He drops his head on my thigh, and I grab the blue washcloth from Molly's outstretched hand and place it on his head.

A few moments later, she swallows hard and whispers. "I'm ready." She holds out her arms, and I lift Chad up and walk him to her. He screams again. "No, Harvey."

My eyes widen as he curls into my arms.

She dips her chin and walks to the door, kissing Molly's cheek and thanking her for looking after Chad.

Inside the limo, I peer at Jemima, noticing her pinched expression. "Are you okay?"

I'm on one side of the limo, her on the other. Chad is in the middle of us, still moaning in pain.

"Yeah, once the medicine kicks in and he falls asleep, he'll be fine."

"How are you so calm?"

My heart is beating so hard with worry.

"He's been sick a few times this year."

I nod as Chad stays curled into me for the remainder of the drive.

When we arrive at her apartment, Jemima reaches for the bag and I carry him up the steps and into her place, heading straight to his bed.

"You need to sleep," I say to Chad.

"Can you read me a book?" He grabs the book on his nightstand.

Kicking off my shoes, I settle myself back on the headboard of his bed. He lies beside me as I read.

A few minutes later, Jemima pokes her head into the room and smiles. "He's asleep."

I close the book and stand, slipping my shoes back on.

She tucks him in, and we walk out to her door.

"I'm sorry for how the night ended. A screaming child and no sex is no one's idea of a good date."

My gaze is fixed on her as I answer honestly.

"This was actually the best date I've ever had."

CHAPTER 22

HARVEY

My team and I gather in the boardroom, with a sleek, glass walled space overlooking the city skyline. The long-polished table is scattered with open laptops and coffee cups, each person absorbed in their screens. There are eighteen of them sitting under the fluorescent lights of the room, while I stand at the front of the table, my own laptop projecting slides. The room hums with quiet murmurs, fingers tapping on keyboards, and pens scraping along paper.

At exactly nine o'clock, I start the meeting, glancing at Silas, one of my employees, who sits with a stack of papers and a focused expression.

"What's the latest on the financials?" I ask.

His eyes flick up from his notes. "Our target company has seen a twenty percent growth in the last quarter."

I nod, taking in the information. "What's the timeline for full takeover?"

"Six to twelve months," he replies, typing quickly. "It depends on how smoothly we can integrate their systems with ours."

"We need to consider how this will impact our cash reserves," I say, scribbling a note on my notepad.

A buzz interrupts me. Jemima's name flashes on my phone. I glance at it, knowing I can't ignore her. She never reaches out, and the curiosity eats at me.

> **Jemima:** *(picture of a slice of cake) I'm planning to eat all this. You'll have to bake more.*

Keeping one ear on the conversation in front of me, I quickly type a response.

> **Me:** *I can bake something else.*

"Alright, I need a risk assessment written by the end of the day tomorrow," I say to Janet, who nods as she taps away on her keyboard.

"Got it," Janet replies, focused on her screen.

> **Jemima:** *I'd prefer you never bake for me again.*

Me: Why?

Jemima: I like it when you're mean. It's easier to hate you.

Me: I'll have to kiss you more then.

My fingers hold the phone a moment longer, the words a little bolder than I intended. I try to shake off the tightness in my chest, but I can't deny the way her reply stirs something inside me, like a dare I can't resist. There's a rush inside. My gaze shifts back to the room, forcing myself to refocus as I try to keep my composure. We continue running through the rest of the agenda and after an hour, it's time I wrap up. "Thanks, everyone. Let's make sure we cover all our bases before moving forward. Meeting adjourned."

The team begins to pack up, and I review my notes on my laptop as they all file out. I take one last look at Jemima's text. She hasn't replied. Finishing my notes, I head over to Esme's desk to handle any waiting tasks and approvals.

After completing my work at the office, I head to Recaredo Events, ready to finish my day there. My mind keeps drifting to Jemima. The kiss we shared is seared into my brain and I want more. Spending time with her makes me feel alive, heard, capable, and appreciated.

She's lived a life much harder than anyone I know, and fuck, she's still crawling her way through the damage. All I want to do is help her. She deserves to be happy. I've never met anyone more deserving. Starting with her bland and non-existent office decor... She deserves to let go of the past. This is her company, and it needs life injected into it. I'm going to pay for it as a gift for her.

I make a call on my way and organize for Susie, my interior decorator, to come over in the next hour. Jemima will be back from lunch soon, and I want her to meet Susie.

When I arrive at the office, I walk past Jemima's. Instead of her usual hard expression, she greets me with a soft, "Hello."

"Do you have any appointments in the next two hours?" I ask, approaching her desk. She swivels her chair to face me, her curiosity evident.

"No, why?"

"I've arranged for an interior designer friend to come by and discuss updating your office."

Raising an eyebrow, she leans back. "A lady friend."

"Jealousy looks good on you," I tease, enjoying the flush of color on her cheeks.

She snorts with an eye roll. "You wish. I'm not a jealous person."

I put my hands on her desk and lean in closer, my voice dropping to a low murmur. "If it makes you feel better, I haven't slept with her. And won't."

"You can do whatever you want, I don't care," she challenges me, her gaze locked onto mine.

"I don't know about you, but that kiss meant something to me," I fire back, the hurt seeping into my tone.

"Shh, Molly's out there," she hisses, her eyes darting to the door.

"Even better. I'm a dirty little secret," I mutter as my frustration boils over. It's not the first time I've felt like we're sneaking around, but this just feels different. A part of me wants to call it out, to demand more, but I know that's not the game we're playing. Yet. The heat in my chest intensifies, and I can't quite figure out why I'm so torn. I should be content, but the secrecy is eating away at me.

"It's not that. Can we refocus?"

I push off her desk, trying to compose myself. "Susie will be here soon. She'll discuss updating this place with you."

Her face changes into a hard expression. "I don't want to change anything."

"I'm paying for it."

She crosses her arms. "I don't need a handout."

"I know. But this place is so boring. It should reflect who you are."

"And simple isn't me?" she challenges.

"No. Not one fucking bit. You're anything but simple."

"What am I, then?" she presses.

I storm back to her desk. "Elegant, strong, intelligent, beautiful... just to name a few. Anything but this." I gesture at the white peeling walls, the outdated wooden desk, and the small, cluttered bookshelf.

"I can do it later. It's not important right now."

"I'm here to help. So let me fucking help. Working in a warm, inviting environment boosts productivity. It will make a better impression on clients."

We have a stare-off, the tension thick, before she finally snaps. "Fine. Let me know when she's here."

God, I want to fucking kiss her challenging ass so bad right now. But I hold back the urge and pull away, not wanting to make a mess of the papers. Leaning down, I try to gently pull my tie from the stack when I hear the unmistakable snap of the stapler. "Dammit," I mutter, looking down to find my tie firmly fastened to the documents.

I try to untangle it, but the more I tug, the tighter it digs into the fabric. With a frustrated sigh, I grab the scissors from her desk, cutting carefully around the staple. Finally free, I smooth out the tie, catching the sound of her soft giggle as I head to my office.

"You know," she calls out after me. "If you'd actually keep it tied, you wouldn't be in this mess."

An hour later, Susie arrives. Jemima comes out when she hears her voice.

Jemima greets her with unexpected warmth, which surprises me. I expected her to say she doesn't require her services.

Molly joins us, and we start explaining what the company is about and its needs. Susie takes notes and asks questions along the way. She designed my office and she's good at what she does.

We show her the empty rooms and discuss the need for two offices now, with the possibility of more in the future. There's one room with nothing in it, and an idea sparks in me. "How about setting up a kids' area! You have spare rooms. That way, when you're meeting with clients, you have this waiting room that's suitable for children," I suggest, glancing at Jemima.

Her cheeks flush slightly, and a shy smile appears.

The earlier Jemima is gone and has been replaced with the softer version. The dangerous version. Her challenging one is safer, familiar... Our kiss changed things for me, and part of me thinks it changed things for her too.

"I never thought about that, but it could be great for the kids."

"What's he into?" Susie asks.

"Basketball," Jemima and I answer simultaneously, exchanging a smile.

Susie turns to Molly to discuss what Hugo would like. Jemima explains she wants to support future hires with children, providing toys for all ages of kids, and comforts to accommodate their needs. She also mentions having options for last-minute babysitting.

My eyes twitch at her offering people to bring in their kids to work, but she explains paying for babysitters or a short-term-only plan. Like for an hour if they need to come in for a meeting or their kids are sick.

As Jemima talks, I wonder how many of my staff could benefit from having help with their kids so they could work and potentially perform better?

I quickly send an email to Esme, requesting her to send out an email with a form for each of my workers to fill out. The questionnaire will include how many kids they have, their ages, if they're facing challenges with childcare, and whether they'd use a program if it were available. This will help me determine if I need to implement something like that within my businesses.

Susie takes detailed notes. "I'll design a concept and show it to you. Now, let's discuss the rest."

For the next hour, Susie goes over colors, textures, and design ideas. Jemima's excitement is palpable, and I find myself captivated by her energy. Her enthusiasm is contagious, and I watch her, mesmerised.

Before Susie and Molly leave, I show pictures of my own office. Their eyes bulge from their sockets. I appreciate finer things, which motivates me to keep working hard.

Returning to my office, I focus on organizing Oliver's events for next year before switching to the new software system setup. I call up any new inquiries and schedule design meetings, eager to share the results with Jemima. I can't wait to show her this.

The shift in the office energy makes my head lift, alerting me to her presence. She stands at the door, her back straight. I go to rise and greet her, but she gives me a subtle shake of her head.

"Chad is sick again. The school just called," she says, her arms wrapped tightly around her stomach.

"Is he okay?" I ask rising, stepping closer, ignoring her earlier warning and gently touching her arm.

"He has a fever. He must be coming down with the flu," she says, worry evident in her voice.

"Take a few days off to care for him. Fuck, look after yourself," I insist, my concern genuine.

She looks from under her dark lashes at me as she whispers, "Thank you."

"Give me your work to do."

She hesitates. "No, it's okay. It can wait."

"Your tasks will only grow. Give them to me. Nothing is too difficult."

"It's not that." She sighs, avoiding my gaze.

My brow furrows, not understanding. "What is it then?"

Her cheeks flush as she looks away quickly. "I don't want to give another guy control over my finances."

I pull her into a hug, her arms immediately wrapping around me. "I understand. But I'm not like him. I'm here to help. You can come back and take over when you're ready. It's temporary."

Her head moves on my chest, probably feeling how hard my heart is pounding. She feels so right in my arms; I don't want to let her go.

"I don't have a choice, do I?"

"No. Chad needs you." I want to tell her that I need her too, but now isn't the right time. Even hugging her is hard to stop when her warm body is pressed against mine. Usually, I fuck a woman and she leaves as soon as we're finished. There'd be no hugging or kissing. It was a scratch I needed scratching, but with her, I want to hold, kiss, and never let go.

"I better show you what I was working on so I can go pick him up."

She pulls away, a visible shudder running through her. I follow her into her office, trying to behave and keep my hands to myself despite the intense urge to hold her.

As she sits down and starts explaining her work, my gaze drifts to her lips. Her focus is on the task at hand, but my thoughts are consumed with how much I want to kiss her again.

These thoughts are so inappropriate, and when I work, I don't usually think like this, hence why I haven't fucked anyone I work with. My casual fucks were always when I went out.

"You've been doing this all on your own?" I ask.

"Yeah, it's a lot," she admits.

"You're so stubborn. I wish you'd told me sooner."

Her head tilts so her eyes meet mine, and the intensity makes my heart race. My eyes drop to her cupid's bow, and all I want is to close the distance and taste her again.

"Take over until I return."

"I won't let you down," I assure her, as I hold her gaze. Her eyes flicker with torment as she murmurs, "I hope not."

"I promise. If you want updates, call or text, and I'll show you what I'm doing."

"Don't tempt me," she says, a small smile playing on her lips.

"If it makes you feel better, do it," I reply, understanding how hard it is for her.

She takes a small step back, but her feet seem rooted to the spot, her shoulders tense as if she's fighting against herself. Her gaze drops for a moment, her fingers fidgeting with the strap of her bag, unwilling to let go, to let me take control.

"Okay, thanks." Her voice falters slightly, but she forces herself to turn, her movements stiff. As she walks away, each step is more reluctant than the last.

"Let me know how he is," I say, genuinely wanting an update.

I can feel the air around us shift. I watch her closely. Her breaths quicken into a pant, her lips parting slightly as if she's about to say something but doesn't. The electricity in this room is at an all-time high, and I can't hold back. Workplace or not, I take the kiss I've been desperate for. I lean in and press a quick kiss to her soft lips, and when she kisses me back, it's everything I could've wanted.

Fuck, I've missed her.

What is she doing to me?

We pull apart, and she walks away. I stand there, unable to move, my heart racing. At the door, she pauses and takes a quick glance over her shoulder, her eyes meeting mine. I flash her a grin, and her pretty cheeks flush a deep crimson color.

I sit in her chair and get started, reading the files a welcome distraction, looking at the words but not reading, unable to focus. This is the only way I'll be able to stop myself from following her.

I've been at her desk working for four hours, but I'm unable to concentrate. I check my phone again, unlocking it with a quick swipe, only to see the same empty screen. No new messages with an update. I click on our message thread, hoping a new one might appear. But nothing does. I google what to give kids when they are sick with the flu, then I call my driver and get him to stop by the stores with a list, from medicine to food. Just as I'm about to have him deliver it along with my card, I change my mind.

I need to see her.

Me: *Is everything okay?*

Jemima: *Sorry, I completely left you high and dry.*

Me: *Yeah, I was about to come down and see if you're alive.*

Jemima: *We're very much alive. (She sends a picture of them watching The Lion King.)*

> **Me:** *I send a picture of her front door.*

A moment later, the door swings open. She runs a hand through her messy bun and asks breathily, "What are you doing here?"

"I brought you and Chad stuff to help him get better," I say, holding up the bags.

Frowning, her eyes drop to the bags. "You know I've got this handled."

My lip's part into a knowing grin. "Oh, I know."

"Harvey?" Chad's weak voice calls from inside.

My eyes dart past her shoulders. She sighs.

"I can't get rid of you now," she murmurs with a hint of amusement in her tone.

"At least someone wants me around," I say, giving her a wink as I enter their apartment. I don't plan to stay long. I just wanted to check on Chad.

The space isn't big, and it only takes a few steps to see him lying on the sofa, watching *The Lion King*. As soon as he spots me, he tries to sit up.

"Stay there." I smile.

Chad nods with half a smile, his cheeks red with fever. He resettles, laying his head back down.

"I got you some things, but I need to get Mom's approval first," I say, winking. His eyes widen a fraction.

Moving into the kitchen, she's stirring something on the stove that smells of onion and spices. As if she can read my mind, she tells me.

"It's chicken noodle soup. Chad's favorite."

"Do you need a hand?" I ask.

"No. But what did you bring?" A small smile tugs at the corner of her lips.

I pull each item out of the bags and place them on the counter. "medicine, Pedialyte, popsicles, Vicks VapoRub, Tylenol, ibuprofen, crackers, pretzels, strawberries, eggs, peanut butter, watermelon, and potatoes."

"This is a weird mix." She laughs, shaking her head.

My eyebrows pull together as I take in the items. "I followed what I found online. Is it wrong?"

She sorts through the things, her movements calm, but there's a softness in her voice when she speaks. "No. You didn't have to do all this." Pausing, her fingers gently brush over the items. "A few of these would've been plenty."

I shrug. "It wasn't expensive."

She steps closer to me. "Not everything is about money."

"Then what do you mean?"

"Most people would only buy a few items."

"I'm not most people," I deadpan.

She shakes her head, her eyes trailing over my body before meeting mine again. My eyebrows lift at her obvious inspection. "Oh, I know."

I lean forward and whisper in her ear, "Don't look at me like that."

"Mommy, when do you die?" Chad calls out, and I'm taken aback by the question.

Our eyes move to the screen to watch as Mufasa falls and dies.

"Not for a very long time, sweetheart," she reassures him.

He seems happy with that and doesn't ask anything else.

"Is that normal?" I whisper.

"Pretty much. Whatever pops into his mind, he asks."

I watch Chad, fascinated. "He's a pretty cool kid."

"He is, isn't he?"

I nod. And I don't tell her I've had a change of heart in my fears about kids. I'm trying to find the best time to tell her.

"I'll go sit with Chad before I leave," I say and walk back to Chad to watch the beginning of the movie with him.

A little while later, Jemima calls out, "Dinner's ready."

"It's time for me to go, but I hope you feel better soon, buddy," I say, roughing up his blond hair.

"Please stay for dinner," Chad begs with sad eyes. What is it about his face and voice that make me unable to say no?

"You can't say no," Jemima whispers behind me, startling me.

"How do kids do it?" I ask, turning to her.

"They know they're cute, so they suck you in."

But as I take in her adorable face and messy bun, I know I'm not going anywhere. Turning to Chad, I say, "Looks like I'm staying for dinner."

With as much enthusiasm as he can muster while sick, he says, "Yay."

"Come join the table, Chad," she orders. I follow her to a small table that's up against the wall with three chairs around it. She lowers the bowls and silverware.

Jemima points at the nearest chair. "Come have a seat."

Soup was also given to me as a kid by my mom and grandma. It was really good, but this is better.

We eat in silence. Chad finishes first.

"Can I leave the table now?"

"Yes," Jemima says. "But dishes go in the sink."

I smile around my spoon at the command.

He takes his seat on the sofa and hits play on the movie again.

After I finish eating, I take my bowl and start cleaning up.

She leans over, touching my hands. "Don't. I'll do it later."

Her face is so close to mine. If I dipped my head, I could kiss her. My eyes drop to her lips, but I refrain.

"Let me help, it will get done quicker," I whisper across her lips.

As her eyes soften and she gives up the fight, we stare at each other for a moment. She snaps out of the daze and grabs a towel to dry while I wash. "When was the last time you washed a dish?" she asks.

"Today."

"I wasn't talking about now."

"Yesterday."

She nods, her lips pressed together, her eyes narrowing in thought.

"Nothing to say?" I ask, my voice light but with a hint of curiosity.

"No, I'm just surprised, that's all." She shrugs, her shoulders relaxed, but I can see the glint of surprise still lingering in her eyes.

"There are plenty more surprises up my sleeve than just my ability to wash dishes, you know."

My eyes twinkle with a devilish smirk.

Bumping my shoulder as she dries the last spoon, she smiles. "One's enough."

But is it? Time will tell.

Once the dishes are done, and Chad is half asleep, I know it's time for me to leave so he can rest. I say goodbye to him, and we fist pump before Jemima walks me to the door.

"Before I go, I want to give you this," I say, handing her the black card. Her eyes drop to it, then back up to mine. "One, nine, nine, one," I add, giving her my password.

Her lip's part, and a squeak comes out before she clears her throat. "What's this for?"

"Take Chad and you shopping tomorrow."

"I can't."

"Why not?"

"He's sick, and I'm not asking for money."

"It's only an hour. One department store..."

She narrows her eyes at me.

"I'm not taking it back," I say firmly, my gaze steady. "So buy yourself a new wardrobe and get Chad anything he needs for school and home."

"This feels wrong."

She's really upset.

"Please do this for me. It will make me feel better knowing I'm looking after you."

"I don't need rescuing."

"I never said that's what I'm doing, did I?

"Not in words, but in actions."

I sigh, unable to get her to see I want to help.

"When's the last time you bought something for yourself?"

She stares blankly at me. The wheels are turning in her head, she's trying so hard. "Before he went away." She exhales heavily.

By *him* she means her ex. The one who should've protected her, spoiled her, and cared for her.

I grab her hand in mine and dust my thumb over her knuckles. "I know this isn't something you're used to, because you're strong and can stand on your own, but I want to show you what being taken care of is like."

She stares at me momentarily before nodding.

I kiss her forehead. "I'll have my driver pick you up."

She waves her hand. "No. I'll do it, but no driver."

I swallow a smile, but I ask, "Why?"

"I don't want Chad thinking your life is normal."

I let out a shaky laugh, ignoring the slight twinge in my chest. Who would've thought a woman wouldn't want to be flooded with gifts. This is a sign that she isn't like anyone I've been interested in.

But she doesn't elaborate, and I hate how much she dislikes my money.

"Thanks for dinner," I say, leaning in to kiss her cheek, when she suddenly moves so our lips collide.

I'm slightly in shock, but her hands grab my waist, pulling me closer, so our bodies are flush. Her silent ask for more makes me lose control. I grab her head with my hands and kiss her ferociously. My tongue skims her lips, begging to enter, and she parts them eagerly. I tilt my head to change the angle so I can kiss her deeper, and before I let my hands roam all over her body, I step back, reminding myself where I am.

"Goodnight, buttercup."

CHAPTER 23

JEMIMA

THIS MORNING, I TOLD Chad we were going shopping for toys and clothes, and his face lit up with excitement. I can't help but remain hesitant in this situation. I get Harvey is just trying to help, and I appreciate it. With little things, sure... but a fucking credit card and a spending spree is a bit much though.

But when I looked at Chad, who had the flu, just lost his dad, and has been wearing old clothes that don't fit him right because he's had a growth spurt... I have to. For him, I have to swallow my pride. What kind of mother would I be if I couldn't do this for him?

He needs new clothes and toys. He's had a hard time, and he deserves these things, even if I'm not the one who's giving it to him. Lately, I've been able to pay some of the debts off; it's not a lot, but it's a start.

So today, I plan to let Chad buy whatever he wants. Before we buy necessities like clothes, I head to the one place that will bring him joy, the Lego store.

When we arrive, we walk in, and Chad immediately rushes off. I follow behind in awe of the bright colors and amazing displays. We've been here before, but it never ceases to amaze me.

Chad touches all the boxes, and his eyes are wide in wonder as he looks at everything. It makes my gut twist that he hasn't gotten any new toys, because paying to fix our life, that his father destroyed, is all I can afford.

Chad plays with the pick-a-brick station, concentrating as he carefully selects pieces to build. Half an hour passes by. He finds a Medieval Town Square set and a Lamborghini, his eyes lighting up with his choices. We buy them and then head out to the local department store. As soon as I step in, a security guard approaches, his expression serious.

"Are you Jemima Recaredo?" he asks.

I hesitate with a gulp before saying, "Yes."

"Wait here. There's someone expecting you."

My heart beats loudly in my ears as panic sets in.

"Mom, what's going on? Are you in trouble?" Chad asks quietly.

"No, she's not," a soft woman's voice says with a warm smile. She's in her mid-fifties, wearing a black tailored suit, and she has brown shoulder-length hair framing her face.

"I'm Patti, and I'll be your personal shopper today. Where would you like to start?"

I blink at her, trying to process this information. What is a personal shopper?

"Did Harvey set this up?" I ask, still trying to wrap my head around it.

"Mr. Lincoln? Yes, he said to look after you and Chad."

Trying to clear the emotions running around inside me to focus on her question, I shake my head.

"Can we start with Chad?" I say, knowing I'm not taking his money to buy myself anything.

"Sure. Come this way," she says, walking away.

I grab Chad's hand, and we follow her to the kids' section. Patti asks Chad an array of questions, and soon he's in the changing room, trying on clothes. I take a second to type a message to Harvey.

Me: *A personal shopper? You're dead.*

Harvey: *Maybe buy something for me.*

Me: *There's no brains in here.*

Harvey: *I was thinking lingerie…*

Me: *Chad's here, remember?*

> **Harvey:** *I'll buy it then.*

> **Me:** *Not happening.*

Chad comes out, spinning around in his new outfit, beaming with confidence. He loves it, and Patti adds it to the yes pile that's already filling the basket. He heads back in to try the next outfit.

> **Harvey:** *Please enjoy today. You and Chad deserve to be spoiled, and I have no one else to spoil. No one is more deserving.*

I double tap the message to leave an emoji, hearting it.

I start typing, torn between wanting to handle this on my own and being grateful for Harvey's generosity. The conflict twists inside me. I want to accept it. I want to let him spoil us because, deep down, I know we deserve it. But then there's the voice in my head, reminding me that I'm supposed to be strong, capable.

I backspace, taking a deep breath, but it doesn't ease the pressure building inside me. I have to be honest.

> **Me:** *I don't feel comfortable taking money from you to buy things for myself. But I'll never deprive Chad of this opportunity, and for that, thank you, even though it makes me feel like a failure.*

> **Harvey:** *Please don't. You're an amazing mother.*

After a few more outfits, Chad's finished. Patti takes me to the women's section, and I browse the racks but don't pick up anything. The prices are too high. I find a sweat set that I love, but I don't add it to the pile, then I say I'm done. My phone chimes and I open it.

> **Harvey:** *Patti says you're not buying anything.*

> **Me:** *Is she watching me?*

I look up at her blank expression. My phone chimes, pulling my gaze down to read his message.

> *Harvey:* Yes. I want you and Chad to have a whole new wardrobe. And Chad to have toys and games.

I tuck my phone away, then turn to Patti and tell her to add a few more things of her choosing for Chad. That should do it. An hour later, my phone buzzes with a new text message.

> *Harvey:* What did you buy for yourself? Show me.

> *Me:* Nothing.

> *Harvey:* Naughty girl.

> *Me:* Chad has a new wardrobe and Legos.

> *Harvey:* I'll order you a new wardrobe since you don't want to listen. Patti will know what you like.

Me: *You wouldn't.*

Harvey: I did.

I stare at his words. He's just ordering me a wardrobe like this is normal behavior.

Me: *You're insane.*

Harvey: I like you.

Me: Doesn't mean I need a new wardrobe.

Harvey: You don't like flowers, or when I baked you a cake, or literally anything I do for you.

Me: Then why do you hang around like a bad smell? (Winking face emoji)

Harvey: Because I know you like me too. Who kissed me last night?

Me: I was delirious.

Harvey: Whatever you need to tell yourself. Now show me Chad's toys.

I walk over to Chad, take a few photos, and hit send.

Harvey: I want to see it after he builds them. Does he like the Lambo?

Me: Why? Are you planning on up-grading your car?

Harvey: I'll have you know mine is worth more than that one.

Me: It's just a car.

Harvey: You know it's not. But I'll get Chad in both cars to see which he prefers.

Me: You can't put car seats in them.

Harvey: Well, looks like I'll be researching what car seats are best in a Lambo (Winking face emoji)

Me: You're crazy. I'm going.

Harvey: Speak to you soon, buttercup.

I've worked from home for a few days while Chad fully recovered. He could've gone back earlier, but I think he wanted some time with me, and I couldn't say no enjoying a few quiet days. Now that he's back at school, I've had plenty of time to watch the office renovations. As I approach the door, the sight of the big changes makes my heart swell. When I open it, my jaw hits the floor. The whole office has had a refresh, new paint, chic accessories, vibrant artwork, stylish ornaments, and scented candles filling the air with warm vanilla scent.

I wander through, taking it all in, starting with Molly's desk, which now feels open and inviting. Before, it was taller and more enclosed, creating a barrier that cut off the view of everything behind it. I move to the new offices, which are vacant, but hopefully soon will be filled with new employees. Then I check out the kids' zone, which is bright and eye catching. I can picture Chad happily building blocks or watching TV.

Next, I move to the break room, which has a new table and chairs ready to accommodate our growing business. Too excited to wait any longer, I head to my office and see the two new floor-to-ceiling bookshelves, new filing cabinets, a desk, and a chair. There's even a gigantic floor-to-ceiling mirror and a plant that brightens the room. My once dull and minimal office has transformed into a warm and inviting space.

Harvey is spending the morning at his company, and he'll come in later today. Now that I've had time to reflect, I can't deny that it was nice having him spoil us. Even the text messages he sent were a highlight, a small reminder of how much he cares. But I haven't seen him in a few days, and I miss hearing his voice.

When I begin work, I notice Post-it notes around the office, with Harvey's handwriting telling me not to freak out because he filed things differently but thinks it will be better. Honestly, I trust him. He's better at business than I am. But even his notes couldn't prepare me for the amount of work he's already done. There's barely anything left for me to do.

How did he do it all so fast? It was taking me forever to go through each invoice.

He's a pro, and I can't be down on myself since I'm still learning. Yet, I can't help the niggle in my head that tells me I'm not cut out for this. But I'm determined not to let it get me down.

As I begin working, Molly pokes her head in. "Your three o'clock appointment has arrived. He's kinda hot. If you find out he's single, maybe slip him my number."

I giggle. "Molly, no. I can't do that. He'll think I'm hitting on him."

"You can tell him you're already dating someone else."

"I'm not dating anyone," I whisper under my breath.

"Yes, you are. Harvey."

"We're not dating," I say, crossing my arms.

"You like him."

"We're not dating," I say more firmly, even though I don't sound convincing. I've only kissed him twice, and it could be a fluke that we share such great chemistry. We'd need more than two kisses to see if this is worth exploring.

The fear of abandonment is something I don't want to go through again. I feel like I'm not good enough and need to learn how to do life alone.

"You should."

"You'll be the first to know if my status changes. Now let Finn in."

She points at me. "Give him my number."

"No promises."

"Please. It's a tough world out there, being a single mom and all."

"Molly, please, any guy would be lucky to have you. You're the one who doesn't let them hang around long enough."

"I never asked for a boyfriend, just a good time."

I smile as she wanders off. We are so different. Hookups were never my thing, even in high school. I don't waste my time unless the guy is worth it and I can see a future. Now, my situation has only made it harder. I'm more protective of myself and Chad.

I close the app as a shadow appears in the doorway. The guy is tall and fills the doorframe. Swallowing the lump in my throat, I say, "Hi Finn, please take a seat."

"Thanks for meeting with me, Jemima."

The room feels smaller the moment he enters. I can see why Molly likes him, but he's not making my stomach flip or my heart race. If anything, I feel nauseous. His aftershave is overwhelming it makes my eyes sting with its peppery tone, as if he's sprayed the whole bottle or something.

We discuss his upcoming event. He's the executive director of JFK Airport. The uneasy feeling intensifies, but I dampen it as I focus on writing notes and asking questions. He's very organized, preparing six months out, a spectacular Christmas party. The budget is endless, and if Harvey's money intimidated me, Finn's makes Harvey seem normal.

When we finish discussing everything, I rise to shake his hand and see him out. But he steps forward and crowds me. My hands start to sweat. Molly has already left for the day to pick up Hugo from school, leaving just me and him. I'm not worried about my safety as much as I'm worried he'll try to make a move.

"Are you single?" he asks, stepping closer with a cocky smirk.

"Uh...no. I mean..." My brain short-circuits as panic sets in. Molly's dying for his number, but asking him will definitely send the wrong message.

"Buttercup, there you are," Harvey's voice calls with a hint of irritation. He steps quickly beside me and wraps his hand around my waist, pulling me into him.

CHAPTER 24

HARVEY

THE EMERGENCY SAFETY MEETING at work held me up today. It's just after three when I finally finish my call. Molly isn't at her desk when I walk in, but I can hear voices. One deep male, and the other, Jemima's. For a second, I think it's Danny, but as I walk closer, the unfamiliar voice becomes clear, but it's not a voice I recognize.

I enter her office doorway and freeze. The image in front of me causes me to grind down on my molars. The guy is standing way too fucking close to her. *Does she know him?*

Her tight expression and the way she tries to pull away makes something inside me snap. I'm not in control as I stride over, wrap my arm around her waist, and pull her toward me.

It's totally inappropriate. I don't know what's come over me.

"Hi," she says softly, clearing her throat. "This is Mr. Hernandez, the executive director of JFK. He wants Recaredo Events to organize his Christmas party."

I thrust out my spare hand, forcing him to step back to take it. "Nice to meet you," I say, swallowing my hatred toward him. He's still gazing at Jemima like he wants her, but she's sinking into my hold instead of pulling away.

"Nice to meet you Mister?"

"Oh, where are my manners? This is Harvey Lincoln," Jemima says.

Finn's expression changes, and his focus shifts to me. "I've met your brothers, Evan and Oliver."

I nod. "If you enjoy working with them, I'm sure we could get The New York Press's coverage of the event if you want?"

His eyes light up. "That would be wonderful."

I grab my wallet, find a business card, and hand it to him. "Email me some details, and I'll forward them to him."

"Thanks for your time, Ms. Recaredo and Mr. Lincoln."

"I'll walk you out," Jemima offers, but I tighten my hold on her. She scowls at me.

"It's okay, I'll see myself out," Finn says.

We shake hands, and he turns to leave. I wait until the front door closes before I let her go.

"What's gotten into you?" she asks, with a slight annoyance in her voice.

I rub my jaw. "What the fuck was he doing so close to you? Doesn't he know that..."

"Does he not know what?"

"That... that's unprofessional to do so."

Her lips curve up. "Harvey, are you jealous?"

"Yes, seeing him standing so close to you is making me fucking crazy. I've never been possessive, but with you, I can't help it."

Her lips twitch as her face morphs into a softer expression. "I've never had that before."

"No?"

She shakes her head, sighing. "No. No one cared about me that much."

"Well, if you were mine, I'd be telling the whole world to back off."

I can't believe the word "mine" just left my mouth. I just mean I would do anything to protect her and Chad. Having a child isn't the obstacle I always believed it to be. In fact, Chad is cool and fun. I enjoy spending time with them. It gets me thinking about how much I want a family like this.

"A few kisses and you think I'm yours," she breathes with a hint of amusement. She moves closer, her body inches from mine. Is she making fun of me, or is she flirting with me?

"What would it take, buttercup?" I ask, closing the distance between us. Her eyes fill with longing and lust, mirroring my own.

Fuck, I want her.

She licks her bottom lip, and I follow the movement with my eyes and a groan.

"A lot more."

I lift an eyebrow. "Like? Another kiss."

She nods lazily. The air is thick with tension, and we've both been wanting more, so I don't bother asking more questions. Grabbing her waist, I pull her to me, bringing my mouth down on hers. She threads her fingers through my hair, hungrily pressing me closer. She tastes and feels amazing, bringing back memories of our first kiss. I push my tongue against her closed lips, desperate for entry. She opens up, and I sweep my tongue into her mouth, tangling with hers.

The way we move so effortlessly is proof of how well we fit together. My hands move to her lower back, curling with every flick of her tongue. She's desperate, and I hiss out her name. "Jemima."

"Don't fucking stop," she says.

I can't help smirking into her kiss. "I wouldn't dare."

We kiss again, but my hands move to her shoulders, slowly pushing her navy suit jacket off. She doesn't resist; instead, she helps rip it off.

"I've thought about this moment so many times," she murmurs.

"Me too, every night."

She brings her fingers to my suit jacket and copies me. But I don't rush. I savor her undressing me.

"You like me undressing you?"

"So fucking much," I growl.

There's something about wanting her to control me. Her confidence gets me harder. My hands move to the buttons on her white shirt, and as soon as they're undone, I pull her shirt from her skirt. She moves her hands to my half-removed tie and whips it off in seconds. As she unbuttons my shirt, her fingers trail over my body as if mesmerized by it.

"Are you okay?" I ask, my voice lower than it was a few seconds ago.

"I'm just taking a second to make sure you're real."

I laugh. "I'm definitely real."

Her fingernails graze my stomach until she's tugging my shirt from my pants and then moving to unbuckle my belt.

She removes it swiftly and grabs my pants to take them off. Enjoying her eager touch, I kick off my shoes so my pants can fall. I stand in my briefs as her hands skim my body until they land on the waistband of my boxers. She's breathing heavily as she peeks up at me, pausing to wait for my permission.

"Take them off, baby."

Biting down on her bottom lip, her eyes drop as her hands push over my very obvious erection. The moment it springs free, she gasps.

"Fuck. You're killing me," I rasp, as my briefs hit the floor, leaving me standing completely naked. She has the audacity to smirk at me, but I'm the one who should be smiling.

"It's my turn." My fingers twitch as they touch her shirt buttons, loving the skin that's revealed. She's so beautiful and about to be all mine. Her chest rises and falls rapidly with every button I pop, as if she's nervous.

"Harvey," she whispers.

"You have no idea how much I've fantasized about you." I slide my hands under her shirt and slip it off her shoulders, watching it fall to the floor. It leaves her in a plain black bra, navy skirt, stockings, and pumps.

"It's even better than I imagined," I say, reaching for her skirt. "You're incredible." Slipping off her skirt, I leave her in just her stockings. I push them down, taking a moment to savor her sexy body. But her eyes look sad? And her fingers twist in front of her.

"What's wrong?" I ask, lifting her face with my finger. She swallows hard, her hesitation bothering me. "What? Tell me," I push.

"I'm not what you're used to," she breathes shakily.

I'm trying to understand where her confidence went. Did I say something wrong? But I come up empty. "What do you mean?"

Chapter 25

Jemima

"Why would you want me?" I ask, as the reality of what and where we're doing this sinks in. It's not in a tearful plea... No, I haven't cried since my ex fucked me over. I swore I wouldn't let another man have that kind of power over me.

I look down at my loose bra and briefs, taking in my small frame, and whisper one of my fears about us. "I'm too old for you."

His hands skim the backs of my thighs, and I try to push away the demon on my shoulder telling me that they hold no muscle tone. When he reaches my ass, I can't help but think about how it doesn't compare to women in their thirties... Mine is practically non-existent. Pancake ass? Yeah, that's me. Plus, I wear full briefs, the kind that hide my ugly C-section scar. I swallow the bile rising in my throat, feeling humiliated.

"You're not too old for me," he says, his hands moving up to my waist to hold me gently.

I wrap my arms around myself. "I am. I've had a kid."

"So fucking what?"

Pain hits my chest. "I don't have a body like a twenty- or thirty-year-old."

"I don't want them."

I snort. "You have no idea what's underneath here."

He stands in front of me, gliding his hands from my ass, up my lower back, skimming the sides of my breast, until they reach my neck. Using his thumbs to tilt my head up, he forces me to meet his gaze. I expect to see revulsion, but what I find scares the fuck out of me... Raw, burning desire. The intensity makes my knees buckle, and I nearly collapse.

"Are you doing this because you feel sorry for me?"

Or to get my company...?

He shakes his head so slowly. His breath tickles my face as he leans in to kiss the tip of my nose.

"I don't feel sorry for you."

I stare at him, waiting for this to be a prank.

"Why are you doing this, then?" I ask, wondering if I'm just another number in his book of girls he's fucked.

"Because you drive me mad."

"Well, that's no reason to kiss me."

"Who says I'm going to kiss you?"

My mouth opens and closes, but no words come out.

"I won't be kissing you again. This time, I will be consuming you."

As much as I thought I didn't want him, he's wormed his way through cracking splinters of the wall I built, proving himself to be different than any other guy.

"No?" I ask, as he grabs my hand from my waist and walks me to the big mirror.

As I stare at my hideous body in the reflection, he stands behind me. When he presses a warm, wet kiss on my left shoulder, it sends a shiver through me that makes my eyes roll back. His lips trail over my skin, each kiss igniting a spark, until he reaches my ear. Then he moves to the right, repeating the same tender touches. My head rolls from side to side, loving the sensation of his lips and care he's showing me.

His fingers move to my bra, slipping the straps from my shoulders, as we hold each other's gazes in the mirror. As the intensity rises so does my breath. The moment he unclasps my bra, it falls to the floor with a soft thud. My nipples pebble into tight buds from the cool air hitting my hot skin.

He rolls my nipples between his fingers, causing me to moan and arch into his firm pinch. I'm achy and desperate as he massages my breasts.

"Open your eyes," he rasps hungrily.

I hesitate, but then follow his command, watching his hand glide down over my ribs until he touches the top of my cotton briefs. I focus on breathing and not on my prominent ribs, hips, bones, or worse, my scar.

When he pushes the briefs down, I don't hear the sound of disgust. No, his chest rises and falls rapidly as he groans my name. I stand naked in more ways than one. The lights are on, and I'm pushing past all my fears with him. I can't believe I didn't ask for the lights to be turned off so he didn't have to see me.

His hands skim my thighs, hips and waist, and I watch as they touch my scar.

"Beautiful."

I choke but quickly swallow the sound. His fingers are buttery soft and ticklish over my scar. He's entranced by it.

"Chad came from here?"

"Yes. An emergency C-section." My voice is shaky and distant like it doesn't belong to me.

His hand leaves my waist and holds my stomach, while the other hand moves from my scar to the top of my pussy.

"Harvey," I pant, desperate to put me out of my misery.

"What do you want, buttercup?"

"I want you to touch me," I whimper.

A growl rips from his throat. "Fuck yes."

His finger skims down to my clit, where he rubs it in slow, hard circles. When I'm a mess and begging for more, he moves his hand to slide through my wet pussy and he doesn't pause until he sinks two fingers inside me.

"Oh my God. Harvey——" I call out. This feels like an out-of-body experience

His thick fingers move in a drugging way that has me needy.

"Is this what you wanted? My fingers buried deep inside your pussy?"

He quickens his pace slightly and brings his two fingers high up and down along my front wall in a come hither. My legs tremble beneath him... He's hit the spot. He doesn't stop.

"Yes-s."

"Good, because it's exactly what I've wanted to do to you."

Goosebumps erupt across my skin and my walls tighten at his intruding fingers, my orgasm building.

"Your pussy is so hungry," he grumbles in a deep, strained voice as he rubs my clit with the palm of his hand with every thrust of his fingers.

My body is vibrating, and my lower back is aching. I'm so close. He's holding me tightly against him as my legs tremble. I can't miss the way his erection rubs against my back. But he touches a part inside me, and I crumble. The noises coming out of me are so unfamiliar. Pure pleasure with a bit of pain. Tearing my heart into pieces. This is the moment I believe that this thing between us could be real. I can trust him. He's picked me up and cared for me in more ways than one. It's hard to deny my feelings any longer. He never put himself before me. No, my pleasure was what he wanted. And there's something so sweet that sparks a twinge inside my heart. Something I haven't felt in a long time has come back alive.

Warm liquid hits my back, and a final spasm leaves me, knowing he came without me even touching him. There's something extremely sexy and powerful, knowing he was that turned on by my body that he came just from fingering me.

Peering into the mirror, he pulls his fingers out of me and licks them clean, moaning my name. His face is erotic. I twist in his arms and bring my hands to his neck, as his hands settle on my hips. His heavy lust-filled eyes make my heart beat harder. I rise onto my toes, and we kiss... It's a slow, soft kiss. When we pull apart, he's wearing the biggest boyish grin, and it makes it hard to stop a wide smile from taking over my face.

I run my hand through his messy hair. "I've always wanted to do this," I admit, curling my fingers and tugging on it the way I've always wanted to.

"I knew you secretly loved it."

He leans into my hand. "The first time I touched it at Oliver's gallery, I wanted to push it up and kiss you."

He growls. "You should've."

I drop my hands back to his neck. "No, tonight was perfect."

"Yeah, it was, wasn't it." He rests his forehead on mine, remaining silent as we catch our breaths and soak in this moment.

A few moments later, we pull apart to clean ourselves up and then the office. I expected it to be awkward, but it isn't. We kiss and throw our clothes at each other, and the weightless feeling in my body makes me feel like a teenage girl with a school crush on the popular kid.

"When can we do that again?" he asks, after we're both dressed and ready to leave.

This is when my reality of a single mom with minimal help hits me. "I don't know."

I hang up the phone with my realtor. I'm searching for a condo for Chad and me. It feels like a big step forward, but also a reminder of everything I'm juggling. Today, I need to find time to call the bank and fill out forms. Pushing the glass door, I take a deep breath, steady myself, and head into work.

"Why do you look different?" Molly's eyes narrow as she reads my face when I walk into work the next morning.

I quickly look down at myself, checking for any changes. "I don't look different. You're exaggerating."

"Take a look at yourself." Molly points to the small mirror on the wall.

I catch a glimpse of my reflection, and there's a mess of flyaways on my head. I quickly smooth them down, but it doesn't remove the fact I barely slept last night. I've replayed my night with Harvey repeatedly. I tossed and turned, remembering every touch, word and kiss, that by the time I fell asleep, I slept in and was late dropping Chad off.

I take the chair beside her desk. "Don't say anything, but... last night, I was with, Harvs."

"Must be serious if you're giving him a nickname," she teases, raising her eyebrow and leaning in closer.

I lower my voice, glancing around as if some-one——Harvey——might overhear. "No, I'm talking in code."

Molly shrugs, a small smile on her lips. "Well, I like the nickname. And he's not here, so tell me everything."

My body temperature rises at the memory, and I struggle to find the words. "It was... mind-blowing. I've never been with a guy like him."

Harvey is not like the men I've known, and I have to stop trying to make him fit that mold. He's different... *better*. I can feel the shift inside me as I realize how much I've been holding him to an unfair standard, comparing him to the past, to the mistakes and disappointments that came with it. But Harvey isn't that. He's something more, something I'm not used to. It's hard to let go of the walls I've built, but I can feel them crumbling a little each time he proves me wrong.

Her eyes widen as she sits back. "What do you mean?"

"He was solely focused on me... showering me with compliments and making sure I felt amazing the whole time. And his mouth... God, his words."

Molly's lip's part, and the biggest smile takes over her face as her hands rub together. "Are we talking dirty talk, or...?"

I rub my temple, trying to will away my embarrassment and not be shy about how good he was. But I'm sure my face is bright red with the memory...

"Goddamn," Molly says in awe. "I've always wanted a guy to do that without me having to ask."

A shiver runs down my spine, the intensity still vivid in my mind. "I've never had that before. But it's——"

"Hot," Molly interjects.

"He wasn't just saying it, he was showing me. It made my insecurities disappear, and I was able to fully enjoy the moment."

Molly's face softens, knowing what I mean. She's aware of how insecure I've been about being a single mom because she is too.

"I'm so glad you found someone who can show you how gorgeous you are, my friend."

I pull her into a hug. "Thank you."

"I'm so happy for you," she whispers in my hair.

I'm happy for me too. I just need to figure out how Chad works in this equation. I'm not ready to tell him I'm dating Harvey; it feels too soon. I want to take things slow with

Harvey. But I can't help but wonder: will Harvey want a long-term relationship with me, and will he be willing to take on Chad too?

CHAPTER 26

HARVEY

THE NEXT DAY, I'M in the shower, my hands press against the cold white bathroom tiles in my ensuite, the scalding hot water pounding hard on my back. I can't shake the vision of her... vulnerable and wounded... standing in front of me. It's so hard to see her not be the confident woman I know her to be. I need to figure out how to bring out that confident, feisty Jemima when her clothes are off and it's just us. The sadness in her eyes terrifies me.

Now that she's letting me in, I want more... so much more. But I can't just ask her on a date or have her stay over at mine or vice versa. This is a hard situation, and I've never had to navigate something like this before.

As I get dressed it sparks the memory of her hands gliding through and tugging it, with a twinkle in her eye, an idea comes to me.

We're interviewing potential hires today, and as I drive to work, my father calls to check in. I give him a brief rundown and ask if he and Mom can meet me at the building

I'm considering for the firm. His detailed eye is something I've always valued.

After hanging up, I send Esme an email to schedule the walk-through and call my realtor for an update on the negotiations. When I pull up to the office, I see that Jemima and Molly are already here.

I walk into the building wearing a stupid grin on my face, feeling high... Not like Danny's usual high, but a genuine contentment with my life.

When I smile at Molly, she gives me an unusually wide grin. I frown, but shake off the weird encounter, focusing on seeing my new favorite person. Without knocking, I walk into her office and kiss her. "Good morning," I say, pulling back.

Her eyes widen, and for the first time, she's at a loss for words. "What are you doing?"

I lean, my lips brushing the shell of her ear. "Taking what's mine."

Her breath hitches, but her expression softens. She doesn't hate the idea.

Something has shifted between us.

"I'll meet you to discuss the interviews before the first candidate arrives. I need to check my emails," I say, leaving her office, and swallowing a laugh at her priceless reaction.

Settling into my chair, I work until it's almost time for the first interview. Wanting to make sure she's okay and we're prepared, I print out some questions for her as a guide. Entering her office, I sit in one of the chairs in front of her. "Disappointed?" I ask.

"No, just surprised."

"I told you. I don't want to be a dirty little secret, and I meant it."

It's not like she hasn't already told Molly. What details, I don't know, and I don't care.

"Let's talk about this later." She's trying to keep to business right now or isn't ready to process what happened last night with me.

"Good idea. Let's have lunch after the interviews. We can discuss the candidates and talk about us."

She doesn't flinch as she agrees, "Okay."

"Let's go through the questions you've prepared. I have some you might want to add."

"Won't you be there?" she asks, frowning.

"Yes, but this is your company. I'll sit back and let you do the talking. I'll be there if you need me."

She scratches at her temple and looks over her questions. "There are obvious ones, like asking about previous experiences and why they want to work here. But I also thought about asking them to describe a time when they created an event from scratch. How they approached it and developed the concept."

I nod, impressed. "Ask them about the budget too. Whether they tracked the expenses and if they ever went over budget."

Humming her agreement, she writes this down on a notepad.

"I also have questions about how they handled issues with events."

"Good idea. You need them to be independent, to handle things on their own while you stay in the managerial role."

"Unrealistic clients and how to talk to them."

"Ask for examples. If they don't have any, that's a problem."

She makes another note. "What's the biggest team they've managed, and how did they handle it? Any new marketing tools they've wanted to try or have tried successfully?"

I whistle. "You're really good at this."

"You doubted me?" she bites out, with a teasing glint in her eyes.

"Never." I smirk.

"One thing you should ask is how they handle feedback. Clients will give it, but you need to make sure they're willing to listen to it, bring it to you, and offer solutions."

She points her pen at me. "Good idea."

Just as she finishes writing, her desk phone rings. Molly informs me that the first interviewee is in the meeting room. We rise, and as she rounds her desk, I stand in her way.

"You've got this. Don't use your heart. This is all about your head."

"This is business," she agrees.

"Exactly. Now let's find us some colleagues."

It's strange how the word "us" rolls off my tongue with such ease, but soon I won't be here. There won't be an "us." I try to ignore the way my stomach bottoms out and follow her to the room.

The interviews go smoothly and end on time. I sit back, letting her take the lead, never needing to speak a word. She's intelligent, capable, and knows exactly what she's doing. Leaning back and watching her in action, I'm in awe. She may not have envisioned this as her job, but now that she's here, I can see she was born to lead. She cares about people but won't take shit and that combination is perfect.

After the last interviewee leaves, I walk over to her and spin her around, holding her waist. "You were incredible."

She looks down, then back up, her shy expression one I've never seen before. It's adorable. "Thanks, but they made it easy."

"They were great, and you made them open up. You're going to have a hard time narrowing it down."

"Were there any you think I shouldn't take to the next round?" she asks as her eyes drop to her notes.

I grab her files to carry them for her.

"Maybe the second to last one. Some of their stories weren't as strong. You want people who've faced major problems and fixed them."

She hums thoughtfully, nibbling the end of her pen as she reads her notes.

"Let's go grab some lunch and we can chat more," I suggest, knowing we both need a break.

"Good idea," she agrees, looking up at me with a small smile.

"No Molly. Just us two." I wink.

She hesitates, and her brow furrows slightly. "I feel bad," she whispers.

"We can bring her something back." I try to make her feel better, not wanting her to feel guilty.

"If we bring her a bagel with cream cheese and a coffee, I think she'll get over it." The tension eases from her shoulders as she chuckles.

"Deal. I'll meet you out front. I have to make a quick call," I tell her, a small grin tugging at my lips.

As she walks off to her office, I book a reservation for us at a unique spot called Spin.

CHAPTER 27

JEMIMA

WHEN HE OFFERED LUNCH, I couldn't say no. Firstly, I want to spend more time alone with him, but secondly, my brain is fried from all the interviews. Luckily, my afternoon work is now clear that the main task is done. I will call everyone for trial periods over the next couple of weeks. Then decide which members I'll keep. I'm hopeful I'll find two good employees.

We head downstairs, and I raise an eyebrow when I spot his car. "I thought we'd just go somewhere nearby."

His smile is mischievous. "I have a better idea."

"Of course you do." I sigh, but a smile tugs at my lips.

He opens the car door, and I slip in. We don't drive far, and when we pull up to a bar, I can't deny my bubbling excitement.

As we enter, the staff greets him by name straight away.

"Do you bring all your dates here?" I joke, ignoring the hardness in my stomach.

"Sure do," he replies nonchalantly, which makes my jaw drop.

He quickly chuckles. "Kidding. I come with my friends and brothers sometimes."

My shoulders drop away from my ears, and we're led to a private table in the corner. There's a big, dark wooden bar along the back, and it's filled with people. It seems like a popular hangout spot. The warm lighting in here makes it difficult to see any familiar faces. Walking past the ping-pong tables brings a smile to my face. I snap a quick picture and send it to Mom with a message: *Look what I found in Manhattan.* I know she'll appreciate the character and charm of this place; it's the kind of spot she'd love to visit. We used to play when I was a kid.

I put the phone away when the server approaches and takes our drink orders. Harvey opts for a beer, and I get a Coke. The way we're seated, our thighs brush, and I can feel the heat radiating from his body. The urge to reach out and hold his hand is strong, but something is bugging me.

"I had a big delivery of clothes last night," I start as the server returns to deliver our drinks.

"Mmm," he mumbles, before signaling the server that we're ready to order and asking for it to be delivered to our ping-pong table.

"I haven't even looked at the menu," I whisper, a bit flustered.

"Look, then yell at me," he teases with a wolfish grin. He's clearly enjoying my discomfort.

Pinching my lips together, I glance down at the menu, quickly deciding on a four-cheese pizza. Since Harvey's been around and the business has started picking up, I've been able to buy more food for myself, which has been helping with my sleep and the dizzy spells I'd been struggling with.

Once we place our orders, we carry our drinks to our table, the soft music playing around us.

I ignore the buzzes through me, knowing I'm playing a game I haven't played in years. Deciding it's time to address the elephant in the room, I take a deep breath.

"I don't like you buying me a whole new wardrobe."

He grabs a ball and hits it to me. "But you didn't spend enough the other day."

I hit it back. "I did… on Chad."

"Not on yourself, Jem."

I miss the ball, and it drops on the ground. "Don't call me Jem," I blurt out, sharper than I intended.

His eyebrows knit together.

I pick it up and hit the ball again. "My ex-husband called me that."

He stiffens and misses the ball, caught off guard. But he's never called me that until now.

"Chad's was a lot of money," I say as he hits the ball, and I hit it back.

"But I asked you to spend it on yourself, and you refused."

Grabbing the ball, I lower my paddle to the table and pull out my wallet, sliding his black card back to him. He shakes his head, leaving it on the table between us. "Keep it."

"No," I say firmly. His posture stiffens, his hand still resting near the card, as if he's challenging me to push back. His gaze never wavers, a mix of determination and something unreadable flickering in his expression.

I stare at him with a tightness in my chest. I feel hot, like the walls are closing in around me. This is too much. "I need some air," I murmur, immediately heading outside. The fresh air hits my face, and I breathe deeply, trying to calm my racing heart.

He's beside me in an instant, his eyes wild and frantic. "Are you okay?"

"No, you can't keep rescuing me," I say, my voice trembling.

"I care about you," he replies softly.

"I know, but I promised myself I'd never depend on a man for money again. So please, don't make me take your card." My voice breaks as I plead.

Guilt flashes across his face. "I had no idea."

"I'm not ready for this step."

He's only trying to be nice, but he needs to understand how smothered I feel and like he's trying to control me.

"I can go slow," he assures me, his voice gentle.

"Not too slow..." I tease, trying to lighten the mood again.

His eyebrow raises, stepping closer until our shoes touch. He takes my chin in his strong hand, lifting my head up to meet his gaze. When he kisses me, I melt into him, feeling his warmth seep into my skin.

It's been so long since I've felt desired, and my whole body responds to his tender touch.

When he pulls away, I whimper, not wanting him to stop. He chuckles softly, his eyes filled with longing as he gazes down at me. "Do you have any meetings this afternoon?"

I sigh, remembering the responsibilities waiting for me. "I need to work."

"And I need you," he says, and the words send electricity through me.

I blink at him, stunned. No one has ever said that to me before, and I can't deny the pull I feel toward him. I want more. I'm not usually one to take risks, but with him, I'm willing to jump off the cliff and see where we land.

There's nothing pressing that can't wait an hour...

"Where are we going?" I ask when we abandon the food.

He grins. "My place." Taking my hand, he walks me back to his car. I don't argue. The thought about food is completely forgotten because I'm only hungry for him.

"At least you didn't say a motel, but I guess your penthouse is the same thing," I joke as I get in the car.

His eyebrows lift, amusement sparking in his eyes. He leans in, bracing a hand on the car's roof, his face inches from mine. "For the record," he says, his voice low and deliberate, "you're the first woman I've ever brought back there."

With a wink, he shuts the door, leaving me stunned as I settle into the leather seat, loving that new piece of information. I trust him. He's never lied to me, and for once, I want to be selfish and indulge in what I want. I deserve this.

Twenty minutes later, we step into his penthouse, and the familiar scent of him hits me. It's comforting, and the energy between us intensifies. My eyes drift over the light wooden floors and the open-plan space, where floor-to-ceiling glass walls offer a spectacular view of New York. Sunlight floods the entire floor, casting a warm glow over the cream leather sofas that look invitingly cozy to sleep on, yet I'm sure he wouldn't need to sleep there.

Soon, I'll have my own place. Nothing grand as this, but it'll be all mine.

I take in the large wooden dining table, big enough for eight, and a sleek kitchen along the back brick wall, with dark wood, marble countertops, and chandeliers hanging above the island. When I came here the first time, after I fainted, I didn't get the chance to have a good look around. Today, I soak it all in.

"This is insane. How long have you lived here?" I ask, unable to keep the awe out of my voice.

"Since I moved out of my parents' house," he replies casually, as if it's just another part of his life, something that's always been.

"To be born into money," I murmur, momentarily lost in thought. I wonder what that must be like to never have to struggle.

He shifts slightly, his tone changing, becoming more serious. "I've worked hard since I was a kid, always trying to prove myself. Fuck, I still feel like I need to," he says with a huff.

My heart breaks for him. Despite his money, he's always been so supportive, offering encouragement when I needed it most. "You deserve everything you have. I've seen how much you work and how much you care about your businesses."

"Well, I was kinda forced to help yours, but I'm glad I did; otherwise, we wouldn't be here," he says, the teasing edge in his voice returning. But then his hand reaches up to trace my bottom lip with his finger, and the tenderness in the gesture makes me forget everything else. His eyes darken with desire, and I feel the electricity spark between us.

Our gazes lock, and everything fades away. He leans in, capturing my mouth in a firm kiss. For once, the world feels peaceful, and I let myself follow my heart's desires. "Harvey?" I whisper against his lips, my breath shallow.

"Yes, baby," he murmurs back between kisses, the intensity of the moment consuming us both.

"I need you."

He groans into my mouth before pulling back slightly, but he keeps our bodies pressed together.

"Take me," I command.

Without hesitation, he grabs my hand and leads me up a flight of stairs near the kitchen. If I thought the view was stunning downstairs, it's even more magnificent up here. His beige leather bed faces the city scape, no plaster walls to block the city views. He moves to hold me, but I've had my fill of the view. What I want now is him. I want to be consumed by his affection, to forget the everyday chaos that is my life right now.

I twist in his arms to face him, and he shrugs out of his jacket. My hands move to untuck his shirt, eager to strip it away. This time, I'm not slow... I want him naked as quickly as possible.

"In a hurry to leave?" he teases.

"Not at all," I reply, my voice husky with desire. "I just want you naked as fast as possible."

"Well, let me help with that." He grins and rips his shirt off.

"Your shirt..." I gasp.

He shrugs. "I can grab another one."

Right, we're at his place. "Be careful with mine. I don't have any spare clothes."

"You could borrow a shirt," he offers.

"And what do I tell Molly or Chad?" I raise an eyebrow.

"Molly won't care, but Chad... yeah, that's awkward." He looks a bit nervous at the mention of Chad.

I smile, amused. "Exactly."

Chapter 28

Harvey

My hand slides carefully over her clothes as I carefully remove each piece. I watch as her hands drop from my chest to the sides of her body. She watches my hands undo the delicate buttons on her shirt and zip down with care.

Our clothes are all off in a matter of seconds. The confidence in her now as she stands here is different. She's not trying to hide her body or stop me from seeing her completely naked like last night. Instead, she stands tall and presses her breasts out toward me. Right now, I want her to only feel, and not think about anything. She needs to understand how much I've fallen for her and how much I love her body. I'll show her how desperate I am to please her.

Her fingers trail from my shoulders down my chest, brushing over the patch of dark hair before skimming my stomach. She slows to a tease near my erection, then drags her nails back up, leaving me burning for more. I can tell it's affecting her too—her cheeks are flushed pink. It doesn't stop her from gliding her hand through my hair and tugging on it hard to tilt my head back, exposing my neck. I swallow roughly as I wait with anticipation for her next move. She moves her mouth to the base of my neck and kisses, sucks, licks and bites her way up to my jaw, leaving little marks along my skin. Then she starts along my jaw to meet my mouth, where she nips at my lip and I lose it, capturing her lips in a growl.

Lifting her into my arms, I carry her to my bed, where I lay her down delicately. She looks beautiful laying on my gray blankets. Her hair fanned out messily around her head, I kiss her this time, along her jaw and neck. I run my palm over her chest and squeeze her breasts before moving down over her stomach and then over her mound and slowly making my way through her wetness. She bucks her hips, desperate for my fingers again, but I fight against her to bring her the best pleasure today.

She has the prettiest pussy I've ever seen. "I want to taste you, buttercup. Will you let me?" I ask in a deep, gravelly tone.

"Yes-s," she begs on a wobbly breath.

The memory of how she felt in my arms last night instantly causes my body to overheat, just like the way her hooded eyes look right fucking now.

My thigh settles between her parted legs, my hands gliding over her hips and thighs, savoring every single bit of her. I kiss her, starting at her lips and following an invisible path to her scar, my touch soft. Gently laying kisses on top of every inch, I admire its beauty to bring a child into this world, one as clever and as kind as her.

She whimpers, and it's a sound I haven't heard before, a mix of pain and pleasure. As I look up, there's a trickle of a tear leaking from the corner of her eye.

I kiss the top of her pussy, inhaling her sweet scent at the same time. She moans when I place a kiss a little lower. The single tear still bothers me, but as if she can feel how tense I am she speaks.

"Such a good boy."

I lift my mouth from her with a smirk. "One kiss and look at you. Opening up like a flower."

"Don't get ahead of yourself," she says with a feisty tone, rolling her head back on my bed.

"Inside, I knew there was something good between us. Calling me your good boy makes me fucking crazy."

"Prove it," she challenges, her eyes daring me to show her.

Leaning down, I flick my tongue over her clit before glancing up at her flushed face, parted mouth, and closed eyes. I bring my mouth back to her pussy, but this time, I push two fingers inside of her at the same time. Enjoying the way her tight, warm pussy grips me. I continue giving her clit attention while I finger her. Her breathy moans are coming out faster. With each swirl of my tongue on her swollen clit, her back arches, and she pushes her breasts up to me. A silent beg for attention. My hand skims her stomach until I find the left nipple and tweak it, causing another whimper.

"Please don't stop," she commands, gripping a handful of my hair and bringing my head between her thighs to where she wants me.

"Never." My head settles between her legs, my hands on them firmly to keep them parted as she moans at every thrust of my finger or every suck of her clit.

Her thigh muscles tremor, just before she tightens her grip on my hair as she cries out. "Oh my God, that's so... good."

It doesn't take long and she's rocking her hips, chasing her orgasm and calling my name.

"Is this what good boys do?" I curl my fingers over her G-spot as I rub her clit with my tongue, loving every moment of this. My cock is harder than ever.

"Yes," she cries, rubbing her pussy harder on my face. "I'm so close."

"Come. Let me taste you," I beg before licking her clit just as her orgasm tears through her and I feel her coming on my tongue.

When her body stops convulsing, I crawl up, and her blissful face is hot as fuck.

My cock is leaking, and I don't want to come without being inside her, so I grab a condom from my bedside table and roll it on.

As soon as I'm back on the bed, she pushes me until I'm lying down. This shift in power is a delightful change. I let her have her moment. She maintains eye contact as she grabs my cock, lifts her hips, and slowly takes me in. As I watch my dick enter her, it's intoxicating. She's tight like a vise, but she sets the pace, edging herself ever so slowly down to when she's almost taken all of me. Her hands rest on my stomach for stability.

I watch the last bit of me go inside, and when she's fully seated, I wait a minute before she adjusts. As she rocks her hips, I rock the opposite, and that friction has her moaning my name in a long drawn-out pant. "Haaarveeey."

"So fucking tight."

My hands are on her hips as she rocks faster, and I feel her thighs tense around me as she quickens her pace. She's chasing her orgasm, and it isn't long before she's quivering and calling out.

As her orgasm rolls through her, mine hits me hard, and I grip her hips, holding her there as I empty.

Her eyes flutter open, and a sexy smirk lifts the corner of her lip as our gazes meet.

She trembles when I pull out, dropping her head in the crook of my neck, trying to suck in deep lungfuls of air. I run my hands up and down her back.

Disconnecting briefly so I can dispose of the condom, I come back and pull her up farther on the bed so I can hold her.

"Here I was, thinking you were cocky and controlling," she says, breaking the silence.

I click my tongue. "There's something blissful about handing over control. It's so fucking freeing. And baby, you need someone to take control over you every once in a while, to free your soul."

She gives me a look, as if to say, *how the fuck would you know...*

She opens her mouth to say something, but just then her phone rings. Her eyes widen in surprise, and she quickly stands up, heading downstairs naked to grab it. I get up, following her, watching her as she reads the screen. Unable to hold back, I ask, "Who is it?" My frown deepens when I notice her expression shift, turning cool and distant.

"Butch's parents."

"What do they want?"

She lifts her gaze from her phone to me. Her eyes are wide and scattered.

She paces the room. "I don't know. I'll have to call them back to find out, but if I had a guess, they want to see Chad."

"Do they know their son did drugs?"

"They found out the same day I did."

Why am I acting like he's my kid? I need to sit back and let her handle this. Although I know next to nothing about him, I can't stop the hatred I feel when he's mentioned. And I know enough to make me want to protect Jemima and Chad from anything associated with him... including his parents.

CHAPTER 29

JEMIMA

WE HEAD BACK UPSTAIRS, where his fingers brush my cheek in a sweet, unexpected touch, making my chest ache for more. I wish I could just be a young woman who grabs one of his shirts, watches a TV show or movie, and then falls asleep in his arms. But instead, I have to deal with real-life problems, so I call them back.

The conversation is short, and I agree to organize a meetup.

I pick my clothes off the floor, lost in thought when Harvey's arms pull me up to stand. He hugs me close, and I wrap my arms around his middle, savoring the beat of his heart and the warmth of his skin against my cheek.

How did he know I needed comfort?

We stand in the middle of his bedroom, and my eyes shift to take in the view. This is the push I need to keep going in the direction I've found for myself. While my ex tries to remind me of my past, Harvey shows me a different path.

"You ready to get back to work now?" I ask.

"No. I've been trying to figure out a way I can convince you to stay locked up in here with me so we can stay in this bubble longer."

I pull my head away from his body to gaze up at him. His face is contorted tightly.

"As much as I'd love that, we can't. We could do this again if you're interested?"

His expression softens, as a small chuckle escapes him. He kisses the top of my head. "Of course I'm interested."

"I'm not sure how to do this..."

"You mean date?" he asks, raising an eyebrow.

That seems serious, and before we label this, I need to test the waters with Chad. "Yeah. Could we hang out with Chad and see how it feels?"

"We could go to a basketball game?" he says, searching my eyes.

Inside it kills me to swallow my pride and let him do something extravagant because I know Harvey will get the best seats. "Sounds great," I say with a smile. The way his eyes light up makes me regret not giving in sooner. He genuinely wants to hang out with us.

"Now, are you sure we don't have time for another round?" He kisses my jaw and down my neck, sucking and biting, and my knees go weak. His erection has been pressed against me, and I'm amazed at how quickly he's ready again.

Have some fun... I hear Molly's voice say in my head. *You won't get another opportunity for a while.*

"Unless you don't think you can make me come in the next five minutes?" I challenge.

He picks me up, throws me on the bed, grabs another condom, and crawls over me, positioning his thighs between mine. Lifting one of my legs onto his shoulder, he presses a kiss on my inner ankle, making my body tremble. He repeats the action with my other. With both of my legs on his shoulders, he leans over. I watch his face... his heavy, hooded eyes focused on my pussy. His hand rests on my left hip, and with his right, he guides his cock inside me. This time, he slides in without waiting for me to adjust.

The fullness feels incredible, and my body softens with the memory of him. He begins to thrust into me, and this angle lets him go so deep, his pelvis pressing against my swollen, achy clit. It doesn't take long before my limbs start quivering, my lower back heating up.

"Harvey, don't stop."

"Never, buttercup," he grunts as he comes.

I crumble at his words, my orgasm tearing through my body until my body collapses. I never thought I'd find a partner again, let alone someone like this.

He pulls away, and I watch his powerful body as he throws away the condom. Then he comes over with my clothes. "We need to get some water and food for you to eat. I've got nothing here, so I'll grab us something on the way back to the office."

"We should've had lunch first."

I'm so weak now I'm a little dizzy when I stand to get dressed. I sit on his bed as I do.

"Next time."

I'm too tired and hungry to argue.

Going to his closet, he comes out with a new shirt, and that simple knowledge is sexy. I've never had a guy rip his shirt during sex, never been that lost in the moment.

He catches me watching him and flashes a wolfish grin.

"Let's go, buttercup."

"Why do you call me buttercup?"

He smirks. "Those flowers I brought you smell as sweet as you do and the nickname for them is—"

"Buttercup," I finish his sentence with a smile.

After we return to work, we head to our separate offices. It's funny how easily we slip in and out of roles. Nothing with Harvey ever feels forced.

I'm going through my emails when a call from my realtor comes through. She tells me she has two condos that would be a good fit for me and Chad, and they'll be available to move into within a few weeks.

That news worries me. I've only just found my footing with my company, and now I might have to move during a time when I'm needed here.

After work, I pick up Chad and we head to see the properties. As we pull up to the first one, I notice the clean, tree-lined streets and the well-kept homes around it. It's also bigger than I expected. But when the agent mentions the price, my chest tightens. It's above the pre-approved loan amount I was quoted. I don't want to take a big risk, so I focus on the smaller one we see next. This one is cozier, with polished wooden floors, a kitchen the right size for us, and full-length glass windows allowing the sun to beam in...just like Harvey's. Chad is darting to every room, gushing and pointing out where he'll store his toys and how close we'll be to the park where we saw Harvey running. His bedroom and the living room are bigger, and there's a spot for a small desk and a laptop, so I could work from home sometimes.

I picture us here, with his school not far away. The safe neighborhood, the many parks for him to play at, and views from every part of the house. I know I need to take this place; I'll never find something this good within my budget. The agent runs through all the details, and I tell her I'd like to submit an offer.

Later that afternoon, I grab some pizza with Chad and decide to watch a movie. I casually mention that his grandparents want to see him over the weekend. My stomach is in knots, as I brace myself for questions about his father, but he doesn't ask; he just agrees to catch up with them. I release a breath I didn't know I was holding.

After tucking Chad into bed, I send Harvey a text about how I put in an offer on a place.

My night on the sofa is restless as I worry what Butch's parents might say in front of Chad and whether I should call them to talk about it.

I get up the next morning at five a.m., make my coffee, and get ready for the day. I can't wait to leave this place and sleep in a new home, with a new sofa and bed, and no memories of my past. Even though there are many good memories, especially recent ones with Harvey, like him bringing over food when Chad was sick or picking me up for our date. I'll make fresh memories in the new place. I just hope I hear back soon about the offer.

As I stand in front of the bathroom mirror, adjusting my blouse, my thoughts turn to Harvey. What would it be like to date a man like him? A man who's not only successful but genuinely cares about me and about Chad. It's hard to wrap my head around the idea of someone so well-off wanting to be a part of my life, wanting to build something with me, with us. He's been so patient, so supportive, and the way he treats Chad like he's his own, it's... it's more than I ever thought I could ask for.

Maybe this is the fresh start I've been waiting for. A new house, a new chapter for Chad, and the possibility of a life with someone who sees the value in not just me, but everything I'm trying to build. I've worked so hard to get this far rebuilding my family's business and putting Chad first, but the idea of having someone like Harvey by my side, someone who's as invested in the future as I am... it's almost too good to be true.

But it feels real. I just have to let myself believe it.

Chapter 30

Harvey

THE FOLLOWING WEEKEND, WE walk into Madison Square Garden, the air buzzing with the chatter of fans all around us. As we weave through the crowd, the smell of pretzels and popcorn fills the air, mixing with the electric anticipation that pulses through the walls of the stadium. When we find our seats, Chad eagerly sits between us, his eyes wide, and he immediately turns to Jemima and asks if they can switch seats so he can have a better view of the court. She agrees, and as she moves, I can't help but smirk, tempted to reach out and hold her hand. But I hold back. Chad's right here, and I don't want to make her uncomfortable. I want to make sure she knows this is at her pace, not mine.

"How did it go with the grandparents today?" I ask, my voice low.

"It was alright. A bit awkward at the start, but then it was normal," she replies, her eyes flicking to Chad before returning to me.

"I bet. Did they ask about him or mention his name?"

She shakes her head, her expression calm, but her fingers fidgeting slightly. "No, but I called beforehand. Told them what Chad knows and doesn't know."

"And they were okay with that?"

"They understand it's about what's best for Chad. It's not about us."

I reach out, resting my hand on her shoulder, giving it a gentle squeeze. The tension in her muscles tells me how much she's been dealing with, and I've been dying to be close to her. But work has pulled me away, and she's been busy with the second round of interviews. We both have so much going on.

"Have you heard from agents about your offer?" I ask, remembering our text conversation about the condo.

"Yeah, we're in negotiations. Hoping to move to inspections soon."

I nod, then turn to Chad, who's completely absorbed in the game preparations. His eyes are fixed on the court, taking in every detail. Seeing the game through his eyes makes me realize how much I've taken for granted, the bright lights, the rowdy crowd, and the energy of this place. It's all new and overwhelming for him, and I can't help but smile at the memory of my first game at his age. I glance over at Jemima, and she's just as entranced, her face lit up in wonder.

Around us, all the fans are wearing team colors, either blue and orange, or black and white. I spot a vendor selling jerseys and head straight for it. The vendor grins as he hands me three shirts, commenting on how good we look as a family. I can't help but smile as I glance at Jemima. She shuffles from foot to foot beside me, her eyes flicking to the vendor, and her mouth parts as if she's about to say something... but she doesn't. Instead, she takes the jersey I hand her and slips one on. I help Chad into his, then ruffle his hair as he beams up at me.

With our new jerseys on, we blend into the crowd as we grab some food.

Hot dogs in hand, we settle into the chairs as the air around us grows with more charge in the anticipation of the team to hit the court. The billboards and neon lights stand out.

"What are those?" Chad asks, pointing.

"Cheerleaders," Jemima answers.

"Or do you mean the mascot?" I ask.

"No silly, I know what that is." Chad laughs, like I said something funny.

We watch and cheer as the mascots goof around. When the players finally come out for warmups, the stadium erupts into the loudest cheer. Chad sits up. "Cool, bro," he says, his grin spreading wide.

I look over at Jemima and notice a hint of a smile lifts on the corner of her lips. The music pumps through the speakers, loud and upbeat, and Jemima leans closer to Chad and asks, "Are your ears okay?"

I didn't think about his ears...

"Do you need me to find earplugs?" I offer. "I'll get some delivered if they don't have them here."

"No, I love it," Chad responds, his eyes never leaving the court.

"Well, if you change your mind, just let me know," I say, the protective edge in my voice surprising even me.

The game starts, and we're all swept up in the fast-paced action, our eyes glued to the players as they sprint across the polished wood floor. A timeout is called, and the camera labelled the "Kiss Cam" starts scanning the crowd. It swings our way and lands on Jemima and me. The crowd erupts in cheers and encourages us on.

"Kiss him, Mom!" Chad shouts from beside her, his voice clear and full of innocent command.

Jemima's eyes widen, darting from Chad to me.

"You better do what he says," I whisper into her ear, my heart pounding as I flash her a crooked grin.

Her eyes lock onto mine as a flush spreads across her face and neck, her hesitation only lasting a second before she leans in, and our lips meet. The crowd roars, Chad cheers, and for a moment, it's just us. When we pull away, I can't help but grin. The camera moves to another couple. I stare at Jemima, but she turns to Chad, checking on him.

He just encouraged us to kiss. Does this mean he's okay with us? My head is spinning, trying to process the moment. I've never needed anyone's approval like this before, but Chad's reaction means everything.

My chest puffs, and who knew that a kid could make or break your day based on simple things.

The game resumes, and the intensity heats up as the final minutes tick down. We're down by two points. Chad jumps up and down in his seat, shouting encouragement, and Jemima and I chime in.

In the final minute, we get ahead and win. The stadium erupts in cheers, and Chad throws his arms around me, shouting, "We won!"

"Yeah, we did," I say, hugging him tightly. I glance at Jemima, a contorted expression on her face.

As we leave the stadium, the atmosphere is still buzzing. "That was so cool! I want to go to the next game." Chad's voice is hoarse from all the cheering.

"You can't go to every game, but I'll take you again some other time," Jemima offers.

"Will you come too?" Chad asks, looking up at me in question.

"If you want me to," I reply, my heart swelling.

Jemima smiles, and Chad's eyebrows pinch. "Yes, of course."

We get into my car, and Chad settles into the car seat I had fitted just for him. He asks if we can drive a little faster on the way home, but Jemima quickly shuts that down.

When we arrive at her place, I walk them to the door, waving goodbye as they head inside. As I turn to leave, my phone buzzes in my pocket.

Danny: *I need another ten thousand.*

Surely, he didn't blow through ten thousand dollars already?

CHAPTER 31

JEMIMA

THE NEXT DAY, I file the final paper, feeling the weight of the moment as I lay it down. I let out a long breath, sinking back into my chair, the tension in my shoulders finally starting to unknot. The neatly stacked financials sit in front of me. Everything is up to date, and with a new system, thanks to Harvey. I feel like I'm on track to make a really good profit.

I have two short meetings today, one with Jeremy about a party for his hospital event, and another with someone in a different state. I'm unsure if it's something I can offer, but I figured I'd discuss and see if there's any way to make it possible.

As I'm preparing, the sound of heavy footsteps brings a smile to my face before he even enters the room. The giddy feeling of a teenage crush never seems to get old. The first time we kissed on my front doorstep, Chad was blissfully unaware... but at the game, he encouraged it.

Now I wonder will Chad feel confused? And what does it mean for my future with Harvey?

Harvey walks over to my side of the desk, grabs my chair, and turns it to face him. Leaning forward, he cages me in, and a piece of hair falls between his eyes. My hands itch to move it, so I push the hair back, keeping my hand on his head. He flashes me a half smile before leaning in and capturing my lips with his. I grip the back of his head harder at the base of his neck.

"Good morning," he murmurs across my lips.

"Morning," I breathe, still trying to catch my breath. I want to tell him he shouldn't do that at work, but I'm the boss, and soon, he won't be here. So, I indulge in the affection he offers. An innocent good morning kiss isn't going to stop me from working. Why did I ever think I had to choose?

Because of my past trauma.

But no more. I kiss him briefly before he pulls back.

"I saw the meetings scheduled for today that I should attend, but I might need to duck out early. I have a meeting with my dad."

I nod. "Why are you meeting him?"

"I want him to see the building where I want to open the consulting firm."

"That's exciting," I say.

The way he talks about his dad and how he wants his opinion makes my heart bleed for Chad, since he won't have that. It's too early to know if Harvey will be that person, but God, I want it so badly that it worries me. He's been great with Chad since their awkward first meeting. If Chad had Harvey as a role model, I wouldn't be mad... Harvey is sweet, caring, ruthless in business when he needs to be and, most importantly he's been trustworthy.

"I want to go through the business's mission and vision, as well as your long-term goals. I think refreshing them will keep you on track for this place."

I raise an eyebrow, biting back a smirk as he shifts back to business mode, as if he didn't kiss me like a lover moments ago.

"Sure, I'm ready when you are."

"I'll go check my emails and be right back."

I watch him leave, and the sight of his swagger in a suit makes me feel like I'm floating on a cloud of lust.

I'm about to leave the office and lock up because Chad has basketball practice tonight. I can finish the paperwork from today's meetings later. Molly has agreed to be my point of contact so I can fly over and meet Mr. Baird. I'll book the flights tonight... just a day trip, maybe an overnight stay, which makes me a bit nervous. But I have to remember I'm the CEO, and I've already changed Chad's life for the better. Once I've chosen my trainees and they've settled in and proven themselves, they'll take on tasks like this for me.

Harvey has left to meet his dad, and Molly has finished for the day. I'm about to pass Molly's desk when Danny walks in. I blink, wondering if this is real. I've been calling and texting on and off, but he never answers.

"Hey," he says, scratching his forearm.

"Where have you been? I've been trying to call you." I hug him, and he hugs me back, a little too roughly.

His eyes have a blueish tint to them, and he rubs at his mouth.

"Yeah, I wasn't allowed to contact you."

The hairs on the back of my neck rise. "You weren't allowed to?" I ask, wondering who would do such a thing and why?

"No. Your boyfriend," he says with a curl to his lip, "told me to leave and never contact you."

I stare at him, dumbfounded. Something feels off, and I can't shake the feeling that there's more to this than he's letting on. With so many questions racing through my mind, I start with the most pressing one.

"Who?"

"Harvey Lincoln. He paid me ten thousand dollars to stay away from you." His jaw tightens, and his shoulders are rigid, like he's bracing himself. He glances at me, then quickly looks away, his fingers tapping nervously on his leg.

Harvey paid him behind my back? I rub my forehead, trying to piece things together, but nothing makes sense.

"He bribed me to leave so he could take over your company."

My eyes sting and my throat aches. So he wasn't interested? *Have I been played all along?*

I blink furiously as I turn my head away, needing a second to breathe before turning back to him. "What made you change your mind?"

"I didn't want him to hurt you. I like you."

That doesn't sit right. There's something he's not telling me.

"I see you've had a makeover. Was that his idea?" His eyes move past me.

"Yeah," I say, my voice flat. I clutch the paperwork tighter, my fingers digging into the edges. My shoulders stiffen, and I uncross my arms over my chest, a shield between us. The familiar walls start to rebuild, brick by brick, shutting him out.

"Must be nice to have money and take over someone's business," he mutters under his breath.

I can't respond yet. I'm too busy trying to process everything he's said. It's not adding up.

"I need my job back," he asks, eyes fixed on me. "I've been interviewing new employees," I reply, my tone sharp. He can't just come back in here after leaving without a word and expect his job back.

He lets out a laugh, shaking his head. "Your dad would've never treated me like this. I was practically family to him. He trusted me. If he could see how you're handling this after everything I did for him, he'd be ashamed. And honestly, I think he'd be worried about you too."

I tense, but he doesn't stop, stepping closer. "You're letting people take advantage of you, and now you're letting go of the ones who actually care. Is that what you think he'd want?"

My jaw tightens as his words sink in. "Don't you dare bring my dad into this," I say. "He's not here to speak for himself, and you don't get to guilt me into anything by throwing his name around." I swallow hard and force myself to stay steady. "I'm doing the best I can, and if that means making hard choices, so be it. This isn't about taking advantage or letting go, it's about moving forward."

My gut is telling me something about all this doesn't feel right. So I'll be keeping my guard up. I don't want anyone I can't trust working here.

CHAPTER 32

JEMIMA

"I think you should go," I say, pointing to the door. Luckily, he moves toward the exit.

"I'll talk to you later," is all he says.

I stand there for a moment, exhaling heavily, ready to find out what the fuck is going through Harvey's head.

But as I turn to leave, Harvey stands tall, his annoyingly sharp jawline and bright eyes making it hard to look away. My heart squeezes, but I gather my strength and swallow down the confusion and hurt. "I forgot the keys." He walks up to me and leans in for a kiss, but I turn my face, letting his soft lips brush my cheek instead. Frowning, he pulls back. "What's wrong?"

"Did you pay Danny ten thousand dollars to stay away from me?"

"Yes," he says, not even blinking.

My chest tightens. I feel like I can't breathe. "Why?"

"I did it for you," he answers, his voice calm, too calm.

But something feels off. My stomach twists, and I can't shake the knot forming in my gut.

"Harvey." I step closer, trying to keep my voice steady. "I'm asking you again. Why did you pay Danny?"

His shoulders sag as he lets out a long breath. "Because I caught him using drugs. Not just in your bathroom..." He gestures toward the men's room. "But he was stealing money to feed his habit. And he was buying from your ex."

I blink, trying to take it all in, but he keeps going.

"I paid him off to protect you," he says, his voice softer now. "I didn't want you getting dragged into his mess. I wanted you to focus on making this business a success, not cleaning up after someone else's mistakes."

We're standing so close, the space between us tense with unspoken things. His eyes don't leave mine, and I can feel the weight of everything he's trying to say. I'm in shock, but I force myself to speak.

"So, you can get your money and leave. I get it." My voice cracks, sounding foreign to my own ears.

"No. I did it to protect you." Voice strained, his eyes widen with shock. "I'm sorry I didn't tell you..." He starts and reaches out to comfort me.

I put my hands up, stepping back. "Don't touch me."

Standing there, his shoulders slumped, hands by his sides, he stares down at me. My breath comes hard and fast. I can't believe he never mentioned any of this.

"You could have told me one thing. Yet-t you hid all of that information," I say, voice trembling. "Were you ever going to tell me?"

"Of course," he says softly.

"When?"

"Soon."

Not soon enough.

"You should've told me when you found out." My arms cross defensively, my posture closing off as the hurt builds inside me. I can feel the distance between us growing, despite how close we stand.

"It wasn't the right time. Look at what you've accomplished."

"You don't get to choose when to tell me things. You were supposed to be honest with me." My body shakes with the intensity of my emotions.

"Butter——" he starts, but I cut him off.

"No!" I snap. The nickname slices through me like a knife. "You don't get to call me that."

Why does it hurt more now that he's in front of me? I wasn't even this broken when my husband went to jail. Why do I feel like crying? I don't cry. But what did I expect when I handed over my heart. I was a fool. A stupid, lovesick fool, acting like I'm thirty-four and not forty-two. My error.

I straighten, reclaiming what little control I have left. "I don't want you back here. Pack your shit and go."

"But——"

My throat constricts, but I push through the pain, my voice sharp. "No buts. I don't want to hear it. You had plenty of opportunities to tell me any of this, and instead, I found it all out now."

Despite the tightness in my chest, I manage to keep my voice steady, though my hands tremble at my sides. The control I'm holding on to is slipping, but I refuse to let him see it.

He paid Danny ten thousand dollars.

Danny was doing drugs.

Danny was stealing from the company.

Danny was buying from my ex.

I can't deal with the double betrayal. I just want to go home and hug Chad, the one person I can trust with my heart.

He doesn't move, but the tears welling in my eyes make it clear I need to get out of here before my body betrays my determination.

"Lock up when you leave and have your driver drop the keys to Molly. Don't call me again."

"I'm sorry, Jemima." His face falls, and for a brief moment, his eyes flicker with regret, but he doesn't argue. As if my words are finally sinking in, his shoulders sag. He opens his mouth, as if to say something, then closes it, the words trapped.

I'm sorry too. So sorry I trusted you with my heart. And ultimately, you let me down.

I storm out, heading home, my body trembling as tears stream down my face as I reach my car. Inside, I grip the steering wheel as sobs wrack my body.

Picking up my phone, I call my mom. I need to hear her soothing voice and advice right now.

"Jemima. Hi."

"Mom," I choke out.

I hear her gasp through the phone, her voice rising. "What's going on, sweetheart?"

"The guy I was seeing was dishonest with me. He said it was to protect me, but it still hurts..."

She inhales sharply. "Dishonest? To protect you? Darling, listen to me," she says, her voice soft but firm. "If you're this upset, you might need some time to yourself. Focus on you for a while. Meditate, take long walks, maybe get a new shade of lipstick! If it's still bothering you, he's obviously not the one. But if it's just a misunderstanding or bad communication, well, maybe that's something you can work through."

"I don't know what I want," I admit, sniffling.

"That's okay, sweetheart," she says softly. "Take your time. Make lists. Write it all down. Pros, cons, things you can forgive. But the most important thing is this... relationships should make you feel adored, not stressed. Remember that."

He never made me doubt his feelings, but honesty is important to me. He knew that.

"Go home, cuddle that beautiful grandson of mine, and I'll call you tomorrow," she says.

I don't feel better, but I definitely feel okay to pick Chad up now. I just couldn't face him before. I don't want Chad to be affected in any of this.

"Thanks, Mom."

I hang up and wipe my eyes, take a deep breath, and force myself to think of Chad. I know what moms do best. They put on a brave face for their children. I'll greet Chad with a smile, pretending like nothing's wrong.

My eyes feel like they're hanging out of my head as I enter the office. I barely slept. Sometime in the middle of the night, I texted Danny, telling him he was no longer welcome in my life or the company. He tried calling, but I didn't answer and blocked his number. There's no reason for us to ever speak again.

"Molly, coffee break," I call out as I walk in.

She looks up, taking one glance at me before standing and coming around her desk. "You okay, boss lady?"

I shake my head, walking slowly to her. The stupid dam wants to open up again, but I fight the urge to cry. "No."

She gestures for me to sit, and I sink into the chair slowly, trying to steady myself. Sitting across from me, her calm presence keeps me grounded.

"Tell me," she prompts softly, leaning in just enough to show she's ready to listen.

"I can't go over all the details because I don't want to relive it. But in short, Danny was stealing money from the company and using it for drugs."

Her eyes widen as she audibly gasps and covers her mouth with her hand. "How did you find out?"

"He showed up and told me Harvey paid him ten thousand dollars to stay away from me."

She winced. "Harvey found out and didn't say anything?"

"Bingo." I nod, making myself a cup of coffee. Even looking at the stupid machine irritates me because he bought it for the office. I'm not childish enough to send it back.

"So, what happens now?"

I hand her one of the coffees and set it in front of her. "Neither Danny nor Harvey will be coming back."

"Thanks," she whispers to me for the coffee. "How do you want to handle this week's schedule?"

"I'll still go to D.C., if you can take care of Chad?"

"Of course. Stay the night, you need some time to think, and a good night's sleep would do you a world of good."

I manage a small smile as I reach out and squeeze her hand. "How did I get so lucky with you?"

"You'd do the same for me. I scratch your back, you scratch mine."

"Always."

"Come here," she says, standing and waiting for me to follow. We wrap our arms around each other, and the comfort of someone I can trust feels so good. I just wish I had more people in my corner. Just when I thought my lonely life was lifting, I'm knocked back down to reality.

"I need to call the new hires for second round interviews and see when they can start. In the meantime, I'll use my temps to help out."

"What can I do to help?"

"If you call the hires, I'll get started on the temps."

If I can just immerse myself in work and focus on Chad, maybe Harvey will become old news. But as soon as I think that, my heart twinges, betraying my lie. It won't be easy to forget him. He became an important person in my life, and my son's.

How do I tell Chad?

CHAPTER 33

JEMIMA

As I'm about to board the plane, a text from Harvey pops up.

I don't answer, just like all the other ones he's sent me. My head and heart aren't ready to talk to him. I'm gutted beyond words. As much as the anger simmers in my blood, if he were close, I'm not sure I'd be strong enough to resist. He's gotten under my skin and into my heart and I just need time to process Danny and his betrayal.

This overnight stay is exactly what I need; it's a chance to get some much-needed space.

When I arrive at the Baird hotel, I check in and am informed the room's ready. The client I'm meeting owns this hotel, but I was upgraded to the penthouse, which we hadn't discussed. I enter the room, and my jaw drops.

It's as beautiful as Harvey's place. Why does everything remind me of him? He's haunting me, even from afar.

Walking through the suite, I spot the bathtub in the middle of the bathroom. I know exactly where I'll be spending my evening. There's even a box of chocolates and a bottle of champagne waiting for me.

I worked on the plane, so I have an hour to kill before I need to meet Mr. Baird. Once I've ordered some room service, I curl up on the obnoxiously large cream sofa, and find a show I haven't watched in forever. My food arrives, and I relax for a bit before heading down to the meeting rooms.

When I arrive, the conference room is empty. I wonder if I misread the email. He was adamant about me being here in person, insisting that the scale and importance of this high-profile gala demanded precision and a level of detail he felt couldn't be addressed over Zoom.

I set my bag down and pull out my phone to double-check, but a familiar ache rises in my throat, catching me off guard.

Harvey: *Please call me.*

Inhaling deeply, I focus on my emails. Suddenly, Mr. Baird's voice booms through the room. "Sorry, I'm late. I just got in from a flight." I jump at the sudden noise, my heart racing, and quickly slip my phone into my purse.

"That's okay. How was your flight?"

"Long," he says, already moving toward the door to his office. He opens it and steps aside, gesturing for me to follow. "Come in here. I have about forty-five minutes to go through this."

Straight to the point. I thought I knew what blunt was, but that was before I met Mr. Baird.

I take a seat, and he begins explaining what he wants. I share my concerns about suppliers, and he's willing to use mine, covering the shipping and time costs. The availability of the high-end material means I need to secure it now before it becomes unavailable.

"How did you come across me?" I ask.

"I attended Oliver Lincoln's Gallery Party."

"Oh, I'm sorry, we must have missed one another amidst the chaos of the night."

But then again, I was also preoccupied with Harvey.

My heart aches at the memory of that night. It was magical... Nothing like I expected from him. Then again, nothing about Harvey is predictable. I get lost in a daydream of how handsome he looked that night until Mr. Baird speaks again.

"I wasn't there long," he says, his elbows resting on the table, hands loosely folded in front of him. His steady, intent gaze on me.

I hold my pen above my notebook, ready to take notes. "Could you share your ideas for the event?"

After outlining his vision and requesting a few last-minute changes, I nod. "I'll prepare a draft of the design and email it to you for approval, along with the updated quote."

He gathers his things. "If that's all, I need to get going. Thanks for meeting with me."

Before leaving, I pause. "Thank you for arranging the room upgrade," I say, offering a polite smile.

He nods, a hint of warmth in his response. "Anything that a Lincoln asks, I will always try to make work."

My lip's part, and I'm about to correct him——that I'm not a Lincoln——but he quickly stands and says goodbye, already moving to answer his phone. I'm stunned by how much he wants to work with me, but also clear he holds the Lincolns in high regard. I did too, until recently.

Well, one in particular...

After scribbling a few more notes, I head back to my room and change into black leggings and a cream sweater, ready to explore the streets of D.C. The grand, tree-lined sidewalks are so beautiful that I end up walking longer than I planned. I stumble upon the Lincoln Memorial and wonder if this is a sign or just another way to torture me. It feels like I can't escape him.

I grab a smoothie from a cute cafe and continue walking, passing by restaurants that look good.

There's so much art and so many murals here. It's nice to explore a new city, just me. Eventually, I start to feel tired and head back to the hotel. I video call Molly to check in. "How's everything going?"

"Chad just finished his homework. Now they're playing while I make spaghetti. How's it there?"

I smile, thinking about the meeting. "It's perfect. The meeting went well. He wants to move forward with all our suppliers."

"He's covering all the costs?" she splutters.

"Yes." Giggling, I remember my own disbelief when he said the same thing. "I'm drafting a design and quote to send to him tonight. Once he approves, I'll email our suppliers."

"Don't work all night," Molly warns in her sweet, motherly voice.

"I just came back from a long walk. I haven't worked the whole time."

"You promise?"

I roll my eyes. "Yes. I'm planning to grab dinner and then soak in the massive tub."

"Send me pics!" she exclaims.

Another laugh escapes me. Her enthusiasm is contagious. She's seriously the bestest friend, taking care of Chad while I'm here. I'll definitely buy her a thank you gift before I leave. My eyes scan the area looking for something special to bring back.

"Okay, okay. Put Chad on."

"Mom?"

"Hi honey, how was your day?"

"Alright, but did you know Hugo has the new transformer Lego?"

His excitement makes my heart swell. The small slice of mom guilt I carry from working instead of being with him fades a bit when I hear his happy voice.

"No, I didn't. But how was school?"

"Good. Can I get the Lego too?" Chad's voice is hopeful.

I smile softly, shaking my head. "I'll add it to your birthday list. Are you having fun at Molly's?"

"She's letting us have pizza," he grins.

"Oh, that naughty Molly," I reply, chuckling.

He giggles through the phone.

"I better go, but I love you. Behave for Molly, and I'll see you tomorrow."

"Okay, Mom. I love you."

He hangs up, and I guess our conversation is over. I don't bother calling back, as Molly will call me if she needs me. Now that work isn't a distraction, I move to the windows overlooking the city. The view isn't as nice as the one from Harvey's penthouse, and the loneliness hits me harder because I don't have Chad here. I'm alone with my thoughts. I snap a picture to show Chad when I get home, and I also send it to Mom.

> **Mom:** *Oh, darling, I hope you're out there soaking it all in! The city is your oyster! I'm on this noisy bus, otherwise I'd be calling you. Take lots of pictures and make the most of it!*

> **Me:** *No worries. I'm about to head out for dinner anyway. I'll call you later.*

Reminding myself that I'm here for work, I head out to a restaurant with a plan to order a glass of champagne. Celebrating alone isn't the same, but I want to acknowledge how far I've come. It would be nice to have Harvey here, but I can do this on my own.

After dinner, I return to the suite, soak in the spa, and then crawl into the king-sized bed. I'm almost asleep when I receive another text from Harvey.

> **Harvey:** *I hope the upgrades I requested made your stay a little more relaxing.*

CHAPTER 34

JEMIMA

I ARRIVE HOME FROM D.C., having spent the flight working on new event contracts. At the airport, I began drafting an email to all the suppliers I'd need, assuming Mr. Baird gave the go-ahead. As soon as the one-hour-and-twenty-seven-minute flight lands, I check my email and see that he's already responded, and he's signed them all.

I quickly send out the emails and add one to Molly, asking her to book me a return trip and letting her know I'll be in the office as soon as I unpack.

Dragging my small case behind me, I take the steps up to my apartment. My breath catches when I see the tall, solid frame waiting at my door. I've missed his face, and now that I'm looking at him again, I can see he's been struggling too. His beard is longer than usual, his hair messier, and his eyes are sad. The way my heart twinges at the sight makes this so hard. *He needs to go.*

He pushes off the wall he's leaning on, his eyes dropping from my case to my face.

"Have you been waiting long?" I ask, my voice betraying my defeat.

"No, I went to the office, and Molly said you were flying back from the D.C. meeting."

"So, you thought you'd wait here all day until I came home?" I cross my arms, eyebrows raised.

He leans back slightly, his posture relaxed but determined, his hands in his pockets. "If that's what it took," he replies, meeting my gaze without flinching.

"I'm not ready," I say, softer than usual. I understand he's trying, but I'm not ready to let him in just yet.

When he reaches out, my body jerks back. I can't let him touch me; it's too hard. His hand curls back, and he puts it back into his pocket.

"I only did it to protect you. Scared you'd get hurt and you'd lose hope, and I couldn't have that," he says with vulnerability in his expression.

"I'm stronger than I look," I argue.

"What can I do to make you trust me again?"

"I don't know," I tell him honestly. I'm just empty and need more time. Words are just words to me. I used to feel safe and secure with him, but now...I feel hollow.

"I need to go inside and work. I have a lot going on right now," I say, trying to scoot past him.

He stays quiet, his eyes fixed on my face. "I've never lost anything. Losing you made me die inside. But not only did I lose you... I lost Chad too. And you're a package deal, and fuck, I want that. I love you. I love him. I love you both so fucking much. You're the loves of my life. Please."

My knees threaten to buckle at his words. I know what he's saying is true, and my heart aches for my mouth to express the same to him, but he hurt me by betraying my trust. I need proof of change, and that will take more time.

"I need time to think. You hurt me. It's only been a few days." With a shaky hand, I put the key in the lock.

He reaches out to touch me, but quickly retracts his hand. "Take the time that you need. Just know I'm not going anywhere. I'll never give up on us. I made a mistake not telling you, and I swear I'll prove that from now on. I'll always be honest."

I sigh. "That doesn't change the fact that you should've told me."

"You're right, I should have. That's something I will always regret. I'm so fucking sorry."

His sincerity hits me hard in the chest, and my eyes sting. Before I can stop it, a tear slips down my cheek. "Me too," I sniff as I turn and open the door.

I've never had a guy chase me and beg me like this before... This is different. But if I am to take him back, I have to wholeheartedly believe I can trust him. Our relationship only exists that way, and if I can't see myself doing that, then there's no point, even if I love him. Love alone isn't enough.

"I won't give up," he says, and I turn away before I say anything else. The moment I'm safely inside my house, I drop my purse and slide down the door, my ass hitting the floor as I cry into my hands. I stay there for a while, and when I'm blotchy and out of tears, I stand and start cleaning up the contents that fell from my purse.

I pause when I see the card Molly gave me. It was for her therapist.

As much as I want to give Harvey another chance, I need to focus on myself. I need to heal. From everything I've been battling, it's time to call.

I don't waste time or give myself a chance to overthink it. With the money coming in from the business and having paid Pedro and Jade back, I know it's time to spend on myself. As hard as that is, I realize I need this. I hit dial, and when the receptionist answers, I book my first session.

CHAPTER 35

HARVEY

I STAND THERE, STARING at the peeling cream paint, my head hanging low. Slowly, I walk back to my car, feeling like I've left my heart in that apartment. They're everything to me, and without them, nothing else matters. I can still hear her sobbing behind the door, and all I want is to go in, hold her, and tell her I'm sorry until she believes me. I've failed her.

I drive to my parents' house, shattering piece by fucking piece. Knowing she's in pain is killing me. I have to fix this. Fix us. I'm dying inside.

With a heavy heart, I pull up to the modern New York house, ring the bell, and the longtime maid opens the door. My mom will be at work, but my dad might be here or at Grams's. I hope he's here.

"Hi Saylor, is Dad here?"

"Yes, Son, he's in his study," she replies.

She calls me "Son" because she never had children of her own, and she watched me and my brothers grow up. I give her a hug as I enter.

"Do you need something to eat or drink?"

"No thanks," I respond, not even able to think about food right now. The thought of disappointing my dad has my stomach in knots.

I walk across the light wooden floors to his study, finding the wooden door closed. Knocking, I wait until I hear him call out, "Come in."

As I open the door, I suck in a deep breath. He's sitting behind his desk, his head buried in a book.

My dad's office is lined with bookshelves filled with a mix of fiction and nonfiction. His desk is cluttered with papers, and the walls are covered in art and framed newspaper clippings. The familiar scent of leather and old books hits me as I step inside.

"Harvey," he says, glancing at his watch, probably wondering why I'm not at work. "What's going on?"

"I need to talk to you about Recaredo Events," I say as I walk into the room and take the chair opposite him.

He leans back in his chair, folding his arms. "What about it?"

"I failed," I admit the words bitter on my tongue.

His brow furrows. "What do you mean, Son?"

"I couldn't help her," I say, my voice quieter now.

"Why not?"

I rub the back of my neck, gathering my thoughts. "She doesn't want me to help her anymore."

"That's not an explanation. Start from the beginning."

I slump forward, hands pressed to my forehead, head hanging between my shoulders, elbows resting on my knees. "We were working together, and everything seemed fine," I say, my voice heavy. "Then I found out one of her long-term employees, a family friend, was embezzling and doing drugs. I paid him off to protect her." I pause, letting out a slow exhale. "But he came back and told her I paid him off. I should've handled it differently."

My dad's gaze sharpens as he leans forward, his elbows on the desk. "Why didn't you go to the police?"

The weight of his question hits harder than I'd expected. My stomach twists as I drag a hand through my hair, tugging at the ends in frustration. "I thought I was doing the right thing." My voice strains. "I didn't want her reputation or business to take a hit. But it blew up in my face. I should've told her the truth." I force myself to meet his eyes, even though it's the hardest thing I've done all day. "I take full responsibility for that. I was wrong."

His expression softens, but his tone remains firm. "As a businessman, I would advise you to call it in."

I nod, feeling the heaviness of my mistake settle deeper in my chest. "I will."

Reminding me of Jeremy when he's deep in thought, he rubs his chin. I sink into the chair opposite his large wooden desk, my shoulders slumped in defeat. "I tried to win her back," I say, staring at the floor. "It's not about the firm anymore. I don't care about that. I lost her, and her son, Chad. That's what matters."

"Did you fall for her?"

"Yeah," I admit. Rubbing my hands down my face, I let out the breath I'd been holding. "But not just her. Chad too. And I lost both of them trying to help."

Dad's quiet for a second, then he moves to stand in front of me, arms crossed, head tilted to the side like he's trying to figure me out. "You didn't fail."

That's not what I expected to hear.

I snort, looking up at him through furrowed brows. "How? I've ruined everything good in my life." Bitterness seeps into my words. "Feels like all I've done is lose."

"You learned your lesson."

"What lesson?" I scoff, hands thrown out. "That I'm a screw-up?" To me, it feels like I've fucked up everything. She was the love of my life. I told her that, and it still wasn't enough.

His eyes stay on mine. "As your father, I need to remind you that family and love are more important than money."

My heart's pounding hard enough to feel it in my throat. Those words hang in the air, sinking into me. I always knew that, but maybe I didn't show it on the outside.

A small grin tugs at the corner of his mouth. "You can have your inheritance."

"No." I sit up straight. "I don't need the consulting firm."

I need her. Money won't fix this.

"You still went there, and learned about the business, and it's growing. But you found love, and I hope I get to meet her."

"What?" I blink, caught off guard.

"Go get your family, Son."

I feel a smile tug at my lips. He said family, like it's already mine.

"You don't care that she has a kid?"

"I only care that you're happy."

My dad's eyes are misty, and I know he's thinking about Grams and her battle with breast cancer. He wants us all to learn about love and family before it's too late.

"Thanks, Dad," I say as I stand.

"Don't thank me," he replies. "Just do something about it."

My dad's words echo in my mind. *Call it in.*

I pull out my phone, staring at the screen for a long moment. With a deep breath, I dial the non-emergency number.

"New York Police Department, how can I help you?"

"I need to report a case of embezzlement and narcotics possession," I say, my voice steady despite the knot tightening in my stomach.

"Can you provide more details?"

"Yes," I reply, glancing at my dad. He gives me a small nod of approval.

As I give them the information, a strange sense of relief washes over me. Maybe I can't fix everything, but I can at least make this right.

When I hang up, the weight on my shoulders feels a little lighter.

It's time to fight for what really matters.

Dad transferred my inheritance to me, but I can't use it for the firm. My gut tells me it's the wrong move. During my run this morning, I passed the park where I saw her and Chad, and the idea hits me right in the chest. A new project to help single moms or dads start their dream business or turn around a failing one.

I'm heading into the office for an emergency team meeting. For the first time in a while, I feel a sliver of warmth in my chest. She might not know I'm doing this for her, but somehow, it makes me feel connected to her. After the meeting, I'm going to her apartment to apologize again. My dad gave me new hope... not to give up on her because she's worth the fight.

The meeting lasts an hour, and we finalize the name DreamMakers, along with the company's values, mission statement and vision. My idea is coming to life. We're meeting tomorrow to look at new spaces, and I've already canceled the offer for the firm.

It no longer feels right.

Now, I'm on my way to her apartment. My leg has been bouncing rapidly since I left, and I'm running over all the words I want to say. I rush out of the car and jog up the stairs, knock, but she's not there. She might already be at work. I pass Jade and Pedro on my way down.

"Hi. Do you know where Jemima is?"

"She moved apartments," Pedro informs me as his wife eyes me suspiciously.

"Can you give me her new address?" I ask softly.

Jade cuts in before Pedro can answer. "No. If she wanted you to know, she would've told you herself."

I can't help but admire their loyalty to her. They may not be her family, but they sure act like it.

"Alright, thanks anyway. Bye," I say, rushing back to the car, heading straight to her office.

CHAPTER 36

JEMIMA

STANDING ON THE SIDEWALK outside a therapist's office is daunting. I never thought I'd end up here, but here I am, ready to open up. My life has been a mess, and all I want is to get back in control.

I take a deep breath of cool air and open the door, walking straight up to the receptionist, trying to hide my nerves. She smiles at me, and I realize I was expecting this to be scarier than it actually is. "Hi, I'm checking in. Ms. Recaredo."

"Can you fill this out and bring it back to me when you're finished?" she asks, handing me a form.

I take the form and sit down, avoiding eye contact with anyone. Staying in the corner, I fill it out before returning it to her.

Ten minutes later, a woman with short burgundy hair, and bright blue eyes, calls my name. Her sincere smile puts me at ease. Maybe this won't be so bad after all.

"Hi, I'm Laura Martinez," she says, extending her hand as I stand. Her grip is firm but gentle.

"Nice to meet you," I reply, following her into her cozy office. The space is inviting with plants, warm lighting and a vanilla candle burning.

"Go ahead and make yourself comfortable," Laura says, gesturing to the chair across from her as she takes a seat.

I sit down, smooth out my clothes, and fidget with my hands in my lap. Laura looks down and then meets my gaze with a reassuring smile. "What made you seek out therapy?" her tone is soft and gentle, as if she's genuinely interested in hearing my story.

My mind races as I try to figure out where to start. Finally, I take a deep breath and ease back into the chair and go for the truth.

"I can't trust anyone," I admit.

"Tell me why you struggle to trust others," she asks.

"Every time I let someone get close to me, they hide things from me."

"Explain that a little more."

"Well, most recently, this guy kept something from me, saying it was to protect me."

"Do you believe him?"

I picture his face as if he's right in front of me, replaying his words and body language in my mind.

"Yes," I sigh.

"Tell me about your relationship with him."

"We were dating, but not anymore. I told him I need some space."

Why is it so much easier to say this to her?

"I think it's good that you've given yourself time. Setting boundaries is important."

Then why does my chest feel this tight? When I see him, I want to fall into his arms. He's shown me he can be there for me and Chad.

"He's the first guy who feels like he's more than just words, you know?"

She nods. "I hear that, but communication is important in relationships, especially when you're facing hurdles."

"So you think this is a setback?"

"Do you?" she counters.

Did I overreact to him helping me? Probably, but there's just been so much pain. Losing my dad, job, Butch's arrest, my mom being away and the apartment.

"I think so," I admit.

She smiles. "I think having some coping mechanisms in place will help too."

"What do you recommend?"

"There's meditation, breathing techniques, journaling, working out; it's really what works best for you. Next time you feel a hurdle approaching, try one and see which works best."

As I open up to her about my family, my ex, I realize how badly I want to break my trust issues cycle not only for me, but mostly for Chad. He's watching and learning every day, and the last thing I want is for him to grow up carrying the same weight of mistrust. The thought of him facing the same struggles feels unbearable, and it pushes me to keep going. She agrees, saying that breaking these patterns can change everything, even if it takes time. We plan to meet again next week, and though there's a long journey ahead, I feel hopeful for the first time.

I'm determined to give Chad a better example, even if it means facing every old wound along the way.

I arrive at Recaredo Events and head straight to Molly's desk, pulling up a chair beside her.

She smirks. "I'm going to start calling that your therapy chair soon."

I laugh, but it falls flat. My mind is a mess. After a real therapy session, I feel like a wrung-out sponge.

"I went to therapy today."

"Did you go to the place I recommended?" she asks.

"Yeah, I did. So, this isn't my therapy chair, it's the chair I come to when I need my friend."

"I love that you need me," she says with a grin.

I laugh again. "Therapy was good, but there's a lot to work through."

She snorts. "It's an ongoing battle. It usually doesn't go away; you'll be dealing with it long-term. But at least she'll give you the tools to handle it."

"I already have homework."

I need to write a letter to my dad because I recognized some guilt I was holding for not listening to him about Butch. I do think that's some of the reason that I've been putting pressure on myself to make this business thrive.

"I would've been surprised if you didn't. That or I'm more fucked up than you," she jokes.

I chuckle. God, I needed this. I'm feeling a bit lighter now. Ready to drop the next bombshell, I say, "When I got back from D.C., Harvey was on my doorstep."

Instead of looking surprised, Molly smirks. "I figured."

"How did you know?" I ask, puzzled.

"I had my suspicions," she admits.

I shuffle in the chair. "You know I can't just take him back like that," I say, clicking my fingers. "He didn't just hide one thing; it was multiple things."

Her smirk fades, and she nods. "I know, and I'm beyond pissed he didn't tell you exactly what was going on."

"But finding him on my doorstep... it was hard to say no when he's given me so much."

"He did give you the first big job," she points out.

Oliver's party was the start of getting consistent, high paying jobs. I'm grateful for that, but I know he had his own agenda.

"But he did it for himself at first, to get his inheritance," I remind her.

Molly shakes her head. "His brother Jeremy was just here, handing in his event contract, and filled me in. Harvey fell three months short of the deal."

The realization hits me hard, and my chest tightens. I struggle to breathe.

Molly leans forward, her eyes locked on mine as she delivers her next words like a blow. "He won't get his inheritance."

"No," I whisper, disbelief washing over me.

She gives me a solemn look. "Yes. I'm sorry."

A lump of guilt forms in my throat, choking me. He was there for everything. He deserved that firm. He helped transform my business in every way, from the aesthetic look to finding new clients, hiring staff, setting up new software, and even handling the paperwork. He was there for everything. He deserves that business. I need to talk to him and see if there's a way, I can help by talking to his dad.

"Why does it look like you're about to do something?" Molly asks.

"I'll go to him," I say, rising from the chair.

Molly smiles and leans back. "Go to him."

I rush out the door and head straight to his place in my car, my adrenaline pushing me forward. When I arrive, the security guard informs me that he's not there. I quickly google his work address and head over.

As I approach the sleek glass tower, the sun in my eyes, I squint and roll back my shoulders before entering. Inside, it's elegant, with large cream tiles and a large glass desk. Everything is modern and clean. I walk straight to the reception desk and ask for his floor.

She types something, and instead of calling him, she simply tells me I'm on the list. I'm not sure what list, but she directs me to the top floor.

The elevator ride feels slow as nerves rush through me. I watch the floors light up, wishing it would hurry. The higher it climbs, the more the nausea rolls in my stomach. People enter and exit, making time slow down.

When I finally reach the top, I exit and breathe a sigh of relief. Walking up to the receptionist, I remember my manners and introduce myself, asking to see him.

She smiles apologetically. "Oh, you just missed him. Would you like to leave a message?"

With a heavy heart, I say no and leave, feeling defeated and out of ideas. I head back to my office, deciding I'll call him when I'm alone and can sit down.

As I walk along the sidewalk to my building, I turn a corner and bump into someone, stumbling back on my heels. When I tilt my head up, I find myself staring into a pair of familiar piercing blue eyes.

I gasp. "You're here?"

"I was looking for you, and when I went to your office, Molly said you had just left to find me," he says, holding a bouquet of ranunculi in his hands. My chest tightens. What is it about him that gets to me? I'm not one to get emotional, but with him, it's different, even moments like this leave me feeling everything all at once.

CHAPTER 37

HARVEY

SHE'S HERE. AND SHE was looking for me?

I grip the bunch of flowers tightly, then push them toward her. "I'm sorry. I fucked up."

"You already apologized," she replies, looking at me softly.

"I know, but I did multiple stupid things that hurt you. And I realize these flowers and my apologies won't fix it." This is more than just about a bouquet or some words. I need to make her understand that I get how much I hurt her.

"Then why did you buy them?" she asks.

"Because you liked them the last time I brought them."

The corner of her lips twitches just slightly. "Are you sure about that?"

"Come on, at least give me a little credit." I give her a half-smile. Even though it wasn't my idea originally, now I'll have to thank my brother for the suggestion.

"They don't erase anything, but they show me you care."

"Care about you? I more than care. I love you," I blurt out before I can stop myself. Her eyes are glossy and bright. I know I'm laying it all on the line. She could crush me again, but I have to try.

"I love you too," she whispers.

I freeze, stunned, struggling to believe she actually said it. In this moment, everything else fades aways, all I can see is her. I'd follow her anywhere just to have a chance to talk things through.

"Can we go somewhere and talk?" I ask, realizing we're still standing in the middle of the sidewalk.

"My place?" she asks.

I try to keep my voice steady as my heart pounds. "The new hangout."

She rolls her eyes but smiles. "Stop making me feel old and just follow me."

"I'll drive."

"I'll direct."

I hide a smile, relieved that she didn't argue about it today. She pauses, looking at me intensely. I force myself to breathe and resist the urge to kiss her. Just because she wants to talk at her place doesn't mean I'm forgiven yet. But I know she's strong, and I want to make sure she knows she can lean on me, too.

When we reach my new Lambo, she stops, and gasps. "You brought it."

"I did. Do you think Chad will like it?" I ask, picturing his reaction.

"Is that seriously a question? I'm more worried he'll ask to drive it."

I laugh, imagining his little face when he sees it. "He definitely won't be allowed to do that."

She climbs in and looks around the car. I wait, counting down in my head. Five…four…three…two…

"You didn't," she says when she spots the booster seat.

"I did."

"Why?"

"Because I was hopeful that you'd forgive me if I begged you enough and didn't give up on you."

"Doesn't mean you stick a booster seat in your sports car," she teases, raising an eyebrow with a smirk.

"Call it wishful thinking," I joke.

She rolls her eyes, but I catch a hint of a smile. "You've really laid it on thick today."

"It could be thicker if you'd let me," I tease.

Her eyes widen, and her face turns crimson. "You're terrible."

"You said it," I reply, grinning.

"I was talking about how much I'd tell you if I knew you wouldn't be repulsed."

As I drive, she directs me to her place. "I want to hear your thickest," she says, with that glint in her eyes I've missed so much.

"Well, first, you need to stop talking about it because I'm already half——"

"Got it," she cuts me off with a knowing smile.

I smirk, feeling a bit more confident now that I can see I'm getting through to her. "I'd tell you how much I miss you. How much I miss hearing your voice, seeing your face, hanging out with you, even doing the most basic tasks."

"Keep going..." she prompts, and I catch a glimpse of the woman I'm head over heels in love with.

"I also miss Chad. He's the coolest kid I know. When I got my car, all I wanted to do was drive over and show it to him. I know he'd love it, and just seeing him happy makes me happy."

I can tell she knows exactly what I'm talking about. "He misses you. He wants to play at the courts with you again. He says he needs practice."

"I bet it was hard to tell him you wouldn't call."

She looks over at me, her eyes a little sad. "It was."

I keep my eyes on the road, but I feel her words sinking in. This isn't just about me apologizing. It's about figuring out how we can move forward together.

"I want us to communicate better," I say. "I don't want to hide anything from you. I want you to feel like you can tell me anything, even when it's hard."

"I agree. I can't keep holding back either. But we need to be honest, even if it might hurt the other person."

"No more keeping secrets," I promise. "And with that being said, I need to tell you I reported Danny to the Police."

Her lips twist, and she glances at me from the corner of her eye. And for the first time in what feels like forever, I believe we're actually moving forward.

Just then, my phone rings. It's Oliver. I tried calling him earlier.

"Are you still moping around?" he asks.

A little giggle escapes Jemima's mouth.

"I'm not moping," I reply.

"You didn't come to play poker this week, and at Grams's, you sat there looking salty as fuck."

"Alright, alright," I say, rolling my eyes.

Jemima's laugh grows louder.

"Jemima, are you in the car with him?" Oliver asks.

"Hi, Oliver," she says, amused.

"Fucking hell. I'm a dead man. Listen, Jemima, please forgive him. He's been a fucking bitch to be around lately."

"Alright, Oliver, I'm going now," I cut him off before he can say any more.

"I was returning your call," he reminds me.

"Yeah, about work. Not so you could tell Jemima what a loser I've been. Way to go, dickhead."

"You'll get over it," he says with a chuckle.

"Bye." I'll call him back later about the new gallery.

"Well, that was enlightening," Jemima teases.

"You mean humiliating."

"I think it helped."

"You mean being called out is better than me telling you?" I raise an eyebrow, giving her a look.

She sighs. "I need actions, not words. So Oliver dropping that bomb tonight was perfect."

"I'll call him back," I offer, reaching for the phone again.

"No, I just mean… I get that you're sorry, but as much as I want to believe you, it's hard. I'm trying to learn to accept it."

"So, what happens next?" I ask, uncertainty eating at me.

"I saw a therapist," she reveals.

This could either be really good or really bad. I brace myself, wondering if she's about to let me down easily.

I park in an empty spot outside a new brick apartment block, ten minutes closer to my house. The area is nicer, and I feel better knowing she and Chad live in a good place.

"How was that?" I ask cautiously.

"Good," she says, though I sense some hesitation. "We talked about how my past is impacting my future. I need to change from saying I can't trust anyone to saying I'll take the time to trust."

"I'll give you anything you need. Tell me what to do, and I'll do it."

She blinks at me, and I have to use all my willpower not to reach out and touch her cheek, to cradle her head like she's the most precious thing in the world.

Turning away, she climbs out of the car. I follow, and we enter the building, which thankfully has security. *Thank fuck.* I love knowing they're safe here.

Her hands shake as she opens her door. As soon as we enter, I take in her apartment, cozy and cute, just like her. The curtains still allow golden light to peek through, stopping the place from looking like an average boxy apartment with a hint of caramel in the air.

"The view," she says, pointing to the window. "It's nothing like yours, but I'll admit, I got this place because of that. It was my favourite thing about your place."

"Is that all?" I ask, still haunted by our time together at my place. I dream of it every fucking night, wishing it was real. Of course, when I wake up, I realize it was just a dream... again.

"Of course not. It was just one of the highlights," she says, understanding exactly what I mean.

I take a deep breath and try to steady myself. "I want to make this work. Whatever you need, just tell me. I'm here."

She meets my gaze, and I see the hesitation in her eyes. "It's not that simple, though. I've spent so long building walls to protect myself, that I'm only now just started tearing them down."

I nod slowly, taking in her words as I step closer to her. "I get that. I've made my own mistakes. I'm not asking you to let them go right away. But I need you to know, I'm not going anywhere. I'm here, and I'll wait as long as it takes."

Her lips twitch into a small smile.

"I'm so proud of everything you've been doing. It actually motivated me to do something big. I'm going to start a new company called DreamMakers, which is inspired by you." I reach out to hold her hand. "I want to help single moms or dads start their dream business or turn around a failing one."

She frowns, tilting her head. "But I thought you fell short on your inheritance?"

"I told my dad everything and he said that my choices didn't make me a failure. He actually considered it exactly the opposite. He was willing to still give me the money."

She looks at me, her eyes softening, as she threads her fingers through mine, and for the first time in a long while, I see the possibility of something real between us. But I also know it's going to take time. Time that I'm willing to give, no matter how long it takes.

"So, where do we go from here?" I ask, my voice full of hope.

"I don't know," she admits, her voice barely above a whisper. "But I'm willing to figure it out, together."

Chapter 38

Harvey

A week later, Chad's basketball camp is in full swing. Parents aren't allowed to stay and watch because it supposedly distracts the kids, so we'll pick him up later this afternoon. We walk out hand in hand.

"What do we do now?" I ask.

"As part of my therapy journey, I have to try different ways to cope with feelings and thoughts. One of them is exercise, so maybe we could run together?" she suggests.

"Let's go home and get changed," I say. "If you enjoy it, we might need to buy you proper running shoes."

She tilts her head, her brow furrowing. "I need special shoes to run?"

"It's better for your knees."

"I know I'm old, but my knees are just fine," she retorts.

"You're not old. You're perfect."

She rolls her eyes. "Then why are you telling me to get running shoes?"

"To protect your knees from injury."

Her eyebrows draw together. "Let's see if I like it before anyone buys new shoes."

I lean in, brushing a loose strand of hair behind her ear. "Who knew you weren't into shopping?"

Her lips twitch, but she keeps her expression serious. "If I need something, I'll buy it. But other than that, I'm not interested in wasting my spare time shopping."

I step into her space, my hand finding the small of her back, and I pull her closer. "You don't have spare time now that you and Chad are mine."

Her breath catches slightly as she arches her eyebrow. "Is that so?"

I nod, lowering my voice. "Yes, so get used to it."

She rolls her lips to bite back a grin, and my heart feels so fucking full. She's so beautiful when she smiles. I'll do whatever it takes to never see that gutted look on her face again.

We enter her apartment, and she heads to her closet. "What should I wear?"

I follow her, and as she stands there in just her white shirt and cotton briefs, I've never been more captivated. My gaze traces the length of her legs until they meet her amused expression.

"You alright there?" she asks.

"I'm just admiring how fucking lucky I am."

A blush rises on her chest. "I know the doctor mentioned running..."

I walk toward her, locking eyes with hers. "Hmm," she mumbles.

"We could do something else."

"I think she meant actual hobbies," she says, her voice cracking slightly.

"Why can't sex be a hobby?"

"It's not," she argues, but there's no conviction.

"Says who?" I ask, stepping closer until we're toe to toe. I reach out, skimming my finger along the bottom edge of her top, my fingernail lightly scratching her skin. She visibly shivers.

"Harvey," she whispers.

My lips twist as I lift her shirt. Her hands dangle at her sides, not stopping me. "Well, I think we could do both. Your first run can't be long anyway."

Her breath quickens as I pull the white shirt over her head, leaving her in just her cotton bra and briefs.

"I can't be late——"

"You mean *we*," I correct, leaning in to kiss her chest where her heart is. She already owns my own heart, and I hope I own hers too.

I'm desperate for her to give me all of herself, but I know she needs time. I need to be patient.

"Harvey..." she breathes.

"Yes, buttercup?" I kiss her neck and along her jaw, and she tilts her head back, surrendering to the moment.

"Don't stop."

"There she is."

"Shut up and kiss me."

Pressing my lips to hers, I pour everything I am into this kiss. Her fingers dig into my back with a ferocity I've never felt before, as if she's just as desperate for this as I am.

My fingers find her bra and unclasp it. I pull away from the kiss to push the bra from off her shoulders, exposing her breasts. Bending down, I take one of her pebbled buds into my mouth and suck it hard. She whimpers loudly as her fingers thread through my hair.

I bite her nipple softly, then kiss my way to the other nipple, giving it the same attention, before my fingers move to her panties. Pushing them down her legs slowly, I reveal her glistening arousal.

"You need me, baby?" I ask hoarsely, giving away my own desire.

"Yes-s," she stammers.

"Tell me what you want."

Secretly, I love her sassy mouth telling me what she wants me to do, before I take over control again.

"I want you to make me come."

I smirk, lying down on the bed, curling my finger. "Come here and sit on my face."

She narrows her eyes, trying to read me before following my command. When she kneels on the bed, then hesitates, I grab her legs, dragging her up until her pussy is directly above my mouth.

I hold on to her hips and push her down over my face. A deep growl leaves my chest as I devour her. The sweet taste of her pussy makes me thirstier. I eat her out, and at first, she tries to lift her hips, but I hold her tightly against my face. The moment my tongue enters her, she settles in and succumbs to the feeling. Her hand reaches behind to stabilize her as she enjoys my tongue fucking her relentlessly. Hips moving, she grinds down on my mouth, begging for more. And fuck, it makes me crazy. I'm fucking her with my mouth, and before I know it, her body tightens, then relaxes as she orgasms.

I don't stop tasting her until she's spent.

She slips onto the bed, lying on her back, her body flushed, and I throb at the sight. But I want more, so I shift until I'm sitting between her thighs, my hands skimming her hot perspired skin on her stomach until I reach her pussy.

"So perfect and all mine," I say, thrusting two fingers inside her. Her back arches with a loud moan as I move my fingers hard and fast, her hips bucking, trying to ride my hand.

My other hand moves to her right hip, squeezing it tightly, leaving red marks on her pale skin, making me feral. I fingerfuck her so hard, she clenches my fingers.

"Harvey, please. God."

"I'm not God. Do these fingers feel like God to you?"

She quivers as she shakes her head, her hair flowing messily over her face.

"No, they're my fingers inside you, making you feel good."

Moving my hand from her hip to her clit, rubbing it in hard circles has her coming again.

"That's it, baby, come all over my hand. Show me how good I make you feel."

I don't stop until her body goes limp, then I pull my fingers out and hover over her. She flutters her eyes open, gazing at me with those bright honey-colored eyes, and I almost come right there and then.

I lower my hips to line my cock up with her entrance. "Watch me fit perfectly inside you."

We both watch my dick as I sink myself deep inside her pussy. Fuck, she feels like heaven. I've missed her and our intimacy.

I begin to move, rocking my hips and looking into her eyes. Her lips part as she pants, her lips pink and swollen, eager for another taste, so I capture her lips in another hot kiss.

When I feel my own climax, I touch her clit with every thrust. Her toes curl and her legs try to close as she chases her orgasm, so I don't hold back now. I fuck her with everything I have. It's hard, hot and passionate. My orgasm slams into me like a truck and my body stills as I empty inside her.

Fuck!

"I forgot a condom," I rasp in a panic.

She's going to fucking kill me.

"I'm sure I can't get pregnant, don't worry," she says shakily, coming down from another intense orgasm.

I frown. "What do you mean?"

"I haven't gone through menopause yet, but I know it's not far off. At forty-two, getting pregnant isn't simple for me... it wasn't easy with Chad either. It took time, and I know how much of a journey it can be."

I shiver as I pull out of her, then head to the bathroom to quickly clean up, and as I do my mind drifts, and it dawns on me that I want a family with her. Bringing back a washcloth for her, I crawl on the bed and clean her before coming back to lie beside her, wanting to keep talking.

"Do you want to get pregnant? I mean, would you want to?" I ask, watching her closely.

"I always wanted a big family. I wish Chad had a sibling. I never had one, and I didn't want him to miss out, but I guess..." she trails off, biting her lip.

"I'll happily give you a baby." I say it with certainty, leaning forward slightly.

Her eyes widen, and I see her freeze for a moment, her eyebrows knitting together as her mind races. "What?"

"I'll get you pregnant." I don't look away as she shifts uncomfortably.

"But you don't want that right now."

"If you want more kids, we'll have them." I cradle her cheek, bringing her gaze to mine, making sure she knows I'm serious.

"You're serious?" Her eyes roam my face, uncertainty etched into her expression.

"Yes. I'd give you anything." My heart is pounding hard and fast as I try to get her to understand.

Her head tilts, disbelief still lingering in her eyes. "You didn't want kids."

"Not before I met you. The only kid I knew before Chad was a friend's. He was forced to give up a lot because of an unplanned pregnancy. I thought he'd ruined his life."

"You think kids ruin lives?" She tries pushing me off.

I cup her face gently. "No, buttercup. The only thing that will fucking ruin me is not having you and Chad in my life."

Her eyes mist over as she blinks. "So, a baby?" she breathes.

"If that's what you want, we can keep trying." My hand slides from her hip to her stomach, resting over her scar where she already carried one amazing child. At the thought of a piece of her and me growing inside her, my heart swells.

She giggles as I touch her stomach. "I'm not on the pill. I didn't plan on being in a relationship. But I don't know if——"

"It will happen," I cut her off, knowing where she was headed.

"What makes you so confident?"

"I have good sperm," I say with a wink.

She laughs, the sound light and playful. "Is that what you think?"

"It's what I know."

She rolls her eyes at me. "Do you want to make a bet?"

I rub my jaw, a smirk forming, knowing that if we're trying for a baby, I want something else too. "If I win, you marry me."

She blinks at me. I know it's a tough ask because she never wanted to get married again. But I want it all with her.

"I always thought it was just a stupid piece of paper."

"It's important to me," I admit.

She rolls over to look at me. "Really? Why?"

I pull her on top of me, wanting to hold her closer. "I want you and Chad to have my name... Lincoln."

"You don't know the meaning of slow, do you?"

"Not when he comes to you," I say before kissing her, reveling in how she melts into me.

I can't help the surge of emotion that crashes into me as I watch her eyes fill with tears, and she doesn't stop the waves from rolling down her cheeks.

Chapter 39

Jemima

A few hours later

"We need to live together," Harvey announces as we jog along the sidewalk after our warm-up in the bedroom. He suggested we jog along the park so the view would distract me.

It's only my first run, so I'll take any guidance.

Since I've gotten stronger, physically and emotionally, I feel the shift in my life. I've paid off the debt that weighed me down, and for the first time in a while, I feel like I'm truly happy. Looking after myself feels less like a luxury and more like part of who I am now. I finally made the time for a hair appointment, the fresh color giving me a new boost in confidence, which has been slowly growing, from the inside out, and with every day that passes, I feel it growing stronger.

"We will have to do it slowly," I puff out, trying to keep up. How is it that he sounds so normal while speaking, yet I can barely talk as we jog?

"We could start leaving things at each other's places and have sleepovers," he suggests.

I'm concentrating on putting one foot in front of the other, trying not to trip.

Chad has only recently started seeing us hold hands and kiss more often.

The sun beating down on my back isn't helping my sweat situation, and his words are making it hard to breathe.

"I don't know, we need a plan." I gasp for air, finally giving up. I wave my hands in front of me and stop jogging. Walking with my hands on my hips, I suck in deep lungfuls of air.

"Why does it have to be so thought out?"

The tightness in my chest slowly eases. "I don't want to make a mistake."

"Chad hasn't said anything?"

I shake my head, "No, but——"

"Has he acted out?"

"No, but——"

Harvey smirks. "No issues, then. Let's not overthink it and just let things happen naturally."

He stops walking and grabs me, kissing me in a way that makes it impossible to think about anything but how much I love kissing him.

"Unfair!" I moan.

"I know, I'm so cruel," he teases before kissing me again.

When we pull apart, we walk the rest of the path. "Did you want to run home?" he asks.

"No, I'm done running."

"Like, forever or just for now?" He smirks.

"I'm still debating."

"What if I create a plan for running?" he suggests, glancing over at me.

"Like a program?" I raise an eyebrow.

"Yeah." He nods. "You need structure and a goal. I think it might help."

"Hmm," I say, considering. "Maybe we could aim for that city marathon?"

He searches my face. "Do you think that's a good idea? You usually need nine to twelve months for your first marathon."

I shrug. "I need an end date."

He laughs, shaking his head. "So, running isn't going to be your new hobby?"

"No," I reply flatly, "I hate this."

He grins. "What other hobbies could you try?"

"I don't know," I sigh. "I'll have to talk to my therapist."

"I've offered some suggestions——"

"Not helping," I interrupt with a smirk. "I want to find something less painful."

He chuckles, and we walk hand in hand back home. I can't wait to shower.

"What about gym classes?" he asks as we near the door.

"I don't think I can keep up," I admit with a laugh. "What about Pilates?"

"Maybe, but yoga might be better," I say, trying to spit some ideas. I do want to continue to work on not just coping skills but strengthening my body.

"My brother's fiancée, Chelsea, owns a studio. I could ask if she does yoga."

I haven't met all of his family yet, but we decided to invite the whole family to Chad's upcoming birthday. He's excited about all the invites I sent out. I didn't want the stress of hosting and meeting Harvey's family at the same time, so I organized it at Chad's favorite play center.

"Yeah, that sounds good. Maybe she can give me some dirt on you."

"You know all my secrets. Except that you're uncommitted to wanting to marry me as soon as possible."

My mouth opens and closes, but I'm speechless.

"Yeah, with you, buttercup, I couldn't slow down. There's something about our connection that makes me feel weak."

"It's the older woman thing," I joke.

"Maturity and deep conversations are my love languages."

We get inside my apartment, and he pulls me toward the bathroom. I raise an eyebrow. "What do you want?"

From the heated look in his eyes, I know he wants to join me in the shower, but there's something sexy about hearing him say it. It makes me even more aroused, knowing how much he wants me.

I want him desperately, but I hold back. He knows how to get me to cave, but I like that he lets me resist just enough to create the sexual friction I need to really turn me on.

"I want to strip you naked," he says, lifting my sticky blue top and tossing it across the room.

"Hmm, and then?" I ask, my voice shaky as I feel the ache in my lower core.

"Then I want to fuck you against the shower wall. I want the warm water spraying on us, and I want you to scream my name."

I tug his shirt off, and let it drop on the floor. As he turns on the tap, I wiggle out of my running shorts, grateful I didn't choose leggings today.

He pushes his shorts down, and we both stand there naked.

"Fucking incredible, baby," he says, his eyes raking over me.

My knees shake, never getting tired of the way he obviously desires me.

"Shut up and fuck me," I demand.

He gives me a wolfish grin. "You got it, baby."

Picking me up, he shoves me against the shower wall, and I couldn't love him more than I do right now.

CHAPTER 40

JEMIMA

<u>**A WEEK LATER**</u>

"Where are you heading?" I ask my mom on the phone as I walk into the office.

"San Francisco," she gushes. "I'm off to dazzle the city, darling, you know how it is!"

"I miss you. When will you come visit?"

"Oh, honey, you know I never make plans. But just call me when you need me, and I'll be there with bells on."

"Well, Chad's birthday is next month, so I need to plan it. I know he'd love it if you could come."

"Oh, my stars, of course, I'll be there! I would never miss my grandson's birthday bash."

"I have something else to tell you," I say, my voice quieter than usual.

Why is it so hard to tell my mom I'm dating someone? It's not like she'll disapprove, but it feels like it's all happening so fast. Is there a rule against moving on when my ex was a douchebag? It's not like I haven't mentioned him before I told her on the phone that I was seeing someone she just doesn't know it's the same person.

It's not like I was actively dating… No apps, no bars… nothing. Harvey wasn't planned. If anything, he's the opposite of who I thought I'd end up with, which I think is a good thing.

"What is it?" Mom urges when I've been silent for too long.

"Things are getting serious with someone."

Mom shrieks. "What? Is this with the person you were seeing?"

I giggle at her reaction, but a sense of dread washes over me. What if she doesn't approve? Last time, she and Dad ended up being right.

"His name is Harvey."

"Mm strong name, I like it."

I giggle again. Trust my mom to comment on his name. My mind drifts to just how strong he is, lifting me up or pulling me on top of him to eat me out. Yeah, he's strong in many ways.

"He's been great," I mumble.

"How does Chad feel about him?"

My heart races as I think of them playing basketball, watching movies, or video games together. I've been slowly leaving some of Chad's and my clothes at Harvey's place.

"I think Chad loves him more than he loves me."

"Never. He'll always be a momma's boy, but it's fabulous he approves."

"I couldn't be with him if Chad didn't like him."

"Tell me more, darling! I'm dying to know!" she exclaims, her voice high with excitement.

I'm not going to explain to my mom how hot he is with his sharp jawline, bright eyes, amazing body, or how good he is in bed. That's way too much information. But I do want to tell her something important. "He's younger than me..."

"Really?" she exclaims. "By a few years?"

"Eight."

"Ohh, good for you! As long as he's ready to settle down and he treats you like the queen you are, who cares?"

I want to say *he's the first man to treat me the way I deserve* but I don't. I want to keep things light.

"He owns a successful acquisitions company."

"That sounds familiar. A secret agent?"

I laugh, remembering the time he called, and I had to google it to find out.

"He buys part or all of companies."

"He owns a company, and he's thirty-four?" she says, her voice filled with surprise and intrigue.

"Yeah, he's really mature."

"Is his family lovely?"

"I haven't met his parents yet, only his brothers, and they're really kind." I sit down in my office chair.

"Well, then I'm sure they'll be fabulous, darling."

"They're retired too."

"Oh my gosh, something we have in common," Mom yells excitedly.

I see Molly hanging around my office door with papers.

"Mom, I better get back to work. I'll send you the details for the party."

"Call me this weekend, sweetheart. I want to chat with Chad and hear all about his birthday plans!"

"Alright, will do."

I hang up and smile at Molly. "Just told Mom I'm dating Harvey."

Molly's face lights up as she steps farther into the room. "And how did it go?"

"Good, but I want to see her in person. She and Dad had a lot of opinions about my ex, and I need to know she likes Harvey before I can feel totally at ease."

"I'm sure she'll love him. He's charming, you have to give him that."

"Oh, I know. That's the problem. My mom will think he's handsome, but I'm her daughter, and she'll want to make sure he treats me and Chad right."

"So, she's coming to the party?" she asks, her eyes widening as she lowers papers to my desk.

"Yeah. She'll meet him then."

"You know Hugo and I are coming too."

"No plus one?" I ask, even though I already know the answer.

"No. I'm still having fun while I wait for Mr. Right." She wiggles her eyebrows.

"Make sure you let me look after Hugo when you need a date night."

She smiles. "Will do."

Her office phone rings. "I better grab that. Here are the minutes for your meeting at two." I take the papers from her as she walks out to grab the phone before it goes to voicemail.

Since hiring two new full-time staff members and an HR employee, I've been holding regular meetings, thanks to the new filing systems and software Harvey set up. It's made a huge difference in streamlining the day-to-day operations, allowing me to take a step back and concentrate on the bigger picture. I'm able to focus on what I need to do while allowing them to manage. I want a team I can trust. I occasionally like to help with event planning to keep my knowledge up to date. I dive straight into reading the papers of Mr. Hernandez's Christmas party.

When I'm finished, I walk over to Harvey's part-time office. When he first came here, I thought it would be temporary, but now, he's really made the space his own. Despite me encouraging his original idea to open the consulting firm, he shut it down, insisting on focusing on family, DreamMakers, Lincoln Acquisitions, and Recaredo Events.

"Hey, you look deep in thought," I say.

"I need you to look at something." He curls his finger in a come here motion, and then he pats his leg.

My eyebrow arches as I try to read him. "This isn't a prank, is it?"

"No, but I'm up for it if you are." He smirks.

"No, I have a ton of work to do today. I have to head to D.C., but I need to sort out a sitter for Chad."

I glance at my phone, waiting for a response from Jade and Pedro. If they can't do it, I'm screwed. Molly has a wedding to attend, so she can't do it, and I have to get to D.C. to meet with suppliers and the team.

"I can do it," Harvey says as easily as breathing.

I can't help the butterflies at seeing his excited face, but I'm unsure. "I don't know…"

"You need to let me show you that you can trust me."

I hesitate, deciding what to do. Harvey's been nothing but supportive, and Chad adores him. I take a deep breath, knowing this is a step toward trusting him completely.

"Alright," I finally say, meeting his blue eyes. "You can watch Chad while I'm in D.C."

His face breaks into a smug grin. "You won't regret it, I promise."

"I hope not," I reply with a small smile, trying to hide the nausea rolling inside me. But deep down, I know this is right. This is the next step in our relationship, trusting Harvey with the most important person in my life.

He leans in, pressing a soft kiss to my forehead. "Thank you for trusting me."

I nod as warmth spread through my chest. "Just don't spoil him too much."

He laughs. "No promises."

CHAPTER 41

JEMIMA

A MONTH LATER

"We need to make sure the table is set before everyone arrives," Harvey says, fussing with the tableware. I swallow a laugh; I've never seen him so wired.

"Where do you want the cake, Chad?" he asks, and Chad helps him. The two of them together turn me into a puddle. Harvey lowers the cake to the podium in the corner, then grabs Chad's shoulders and squats down to his level. "Are you okay? Is there anything else you want for your party?"

His words and actions are killing me. I'm frozen in place, just wanting to watch this exchange forever. When Harvey babysat Chad while I was away, they grew closer. Chad couldn't stop talking about all the awesome things Harvey can do, and then Harvey would tell me how amazing Chad was.

"No, but when are people coming?" Chad asks.

Harvey grins and checks his watch. "Any minute."

"Cool." Chad wanders over to me, and Harvey straightens up, adjusting his shirt with a soft smile. "Mom, everyone will be here soon," Chad says.

"I know." I smile. "I'm so excited."

"It's my first party," he says, before greeting a school friend. Harvey slips beside me, his pinky grazing the back of my hand.

"You, okay?" he asks.

"I will be," I reply.

"Stop stressing."

"I could say the same thing about you." We laugh together, both of us wanting Chad to have the best day. But we know it's a big day for us too. Harvey met my mom, and I'm about to meet his whole family.

My mom is already here helping set up. Jade and Pedro and Butch's parents declined to come to the party, instead choosing to meet on another date.

I think I have it worse, though, because there's so many people I have to meet, while he only has to meet one. He tells me they'll love me, but I'm older than him and have a kid. It's a lot to take in.

As I welcome the parents of Chad's school friends, I say hello to an older familiar guy with dark hair and an unreadable face. He's holding the hand of a pretty, tall brunette.

"Hi," I greet them.

"This is my older brother Evan and his fiancée Chelsea," Harvey cuts in. I'm relieved by his presence because I didn't see them enter with a child, so I knew they weren't school friends.

"I've heard about you. You own a studio?" I ramble, instantly regretting it. Why am I so weird right now? My composed self is completely gone, replaced by a nervous wreck.

She reveals a dazzling smile. "I do. I'm Chelsea, it's lovely to meet you...."

"Jemima. Sorry, bad host," I say, holding out my hand.

Chelsea slips her hand into mine and shakes it gently. "Not at all. And Harvey mentioned my yoga classes to you?"

"Yeah, I hate running, so I didn't want high impact. He suggested trying out your studio."

"Definitely come down. I'll give you free trials, in case it's not for you," she beams, her face lighting up.

"Thank you," I say, smiling back.

"Oh, hello, hello," another familiar deep voice calls out. He has dark hair and a light beard. It's another brother.

"Hi, come in," I greet.

Evan and Chelsea make room for them, and Chelsea says hi to the other woman.

"This is my brother Jeremy and his fiancée Nova," Harvey introduces.

"Hi, nice to see you again," I say, feeling overwhelmed with everyone, and there is still more to come.

"Make yourself comfortable," Harvey encourages them, and they move away, leaving us alone.

"Do you need water?" Harvey whispers.

"Please."

When he returns with a bottle, I quickly drink half of it at once.

"You only have Oliver and my parents left."

"That's me," Oliver's deep voice says as he approaches, shaking Harvey's hand.

"Nice to see you again, Jem," he says before joining the group, which allows me to greet the final three who have walked up behind Oliver. I'm grateful I just had water because I'm shaking as I look at them.

"Hi, Mr. and Mrs. Lincoln," I say.

"Call us Eliza and Sebastian. You don't need to be formal with us." Eliza smiles.

"I told her not to worry," Harvey adds, his hand touching the top of my jeans. The small gesture makes my body relax a little.

"It's nerve-wracking meeting family, isn't it, dear?" the older woman says beside Sebastian.

"Yes," I say with a light laugh.

"Don't worry about us, we don't bite. We're just thrilled to be here. Where's your little one?" the older woman speaks again.

"Yes, we've been asking Harvey all about him," Eliza says.

I wave Chad over, and he stands beside me, looking up at the three people in front of him. He hides behind my leg slightly, like he did when he first met Harvey. He's waiting for me to introduce him, but Harvey beats me to it.

"Chad, these people here are my mom, dad, and my grams."

"Hi," Chad says in a soft voice, but he steps out from behind my leg and looks over at Harvey. He must see something that brightens his face, and then he runs off to go play with his friends.

"He's lovely," Sebastion says.

"Thank you. Could I introduce you to my mom? She's been asking about you all."

"Yes, please," Grams says, holding her walker.

"Do you want to sit down first?" I ask.

"No, don't be silly. We'll be fine. Bring her here where it's quiet. I can't hear much in big crowds," Grams says.

I nod and go grab Mom, bringing her over. She says hello before they take a seat and start talking about her travels. I can't help but glance over, wishing Dad was here to meet them.

"Are you okay?" Harvey asks.

"Yeah, I just wish my dad was here to meet everyone."

"He would've loved me, right?" Harvey jokes.

I roll my eyes, and the lightness in my heart returns. He's magnetic in how he does that in such a short time.

"Yes, he would have," I say, wrapping my arms around his neck.

His breath tickles my ear as he leans in close, making goosebumps rise on my body. "I would've loved him too."

My eyes prick with tears, and I go to speak, but a throat clears behind him. It's my mom.

As we pull apart, he says, "I'm going to check on Chad and make sure he doesn't need a drink."

Harvey slips away, and I tear my gaze from his navy sweater to my mom's gleaming eyes. She knows. I walk over to her.

"What do you think?" I ask her, nibbling my lip as I gaze over at Harvey talking with Chad.

"He's handsome," she says, a little too loudly for my liking, but I am too eager to hear what else she thinks.

"What about him being good enough for me and Chad?"

Her warm smile makes my heart beat out of my chest. "He's absolutely wonderful! Watching him fuss over Chad today makes me forget he's not actually his father. Honestly darling, it's like he's already part of the family."

"Do you think Dad would've approved?"

"No question. The brains, the family, the heart. God, what's not to love?"

"How was his family?" I ask, still needing to talk to them more, but the bundle of nerves in my stomach holds me back.

"Wonderful. I can see why he's such a gem. They've raised him right, with all the love and care a person could ask for."

"Thanks, Mom," I say, hugging her.

"What will you do about your living situation?"

"He wants to live together. But I want to make sure Chad is okay with every step."

She nods knowingly. "He will be. If he didn't like Harvey, you'd know by now."

I hope so.

"I just want him to know he can always come to me and that he'll always be my baby."

She gives me a warm smile, her eyes soft with affection. "He knows, sweetheart. And how lucky is he to have two people who love and care about him so much"

"True. I'll go mingle before the food is served."

I swallow the lump in my throat and start with his family.

"His brothers are hot," Molly whisper-shouts, leaning closer to me at Chad's party.

"I know, and they're nice," I say as I glance toward Harvey's brothers, who are chatting across the room.

"And of course, they're all taken," she says with a dramatic sigh, rolling her eyes.

"Oliver is single."

She raises an eyebrow at me. "No, I don't think so. They were all whispering about a girl."

I wince, my smile faltering. "Sorry."

"Not your fault. The good ones are always taken," she says shrugging.

"Did you go out with that one guy from the app again?"

"Yeah," she says with a wrinkle of her nose. "He was alright, but not husband or father figure material."

I nod, understanding what she means. Not all men can be good stepparents; it takes a special kind of person.

Her words make me think about how easily Harvey has stepped into this role. And then I think of Butch. We finalized our divorce. I'm surprised he didn't contest it, but I'm relieved to put that chapter behind me. I haven't heard from him since, and honestly, I'm fine with that. He's in for a very long time. Danny's in there too, arrested and charged for criminal possession of a controlled substance and grand larceny in the 3rd degree. It still feels unreal, but at least I'm free to move on.

"Yeah, don't rush it. Have some fun."

She turns to face me. "Did you talk to the therapist about the baby plan?"

I look around, making sure no one overhears.

"I did. She said as long as I feel ready and we keep communicating our needs, there's no reason not to move forward. She also mentioned that trust is something that has to be worked on daily."

She nods slowly, her expression softening. "Do you feel ready?"

I sigh and run a hand through my hair. "About having another baby? No. I have a business, so I'm secure financially, and I know Chad and I will be fine. I just don't want him to break my heart."

Her lips curve into a small smile as she tilts her head. "You love him."

"I do," I admit, my voice dropping to a whisper, "and it scares me."

"That's normal," she says gently, resting a hand on my arm. "Keep going to therapy. You'll get through it. It just takes time."

I chuckle softly and shake my head. "You know, that's exactly what she says."

Her grin widens. "I know because she tells me the same thing."

I laugh, the tension in my chest easing a little. "It's always easier to give advice than to believe it yourself, huh?"

"Exactly," she says with a knowing smile, squeezing my arm lightly.

It's time for the cake, and Harvey steps off to the side to give Chad the spotlight. But to everyone's surprise, Chad pulls Harvey and me closer. We exchange glances over his head before smiling for a family picture.

Everything feels right. It's one of those rare moments when I realize that I'm not alone in this world, there's a family behind me. As the flash of the camera goes off, I feel a weight lift off my shoulders.

Maybe the next step in my life, whatever it is, doesn't need to be perfect. Maybe it just needs to be real. And with this moment, I feel ready to move forward with Chad and Harvey by my side.

EPILOGUE

HARVEY

A few months later

"Morning, buttercup," I whisper as I kiss her. Waking up beside her is the best part of my day. I hear little footsteps approaching, and a smile spreads across my face. Lifting the covers, I wait for Chad's sleepy head to crawl in before the alarm blares.

We're still finding our new morning routine at her place.

A few minutes later, I climb out of bed, but Chad bounces out and runs straight for the kitchen.

I leave Jemima to rest a little longer while I get up to make Chad some breakfast. Brewing a coffee for Jemima, I bring it to her in bed, along with some toast. She's already lost in a book when I walk in.

"I'm so spoiled," she says, setting the book down beside her.

I kiss her lips and head back to the kitchen to make Chad's school lunch. We need to drop him off before heading to work.

Chad is ready for school, but when I enter our bedroom, Jemima isn't there. I hear a strange sound coming from the bathroom, so I walk and find her bent over the toilet. My heart races, and I quickly move to her side, placing a hand on her back.

"Are you okay?"

She dry heaves, and I wince.

"I just all of the sudden was nauseous and, oh my god, I'm late."

"Don't worry about work. I can take Chad, and you can rest today."

She turns to me, a hint of a smile on her lips. "No, silly. My period is late."

My jaw drops, and my eyes widen as the realization hits me.

"Are you sure?"

"Well, I'll need a test."

"I'll go buy one," I say, ready to head to the store after dropping Chad off.

"No, wait." She holds out her hand. "I've got a box under the sink."

I open the cabinet doors and search until I find the box. My stomach twists with nerves, as I hand it to her. She tears it open and tries to stand, but I quickly reach out to support her.

"Do you want help?"

"Can you go check on Chad? Give me a minute to pee on the stick alone." She laughs.

"Right." I step out, making sure everything is ready for school, then return to Jemima.

Running my hands through my hair, I pace the room. "Is it ready?"

"Almost."

I enter the bathroom and see her standing there, looking a bit paler than usual. The timer beeps, and we exchange a look that makes my stomach drop.

What do we do now?

As if reading my mind, she takes my hand. "Come on, let's do this together."

I step forward and see the lines. "What does that mean?"

She suddenly bursts into tears, and my heart pounds harder.

"What's wrong? We can try again, buttercup. Please don't cry, it kills me."

She sniffles. "No, I'm happy. We're pregnant."

"We are?"

Looking at the stick again, then back at me, she nods.

"You're having my baby?" I whisper.

"Yes."

"Can we tell Chad?" I ask as tears blur my vision.

"Maybe we should do it on the weekend," she suggests. "Make it special for him."

"Good idea." I lean in, kissing her softly, feeling so much love and excitement for what's to come.

EPILOGUE 2

JEMIMA

THAT WEEKEND, WE'RE GATHERED around the coffee table, playing Chutes and Ladders.

Harvey is fidgeting in my chair, shooting me subtle looks every few minutes like, *Are we gonna tell him yet?* I smile back, silently telling him to wait.

Chad spins and lands on a ladder, climbing up the board with a big grin.

"Nice move," Harvey says, ruffling Chad's hair.

Chad beams, and it feels like the perfect moment. I glance at Harvey, giving him a subtle nod.

"Hey, honey," I say, keeping my voice light but warm. "We have some exciting news."

Chad's eyes widen. "What? Are we getting a dog?"

I laugh. "Not quite. You're going to be a big brother."

For a second, Chad freezes, processing. Then, he jumps up, pumping his fist in the air. "Yes! This is so cool!" Beaming, he glances between Harvey and me.

"I'm glad you think so," Harvey says with a grin. "We're pretty excited too."

Chad flops back onto the floor, clearly thrilled. "When's the baby coming? Is it a boy or a girl?"

His questions about the baby catch me off guard. I'm surprised, especially since he still hasn't asked anything about Butch.

"It's too early to know." I chuckle. "But we'll let you know when we find out."

After the game, I lean back on the couch, a wave of contentment washing over me. "We'd better get you to bed," I say to Chad, nudging him gently.

"You stay here," Harvey offers, already standing. "I'll take him. I'll be back soon."

"What do you feel like eating when I get back?"

Resting a hand on his chest, I laugh softly. "I don't have cravings yet."

Harvey leans down and presses a kiss to my forehead, his eyes filled with love. "You've changed my life," he murmurs. "And I'll always be grateful for you."

I watch him walk away with Chad; my heart full as I take it all in. Moments like this remind me of how lucky we are.

The End.

BONUS

Jemima's packing our suitcases for a trip to Hawaii. I insisted on a babymoon, wanting Jemima to relax before we welcome our daughter. She's twenty-one weeks now and finally feeling well.

"Now this is a track," I say as she blasts Nirvana's "Smells Like Teen Spirit." Walking into our bedroom, I have her Starbucks hot chocolate in hand.

"Thank you," she says, stepping forward to take the cup from me. She immediately takes a sip and closes her eyes.

I step closer, wrapping my arms around her waist, one hand resting gently over her growing belly. "How's the packing going?"

She sighs and glances at the floor covered in suitcases and piles of clothes. "Coming along slowly."

"Let me help," I offer, brushing a strand of hair from her face.

"If you can pack your suitcase and help me with Chad's, I think I'll be done."

We work together as Chad sits on the floor and packs his toys into his backpack. Soon enough, we're in the car, on our way to the airport. I brought us first class tickets for this trip, and the look on Chad's face when he saw his seat made it all worth it. Jemima grumbled at first, but as soon as she reclined her seat into a bed, she gave me a grateful smile and a quiet, "Thank you."

When we arrive at the luxury resort, we enter the penthouse suite, the cool air a welcome relief.

"Lie down in the AC and read your book," I tell her, pressing a kiss to her forehead. "I'll unpack."

Later, we head down for dinner. Instead of going to the main dining area, I lead them to the rooftop, where a table waits for us under the twinkling stars. Jemima's eyes widen in surprise, and I can see the tension in her shoulders melt away. All I want is her to feel comfortable, loved, and cared for.

We sit down as a family and enjoy dinner under the night sky.

Before dessert arrives, I clasp Jemima's hands across the table, my heart pounding hard. "Jemima, ever since the moment I saw you, I knew you were for me," I begin, my voice steady despite the lump in my throat. "I'm so happy to be part of your and Chad's life."

Her eyes fill with tears. I clear my throat, determined to finish what I want to say. "I don't want to spend another moment without you knowing how much you both mean to me."

I push back my chair and kneel in front of her. She gasps, her hands flying to her mouth. Chad grins, nearly bouncing out of his seat, and I give him a wink, silently thanking him for keeping this secret. Reaching into my pocket, I pull out a small velvet box and open it to reveal the sapphire teardrop ring.

"Jemima Recaredo, will you marry me?"

"Yes-s," she splutters, sliding off her chair to meet me. Her hands clutch my cheeks as she kisses me, and I hear Chad's excited cheer behind us. We pull him in for a hug, the three of us laughing as tears roll down Jemima's cheeks.

When we finally pull apart, I take her hand and slip the ring onto her finger, marveling at how perfect it looks there.

Tears fall as she whispers, "This is incredible. I didn't think I could be this happy."

I rest my forehead against hers and murmur, "You and Chad and soon to be our little girl are everything to me."

Dessert is served, but I hardly taste it. Chad fills the time talking animatedly, while Jemima keeps sneaking glances at her ring, her fingers brushing it, as if to confirm it's real.

As we head back to the room, Chad's excitement bubbles over. He calls out to the receptionist in the lobby, "I'm going to have a baby sister and a new dad!"

Jemima and I laugh, and the receptionist smiles and congratulates him.

Back in the room, we tuck Chad into bed. His eyes grow heavy as he snuggles under the covers, but before he drifts off, he yawns and looks up at me. "Goodnight, Dad."

It takes me a second to respond. The word Dad creates a warmth that's indescribable. I lean down, brushing his hair from his forehead. "Goodnight, Chad. I love you."

ALSO BY

The Gentlemen Series

Accidental Neighbor

Bossy Mr. Ward

White Empire

The Christmas Agreement

Resisting Chase

Saffron and Secrets

Chicago Billionaire Doctors

Doctor Taylor

Doctor I DO

Doctor Gray

Doctor Spark

The Lincoln Brothers

Billion Dollar Mistake

Billion Dollar Revenge

Billion Dollar Dispute

Billion Dollar Vow

ABOUT THE AUTHOR

Sharon Woods writes spicy, feel-good contemporary romance novels. Based in Melbourne, Australia, with her husband and two children. She drinks a lot of coffee, loves to workout, explore new places, and has an unhealthy addiction to reality TV.

Follow Sharon:

Website: www.sharonwoodsauthor.com

Newsletter